DARK HEAT

J. M. Taylor

Genretarium Press

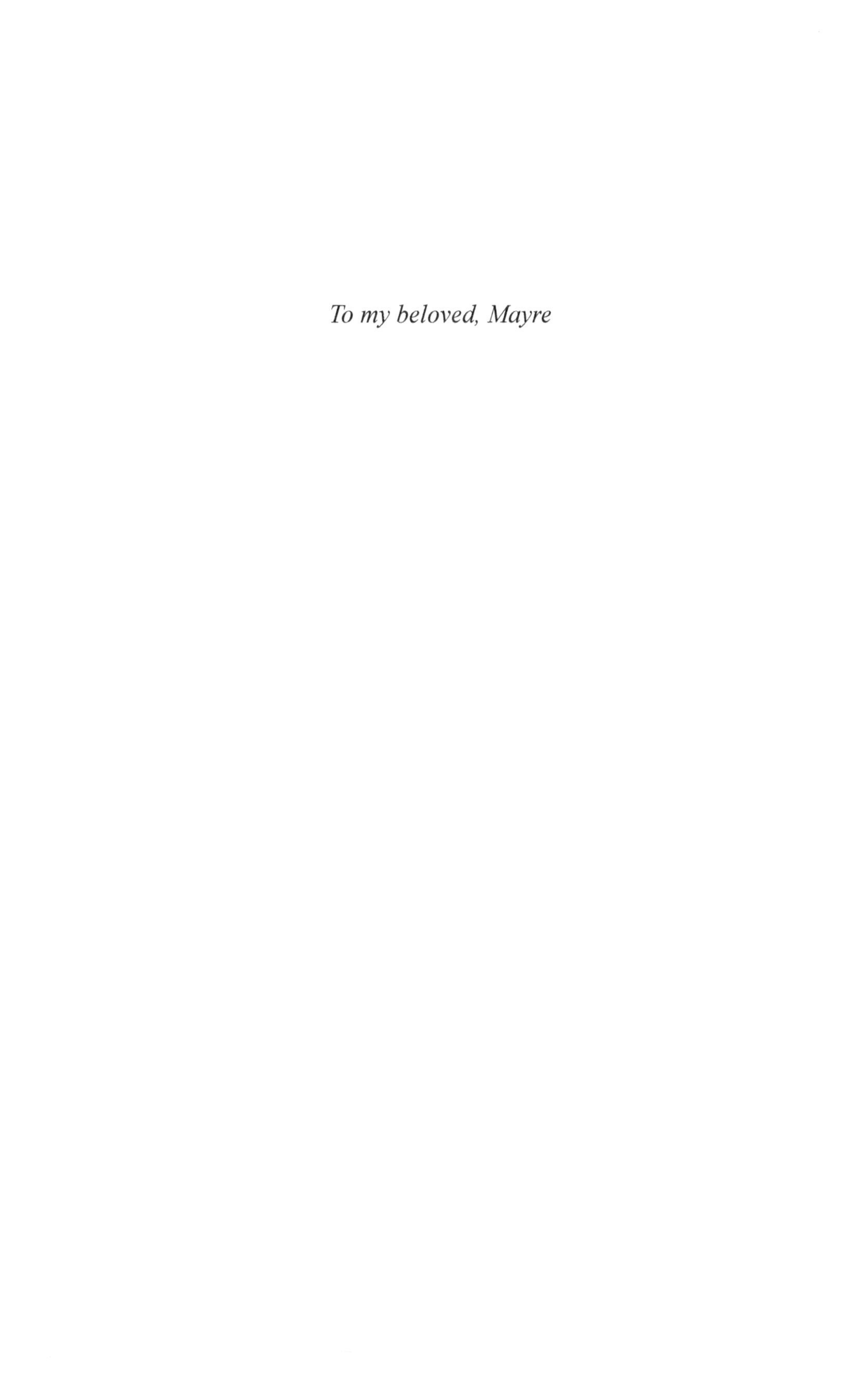

To my beloved, Mayre

Chapter 1

Starr knelt in the dirt, ignoring the July rain. Maintaining the garden was an everyday job, no matter the weather, and besides, the mud would help the seedlings acclimate to being transplanted. Nearby bees ignored the rain as well, happily pollinating the patch of wildflowers that used to be a driveway. Starr's trowel made neat holes for the root balls and stems as she lifted them from a basket she'd woven herself.

The rain's drumming covered the sound of a car until the echo of a slammed door reached her. Without stopping her work, Starr cocked an ear and listened to the rap of boots on her front steps. Not a customer. She knew that gait only too well.

She pictured him stalking through her front hall, like he'd done a thousand times, and it never failed to raise her blood pressure. She'd have to take a dose of cardamom and hawthorn after he left. He probably wouldn't even pause to smell the gumbo on the stove.

The back door opened.

Without turning, she shouted, "How many times do I have to tell you? Knock before you come into my house."

His voice sounded like a rusty engine. "I haven't knocked on a door in forty years. I'm not starting with you."

"What do you want?" She concentrated on catching a Japanese beetle. She admired its iridescent brown shell for just a moment, before she crushed it between the trowel and a rock.

"Get yourself out of the rain, woman, and talk to me like a civilized person."

"Rain won't kill you, and I have work to do."

"Those flies are a plague. Nothing but corruption out here. Get in the house."

Starr dropped the trowel in the basket and stood to face him. Winter Wyman stood on her porch, tall and thin. Beneath a battered Stetson, stringy white hair hung to his shoulders. His piercing blue eyes might have been handsome in a younger man's face, but now they glowed like pale ice in deep crags. His nose curved like a hawk's beak. He wore a dark suit over a white shirt that stayed crisply starched, even in the rain. The tiny string tie had a pearl clasp. The very sight of him sickened her.

Starr folded her arms. "I'll do what I please. This is my home now, and you're trespassing." Still, she carried her basket of clippings toward him, as if she couldn't resist his spell. It made her feel small, but she knew there was no choice in the matter.

"This house is a lot of things, but it's no home. For God's sake, wipe the filth off your legs," he said in disgust. Without waiting to see if she would, he went back inside.

For a few steps, Starr refused. If she wanted to track dirt into her own house, what did he care? But before she reached the porch, she took a few slaps at her knees. There were still black lines in the creases, and a couple of red spots where she'd scraped against pebbles, but it was good enough.

By the time she got inside, Wyman had already arranged himself at the head of her small kitchen table. He sat as he'd stood, ramrod straight, his long waxy fingers neatly folded like a schoolboy's. His

Stetson hung on a hook by the door, and now she saw the nicotine-yellow tinge to his white hair. She put the basket down on the counter, then stirred the simmering stew. Eventually she faced him, and put on her most polite tone.

"Would you like to try the gumbo?"

"You know I won't eat anything with bottom-feeders in it."

"Then how about some licorice tea? I made some special for you."

His grin was forced, but he said greedily, "Now, I would like some of that."

She took a pitcher from the refrigerator and filled a tall glass. She sliced a lemon, putting one slice into the tea, another on the rim. She placed the glass on the table ceremoniously, as though presenting him with a chalice.

"Won't you join me?" he asked.

"You know I don't enjoy it the way you do. Go ahead, drink." Her voiced chilled. "Then we'll talk."

The old man tasted the licorice tea, then drank deep. Starr already had the pitcher at the ready to refill it. He drained it again, but this time she let the glass stand empty.

"You've had your refreshment," she said. "Why don't you go upstairs?"

He folded his hands again. "I want to talk."

She sighed. "About what? Nothing ever changes. He's upstairs, see for yourself."

"I want some explanations. I pay you good money to care for him, and I am disappointed with the lack of progress."

Affecting a calm she didn't feel, Starr tasted the gumbo, then added more Worcestershire. She felt his gaze boring into her, but she counted three more turns of the spoon before she answered.

"I told you, sometimes the injections seem to work, but only for a minute. If I turn off the TV, he screams. He eats well enough, and I clean up after him. What else do you want me to do?"

"I want you to make him whole."

"He needs a doctor for that, real therapy."

"I don't like that attitude. '*A merry heart doeth good like a medicine.*' "

"He belongs in a hospital where they can give him real help."

"How many times do I have to tell you that no son of mine will be put in a loony-bin."

She shrugged her shoulders. It was an old argument. "It's hard to have a merry spirit, old man, with the likes of you skulking around every day."

Wyman struggled to keep his face passive. "Is there any sign at all? Does he talk?"

Starr pushed aside a jar of herbs and leaned on the counter with folded arms. "Since you last asked, yesterday, I've talked a blue streak to him, but no response. When I complain about a mess on the floor, he smiles, so I know he understands me. I think the mad little monkey-man does it on purpose."

The old man slapped the table so hard the glass jumped, but Starr didn't flinch. Wyman's histrionics were as studied as the angle of his Stetson. "You will not talk about my son like that. Whatever he does, he can't help it. I've paid you to make him better, and if he hasn't improved, it's your failure, not his."

"Maybe you'd be willing to take him into your own house, then." She privately enjoyed the look of disgust that washed over his face.

"I didn't say that. But I pay you well enough that you shouldn't have to be letting in your… your…" It always came back to money. Not love of his son, not any empathy for him or anyone else. But Starr could speak his language.

"Clients," she finished for him. "Folks from the neighborhood, just like you. I provide them with a service. It's not my fault if you don't approve of some of them."

"It's disgusting, the fraud you perpetrate on them."

"It's natural. And better than what I have to deal with up there." She jerked her head toward the ceiling. "I'm helping people, same as I help him, same as I help you. And if I had the freedom to pull up stakes and leave it all behind, you'd better believe I would. Now, if you've got nothing else to say, either go up and see your precious son, or leave. I have work to do."

He snorted. "Work. All you do is get your hands grubby."

"I make him dinner, better than he'd get at a hospital." She knew she was arguing against herself here, but she was angry. "And I keep him safe and clean. I give him therapy far beyond what you pay for, but it's not enough to cover all my bills. So I do what I trained to do."

She held his cold blue gaze until he relented. He stood up slowly, like an uncoiling snake. She smiled pleasantly and took his Stetson off the hook, holding it out to him.

"I believe I will visit with him," he said, taking his hat. "But I want you to come as well."

"Certainly." Always give the client what he wants.

She led the way through the house to the stairs. It occurred to her that the wallpaper must be at least as old as herself, and the humidity from her plants was causing it to peel. But she also knew she'd never get around to replacing it. Maybe a dab of glue would hold it.

They mounted the narrow stairs. "Clay," she called. "Clay, you have a visitor." Behind her the old man heaved with exertion. When they reached the top, he stood uncertainly, grasping the railing. She smiled, and when he nodded his readiness, led him to the end of the hall. Through the door, they heard screams from the television, then thumping music.

"Maybe I should come back another time," Wyman said, his voice suddenly bashful.

"I think now is the perfect time," Starr answered, flinging the door open.

The man gasped and Starr shoved him forward. Clay, his blond hair just as long as his father's, sat on the end of the bed with his knees and pants wide open. He stared maniacally at the porno on the television, and came just as they entered. Starr grinned wickedly. Seeing the look on the old man's face made the nasty clean up worthwhile.

"Oh, son," he moaned, "is there none to plead thy cause? Woman, thou hast no healing medicines, only ungodly images."

Clay leered at his visitors, but in his eyes Starr saw no hint of a soul.

After the old man stormed out, thumping slowly, pathetically down the stairs and out the front door, Starr snapped on a pair of rubber gloves. Distasteful as the work was, it was nothing more than bodily fluids, as natural as anything rotting in her compost pile.

She led Clay to a plastic chair, then stripped the sheets and disinfected the floor. She ignored the scene that played on the TV, a man dressed as a Greek warrior fucking a woman who wore nothing but glitter. Did Wyman realize his cash supported subscriptions to five premium cable porno channels? Clay growled impatiently, but she didn't worry about blocking his view. He could stand a minute or two without visual stimulation.

The bed stripped and changed, she left him to his sword and sandal sodomy.

In the kitchen, the gumbo bubbled happily. She tasted it, added some salt. She emptied the licorice tea and lemon slices into the compost pail by the sink and took it outside, ignoring the waiting boots. She liked the feel of the wet grass and mud on her bare feet.

The rain still fell in huge drops. She surveyed the garden, and decided she didn't have it in her to prune anymore. Instead, she cut through the swarm of flies that braved the rain and dumped the compost in the huge bin in the back corner of the yard. The rain hissed on the hot black plastic.

Back inside, Starr checked on Clay. Finding him sedately watching another sexcapade, she showered, scouring herself with a lavender salt scrub until her skin flamed red. She used a stiff brush to clean the dirt from under the nails on her fingers and toes. She changed from her work clothes into an outfit no one in town either deserved or would appreciate. But the pencil skirt and sheer top drew a line between her nursing duties and the life she craved.

She strapped on a pair of heels and checked herself in the mirror. She forced a smile and something about it reminded her of her mother, but it was gone in a moment. She frowned and chose a bottle of lavender vanilla perfume she'd made herself. She dabbed some on her wrists and throat. The scent didn't calm her immediately, but she knew the lavender would work on her in the background.

She checked her image in the mirror once more, then stood at the top of the stairs. She called through the closed door at the other end of the hall, "Clay, stay out of trouble. I got to see if Mac is in a swingin' mood or not."

Chapter 2

Jase Patton pushed his Shelby Mustang through the rain, climbing past 90 miles per hour. Ahead of him was the rural town of Cuthbert, so deep into western Massachusetts that it might as well be New York, probably already asleep this Friday night. The white lines blurred into a steady string. The tires droned like an attack chopper. He had acquired his target, and he was locked and loaded.

He reviewed his objectives. First, he would recover the tablet. That would make him very wealthy. Then he would ensure there was collateral damage. That would make his employer very happy.

"Nothing short of total humiliation," his employer had told him. They had been sitting in a heavily air-conditioned office, watching the swirling brown dust through a small window. "I've learned that he has a bargaining chip." A folder dropped in front of him, and he opened it. He found a grainy photo and a single-spaced history of the object, a flat piece of ivory. It was ancient, very ancient, and well-travelled. Its recent history was violent and bloody. "He got it as escrow in a deal, but didn't hand it over on time. Get it back. How you go about it is up to you, but if he comes out of this with a shred of dignity, I'll have you chained to that rock until the sun scorches your flesh and the crows eat out your eyes."

The chains were already bolted in place. Clear, deep scratches testified to its recent use. He wondered how many others had failed before him. But Jase knew how to take orders. He felt nothing for or against his target. Just another job. But this one could lead to new opportunities.

He left the compound, driving past the rock and its heavy chains. That night, in a motel room hundreds of miles distant from his employer, he closed the blinds and studied the dossier. He opened his laptop and called up a map of the area, He had to zoom in to see beneath the tree cover. Most of the buildings were concentrated around a colonial town common, but the one he was interested in was further out, among orchards and farmland. He clicked through pictures and the official website. A direct attack would never work: this one called for using leverage, not an assault. He'd have to infiltrate the perimeter through stealth.

Now the Mustang devoured the Massachusetts Turnpike in vast gulps. He left Havilah behind, nothing but a college town. Except for the roar of the engine and the humming tires, silence reigned in the car. His eyes were locked on the rainy glare ahead. Even the trees that lined the highway leaned back to avoid him.

He found his exit and cut his speed in half to wend his way through the approach to the town. The sudden deceleration tugged at his gut. The empty road gave way to outposts that signaled the outer limits of Cuthbert: an ancient service station with modern gas pumps, a generic concrete structure that might have housed a drug store or a day care. Warehouse dealerships showcased cars that outnumbered the population. This time of night, there was no telling the difference between abandoned and occupied shacks. Huge oaks towered over everything, many of them shrouded in Devil's Tail vines.

The red glow of neon announced "The Rhode House." He eased off the gas, and the engine whine reduced to a hiss. He drove over packed dirt, rumbling past pickups and a row of bikes lined up like horses at the trough. He found a space in the far corner, near the tree line.

The joint was a long, rambling farmhouse, red paint barely covering tinder-dry clapboards. It had probably been here since before there'd been a road. Someone staggered out, and the jagged notes of old-time country music cut briefly through the air. He pictured a jukebox that hadn't been updated since Dylan went electric.

Inside, Jase found a bar made of plywood, and walls of cracked paneling. The dance floor was scarred with cigarette burns and surrounded by heavily lacquered tables with mismatched chairs. The juke played Johnny Cash: "Ring of Fire."

The drinkers were the odd mix of flotsam that washed ashore in this kind of place, the only watering hole on the edge of nowhere. Bearded bikers in pirate bandanas downed shots in one corner, while preppy students desperate to escape Havilah College argued about literature in another. Random customers drifted in between, sipping their rum and cokes, their beers, their martinis.

Odd that no one paid him any attention, either. A dive like this catered to locals, and he definitely wasn't one. Jase took it as a good omen, and found a spot at the bar between a hipster in a Sinatra porkpie and a guy who looked old enough to have met the Chairman himself.

The barmaid, a wiry thing with short hair that covered her scalp in swirls, gave him an appreciative once-over. Jase returned the smile. But when she raised an inquiring eyebrow, he shook his head. Wordlessly, she gave him the Maker's he ordered and retreated to the other end of the bar. He sipped his drink, listening to bits of conversation floating over him. The bikers were discussing mortgage re-fi. The couple at the table behind him were complaining about church bells ringing. Nothing of interest. Then he heard the hipster say something so odd he had to force himself to keep a neutral face.

"I make it in my basement lab," he said. "I bought most of the hardware on eBay from pharma start-ups that went nowhere but Endsville."

"No one bothers you?" a woman asked.

"It's all copacetic, at least for now," the hipster said. "I can get you some in a couple of days when they're ready."

"I'll think about it, Mac," she said.

"Take your time. I'm making extra beyond his order, just to hone the recipe. But honestly, I can't vouch for the strength of any particular batch. Could be 18-karat. Could be a bomb."

The woman said again, "I'll get back to you."

The finality in her voice was clear, but Mac leaned in, talking fast to keep her in place. "I'll bring some when they're ready, and we can do a trade."

She smiled and patted his hand. "You know where to find me if you need to cure your hangover." Then she fixed him with a stare no one could misinterpret.

The hipster nodded and finished his drink. A martini, by the speared olive that bobbed in the glass. He pushed off the bar, whistling into oblivion.

That left Jase looking the woman dead in the eyes. They were green, and she wore just enough eyeliner to make them glow. Dark curly hair framed her round face. A black cord clutched at her throat. She wore a tight white sweater whose short sleeves showed off her strong arms, and a neckline that showed off the rest. She fit the profile he was looking for. Her smirk was all the opening he needed.

He pointed to her empty glass. "What are you drinking?"

"Margarita, heavy on the salt." Jase waved to the barmaid and gestured at their empty glasses.

"Were you listening in?" She looked like she wasn't too worried about the answer.

"Wouldn't dream of it," he said. The barmaid plopped the drinks sullenly on the bar and retreated again.

He tilted his head to indicate the server. "She doesn't seem too friendly," Jase noted.

"Terry's been like that since she was born, but she pours a good drink." As if to prove it, she sipped her margarita, locking eyes with Jase over the rim of the glass. He found himself falling in.

"You guys friends?"

That broke the spell. The woman flipped her hair over her shoulder, glanced around the room. "Not that close. We were in school together. You interested in her or me?"

Jase grinned, this time for real. "Who said I was interested at all?"

She ignored the question, licked salt from her raised glass. She made a show of moving her other hand along her strong body as she smoothed out a tight black pencil skirt. She seemed to have no hips, and the skirt, just barely covering her knees, revealed strong, straight legs. *She's an Amazon*, he thought. He caught a glimpse of black heels that earned the right to call themselves stilettos. But he also noticed that despite the come-and-get-it outfit, her nails were short and unpainted, with a dark line of dirt beneath the quicks.

"It just so happens that I did hear a bit of what you and Porkpie were discussing," Jase said, bringing his gaze back up to her eyes. They twinkled at his irreverence. "And it just so happens that I'm interested in chemistry myself. Maybe we could talk where it's quieter?"

"Not so fast, Sparky," she said. "I've got nothing to hide. He's not cooking meth, if that's what you're after, and neither am I."

"Sure sounded like you were planning a major delivery. What's your name?"

"Starr."

One of those New Age crystal and incense types. "Of course it is. And what do you do? Faith healing? Tarot cards?"

Starr took a long pull of her drink, again watching him over the rim of the glass. Again, Jase forgot what he was after. She was trouble, and no mistake. But when she answered, "I make homeopathic remedies," he knew he'd come to the right place.

Jase tipped his glass. "I got you, sister. You got a plot somewhere in these hillbilly woods?"

She rolled her eyes. "No, I don't grow weed. There's no money in it now that it's legal here. The commercial growers got in the game and ruined everything. Besides, I get inspected too often as it is. Everything I grow is proven to treat some medical complaint or other, and it's cheaper than buying online. If you're looking for something more… *potent,* you'll have to bark up another tree."

He let his eyes take in her long body. "No," he said. "I like your tree just fine."

She turned to give him a better view. "Just what are you after?"

He made up his mind. "Let's go for a ride and I'll tell you."

Chapter 3

Starr leaned on the bar and cocked her eyebrow. "You're pretty sure of yourself, tiger. My daddy always said not to take rides from strangers."

"He was right. My name's Jase Patton."

"Nice to meet you." She offered her hand. He shook it like a man's, none of that dainty fingertip touch some men used to pretend to be gallant. She returned the pressure confidently, keeping the steady eye contact that had already brought results.

He said to her, "Well. We got that out of the way. I guess your daddy has nothing to worry about. What about your mother?"

She should've seen that coming. She'd opened the door, but hadn't expected him to walk through. He waited patiently, and she showed her teeth to hide her surprise.

Finally, Starr answered, "She took off a long time ago. I don't think you'd be interested in hearing that story." But she had to look away to say it.

"Maybe, maybe not. You coming for that ride, or not?"

She considered his offer. He certainly didn't have any competition. She'd seen him when he first walked in, dressed all in black, stalking like a panther. Lean and muscular, at least half a head taller than her, and she was five-ten herself. His light brown hair was cropped to coarse bristles. The only out-of-place detail was a childish-looking woven bracelet on his left wrist. She was happy to talk to him, flirt a bit, but he oozed danger.

While she considered, she glanced around the room. Nothing new, nothing ever was. It could've been any night of any week for the past three years. Terry glowered from her end of the bar, and that was something to boost her nerves. Jase could be hers, maybe even useful. She wondered how far could it go, and decided to find out.

"All right, mister. Let's go." She stood up, tried to avoid smoothing her skirt yet again, but couldn't resist. "What would you like to see?"

"I'm new in town, and looking to make friends." He finished his drink in a quick gulp. "You can be my guide."

She touched his arm. "Lay on."

"Not finishing your drink?"

"I licked the salt off. That's the best part." She snagged her purse and walked ahead of him, slow enough to tell him she was in control, fast enough to keep him moving. She felt his greedy gaze on her. At the door, she looked over her shoulder. He moved smoothly, his eyes hooded like a snake's. She flicked her tongue through her lips, and slipped outside to wait for him in the dark.

A second later, he was there, hands at her hips, pushing her against the side of the building. His tongue darted across her teeth, then deep into her mouth. He pressed his groin against hers. She put her arms around him, clutching the hard muscle of his back, the curve of his ass. She squeezed once, then broke the kiss.

"A good start," she said. "Where's your car?"

He took her elbow, and Starr wondered just how in control she was. She stumbled when one of her heels hit a rock, but the pressure on her arm was so steady she didn't fall. A wave of heat radiated from her belly along her legs and arms and into her face. What the hell was she doing? She breathed out, steadied her racing heart, and let this man Jase lead her.

An alarm chirped and headlights flashed twice. In the glare, she saw a black Mustang. She waited by the trunk for him to open the door, but he strode straight to his side of the car. The power play excited her. When she unlatched her own door, the engine was already running. She folded herself into the black leather, curling up to watch him.

His hand was on the gearshift, and he didn't bother to look as he reversed and spun the car out of the lot.

"Where to?" he said. He spoke without taking his gaze off the road, but she had no doubt he was somehow taking in every inch of her. Where, indeed? She wanted him, wanted him in her huge, lonely bed. But then there was Clay. How would she explain that? And what would Clay do if she brought home another man? The trees flew by in a dark blur. Then she knew.

"Go this way a mile, and then turn left up the hill."

Jase drove with intense focus, oblivious to her. She longed to touch him, to feel the strength in his arm, but contented herself with rubbing her own thighs together. He completely ignored her presence, but that only drove her deeper into imagining what he would be like when he finally took her in those arms. She was ready to be taken, and held her knees rigidly together to keep from moving any more than she had to.

He took the turn she indicated without slowing, and shifted to power up the incline. Near the top of the hill, he broke the silence. "Now what? There's nothing but trees."

"Over there," she breathed. "The sign that says 'Bell Hill.' "

The fierce headlights illuminated everything like it was day, plunging everything behind into deathly shadows. "Over there," she repeated.

He cut the engine in front of a low timber building with a tower rising from the back corner. "You live here?" he said. "It looks like a church."

"It's not my house," she said. "But I'm the only one who ever comes here. They call it the 'Church in the Woods,' but it's really just a bell tower." *Was that babbling?*

"New one on me," he said and got out. It had stopped raining.

Before Starr opened her door, she fixed her hair in the mirror, then reached down and slid her panties off. Hands shaking, she opened the door, dropping the crumpled underwear into her purse. She studied him from behind. He was looking out over the streetlights of Cuthbert below. A damp breeze riffled through his short hair. She imagined he was contemplating how he would conquer it. If he did, would she play a part? She flipped through the alternatives. She decided yes.

Starr took a long shuddering breath before closing the car door. She forced herself to make slow, deliberate strides toward him. *Not too fast. Make him wait*. She barely succeeded. What was it about him? The strength drained from her legs as he embraced her, this time kissing her neck and sending his hands to search beneath her sweater and along the waist of her skirt.

"Inside," she said, desperately.

He let her go long enough for her to find the key in her purse and put it in the lock. She hoped the darkness hid her shaking.

Inside, she realized her mistake. No one knew she was here, with a man who didn't care at all how much he hurt her. Before she shut the door, before she found the light to guide him to the futon against the wall, he was already crushing a breast with one hand, grappling for the zipper of her skirt with the other. She fought for control, pushing off his jacket, unbuttoning his jeans, pressing her face into the hardness of his chest. Her heel rapped against the wood floor and echoed off the bare walls, the moans of all the lonesome ghosts in her life.

But then he had her sweater off, and her skirt fell to her ankles. She tried to say, "To the back, on the bed," but his mouth was on hers even as one hand reached down between her legs. He lifted her off the ground. She felt her belly lurch, like she was in zero gravity, and then he was inside her. He stood like a colossus in the middle of the room. Each thrust flung her head back, and she dug her stilettos into his thighs.

She ached with pleasure, her arms and legs slick with sweat. When he was through, she told him to take her to the bed. He found the futon mattress and lowered her to it. She lay back, panting. His silhouette hovered over her, a darker patch in the darkened room. Before she could speak, a mechanical whirr wound up behind her like the gears in a clock.

"What the hell is that?" he said. His shadow tensed, ready to spring.

"The carillon," she said. "It's chiming eleven o'clock."

"Let's see if we can make it to midnight," he said, and lay down next to her.

They went well past midnight. He worked her over, biting, heaving, until Starr had to beg him to stop. But when he rolled off her, she couldn't resist snuggling against him, craving strong hands that caressed instead of menaced. But he kept them knit behind his head, and she shivered despite their exertions.

The clock struck one. "End of the witching hour," she said.

"Does it go all night?" His voice was steady, inquisitive, not conversational.

She nodded against his chest.

"Must get annoying."

"Only to newcomers," she said. "There's a faction that wants to make it ring only from nine to five."

"There's always a faction in a town like this."

She stroked his belly. "But it's been ringing the hour every hour since the 1800s."

"That's a lot of ringing."

She twined her legs with his to keep more of his heat close, but he seemed to have lost all interest now that they'd finished. As in the car, it only made her want him more. But he brushed her hand away and she let it rest nearby, hoping he'd change his mind.

What had happened to her? A couple of hours ago, she was a strong woman, able to stand up to the old man, running her own business. Now some stranger fucks her a few times, and she was ready to give him everything. Then again, what could she give him? A bouquet? His questions about the bell tower didn't suggest he was looking for a place to stay, wondering if he could live with that as he settled down. Everything about him said he'd leave when whatever errand he'd come for was finished. And wherever he was from, it was far from here.

"You said you'd tell me what you were after," she reminded him.

"What if I already got it?"

If only. "Tell me," she insisted.

For a minute, she was afraid she'd angered him. But when he answered, she heard something approaching joy in his voice.

"Art," he said. "An object belonging to a good friend of mine was stolen. It's somewhere here in Cuthbert."

Starr laughed. "There's nothing worthwhile in Cuthbert," she said. "Just a rundown old town, a wide place in the road to Havilah. 'Where there's gold,' my father always adds."

"Your father's wrong," Jase told her. "The gold is here. And I came to get it."

She sighed, knowing she had already lost him. "I'm sorry," she said. "If anyone knew about art, it would be a professor in Havilah, at the college."

"No, this is the place. Everyone knows Cuthbert is the hub of the crackademic highway."

Her voice caught, but she managed to whisper, "Then you are in the right place."

"Your Rat Pack friend. What's his name?"

She let herself relax. He didn't know the truth. She said, more easily this time, "Mac? He does chemistry projects just for the fun of it. No, you're looking for…"

"Talis, right? That's the name I got from a kid in Havilah."

She nodded. *Thank God.* "He's a dealer, all right. But he sells just to feed his own habit. He's a loser. What could he have that you'd want?" She dared to reach out again and stroked him. It had the right effect.

"Can you set me up with him?"

"I'll tell you next time the bell rings," she said, climbing on top of him.

Chapter 4

Left on her own after high school, Starr decided she'd never let herself be cowed by some stranger with nice eyes. Not like her mother had.

So now she took control. She straddled Jase and set the rhythm. This time she savored his touch and the heat of his body, instead of fearing she'd get burned. She stared him in the eyes, until he was forced to look away. She laughed wickedly. For the first time in months, she felt clean.

"So," she said, pinning him to the bed like a wrestler. "What is this geegaw you're looking for? Why do you want it so bad? If I like your story, maybe I'll point you towards Talis. But you have to earn it."

He did. But every time he tried to change positions, she put him back beneath her. She was going to take what she wanted first.

"OK," he said when she collapsed, sated, atop him. "Get up. I can't talk with you draped over me like that."

She rolled off and he sat up. The clouds had passed, and his broad, scarred back rippled in the growing light of dawn while he talked.

"April, 2003. Saddam's still in Baghdad, but not for long. As our tanks rolled in, the Republican Guard took up positions all over the city. They didn't have a chance, but no one sent them the memo.

Firefights went on for days, bullets came from everywhere. Imagine a gun in every window in this town. Or RPG launchers, or just rocks and Molotov cocktails. The Guards dug themselves in like termites at their compound near the al-Ahrar Bridge over the Tigris."

She touched his shoulder, but he shook it off.

"Across from the al-Ahrar was the Iraq National Museum. It made for a good fortification, so they built sandbag walls around it and put snipers on the roof. Can you believe it, fucking snipers in the Children's Museum."

"I remember," Starr said. "They looted the whole place. No one bothered to put a guard there."

Still staring at the floor, Jase continued, "Culture takes a backseat in wartime. And Saddam had his soldiers in there, using the artifacts as a shield. Who wants to be the asshole who put a shell through some ancient treasure? But after two days of fighting, the Third Infantry had no choice. There's about a hundred fighters in there with RPGs and machine guns. Shit-awful. So one well-aimed shell from an Abrams tank took out the grenade launcher and another one got a sniper nest. After that, the Americans owned the intersection, and the museum compound."

"An empty museum."

"Not exactly. The staff hid the most valuable pieces during the run-up to the war. And it turned out that a lot of pieces, though nowhere near enough, were returned as soon as the fighting was over."

"Except for one particular item, I take it."

He nodded. "Plenty more than one, but you get the idea. But the piece I'm looking for wasn't looted. See, there were actually three different robberies. The first was just the crazy rush after the Republican Guards were sent packing. Smashed cases in the public galleries, offices trashed like you wouldn't believe. The whole compound stank. A trail of blood from the RPG shooter. That's when the bull's head on the Golden Harp of Ur was destroyed. Luckily, it was a fake on display. You've seen the pictures. The real sucker is like 5000 years old." He stood up, pacing the room. "You could tell they'd decided to become civilians because they'd burned their Baathist cards along with their uniforms." He shook his head. "If you're going to fight for a cause, don't betray it at the last minute."

His detachment left her chilled. She drew her knees up and hugged them for warmth.

"Anyhow," he continued, "after that, professional thieves hit the upstairs storage rooms. No forced doors. They swiped statues, amulets, even tiny beads. Clay tablets with the earliest writing. Someone with keys, someone who knew what they were doing."

"Maybe the keys were left behind."

"Could be, but there were hundreds of locks in that museum, and the keys aren't marked. It would've taken forever to test them all, and no one had that kind of time. That one was bad, but the third wave was the worst: the basement, definitely an inside job. The main door was still locked, and the only other way in was down a hidden stairway and through a brick wall. And that's what the bastards did. They broke in from behind, and got out the same way. They got gold, silver, jewelry, thousands and thousands of the finest collection of cylinder seals. Crushed what they couldn't carry. The simple weight of the metal could buy this town five times over. Add to that the fact that these were made by master craftsmen long before Abraham ever saw a burning bush. Not just Mesopotamian artifacts, either. Stuff from Greece, Rome, the entire Mediterranean."

He quit pacing, watching the huge carillon drum inch slowly in its orbit. For a long time, he didn't say anything, and Starr wondered if he'd fallen asleep on his feet.

"I get it," she said. "Old stuff is valuable. But it's their loss."

The sun had breached the horizon, and the first rays cut across the room, landing on the carillon drum. Its hundreds of brass screws scattered the beams like jewels. Neither of them had noticed its chimes all morning.

"Not just their loss. It's like those Buddhas the Taliban dynamited in Afghanistan. We're talking common human culture, not religion."

She barked a derisive laugh. "Christ, I didn't figure you for some hippie. And that's coming from an herbalist."

"A what?" Jase shook his head. "I don't give a shit about Kumbaya. And it's not a living thing, and it won't put food on your table. But what I mean is, no one person has the right to hide it away. Not there, and not here."

"So what is this piece, exactly?" She felt like she was in a movie, and it made her laugh again. Would someone's head explode before this was all over?

"A piece of the Treasure of Nimrud."

"Nimrud?"

"A city, named after Nimrod, the Babylonian version of Orion. The collection is priceless, of course. But not even Saddam's sons Uday and Qusay could get their hands on it. It was moved out of the museum and hidden around the time of Desert Storm. Huge gold bracelets, helmets, the stuff of dreams."

"So we're back to gold."

He stood by the window, sunlight dappling his skin. She wished he wouldn't. What if someone saw? But no one came up here. And besides, anyone who cared would've seen her leave with him last night. How long would it take for that story to spread? But his next words brought her back to the present.

"Ivory. The panel from the back of a chair, half the size of a vinyl record. A carving of Nimrod himself, in ceremonial armor. In one hand he holds a sword, and in the other, the head of his enemy." He mimed the position, and he looked like a museum piece himself, a Greek nude warrior, or even a god.

"That's it?"

Jase snorted. "Besides the legend that Nimrod was the architect of the Tower of Babel, the value of an ivory carving is astronomical. As near as I can figure, it was smuggled into Turkey with a shipment of guns. After that, it came to this country in a shipment labeled 'Decorative Tiles.' The owner of a chain store said it was an accident of labeling, but before the feds could seize it, the store burned and the panel disappeared. Everywhere it goes, it spreads misery like a curse."

Starr laughed out loud, then buried her face in her knees. "A cursed artifact? Is a mummy going to come lumbering after us?"

He gave her a sidelong glance, and a wink. It was at the same time an acknowledgement of the absurdity of a curse, and a suggestion he wasn't lying. "No King Tut shit. Gunrunners and drug distributors use it as collateral in deals. It's like a credit card. Except somehow, no one ever tries to save a library or feed the hungry with it."

He turned and faced her. He was beautiful and wickedly tempting. "So what's your verdict?"

Starr looked him in the eye, the same hard stare she'd given him at the Rhode House, the same stare that brought him to her bed.

"I can tell you where to find Spyro Talis. I can't imagine him having a treasure like that. But if it doesn't bear fruit, I might have another idea."

Chapter 5

The rising sun broke the spell. The real world intruded with the light of day, and Clay would be needing breakfast. Even on a Saturday, there were customers to take care of, now rumors to contend with. So much for sleeping. Starr pulled on her skirt and sweater, relishing their warmth, but wearing last night's outfit made her feel like a college student making the walk of shame back to the dorm. She stood in the doorway watching him get dressed.

"You coming back here later on?" he asked.

"Buy me a drink, if you want to see me again," she said. She turned the lock. "Close this tight behind you. I don't want to come in and find a raccoon curled up on my futon." He grunted a response that ignored the humor of the image.

His car, she noticed, was spattered with mud. In the daylight it was just another car, not the mysterious and alluring chariot that had carried her off last night. A magic trick, or just the prelude to another disappointment?

It was too far to walk back to the Rhode House for her car, certainly not in heels. Instead, she cut through the woods in her bare feet. The morning air felt good slipping through her tangled hair, and beneath her sweaty clothes. She ducked below a branch, avoiding the pine needle-covered lake that had formed in yesterday's rain.

A channel had formed in the soft dirt, leaving orderly berms of detritus along the edges of the path. The morning sun glinted on wet spider webs that glowed like strings of electric lights.

She loved this time of morning, before Mother Nature had fully awoken. She loved the solitude, the chance to be herself, even after spending the night with someone for the first time in too long. It gave her a chance to start off the day on her terms, before she had to think of Clay, before she remembered why she was bound to him like this. She savored the scent Jase had left on her skin, and replayed the highlights with only bird songs to score the film that flashed through her mind.

She reveled in the cold squelch of the mud between her toes, and it reminded her of a poem she'd once read by Pablo Neruda, about a woman's feet touching the ground. It had an erotic charge that fit the moment, and she wondered if she'd be able to track it down, if she'd even remember to look, once her day got going.

A bright orange mass shone a little way off the path. When she went to investigate, Starr grinned. Just as she'd thought. It was a beautiful chicken of the woods, *Laetiporus sulphureus*, a huge brainlike specimen of delicious fungus growing on the trunk of an old oak. She stepped closer to admire it, and noticed some *Amantia phalloides*—death caps—growing at the base of the tree: life and death mingling in the woods. Nature had her ways. She'd come back to collect her find, after reading up on recipes.

Starr trod back to the path, marking the spot for later. A pleasant static buzzed in her head—the memories of the night before, the possibilities in her future. Then an iridescent dragonfly zoomed towards her and she lost her balance. Her skirt was too tight for her find a steadier footing, and suddenly she was on the ground, connected to the earth in no way Neruda would have rhapsodized. The landing shuddered through her, and all she could do was laugh. She gathered herself on her knees, reaching out for a low branch to haul herself back up. She hunted about for her heels, and realized they were the only part of her outfit that could ever be worn again. It seemed fitting.

Starr emerged from the woods into her dewy garden. It was like the last moments of sleep, when the tattered shreds of a dream were swept away with a waking yawn. Tiny apples were starting to weigh down their branches. The sight of her tomato plots, the circular herb beds, the long rows of garlic just putting out their scapes, eased her back into reality.

She crossed the garden, mounted the back porch, and the transition was complete. Inside, with no sense of romance or memory, she stripped out of her ruined skirt and branch-torn sweater, using them to wipe off the worst mud from her feet. She tossed them in a heap by the basement door to be thrown away. The stilettos clunked in a corner to be cleaned some other time. She stepped into her work clothes, and set to making breakfast for herself and Clay.

Upstairs, Clay still lay asleep, exhausted, she guessed, from another night of finding pleasure in himself. What a couple we make, she thought. Who ever thought they'd end up like this? She put the breakfast tray on the table, turned off the TV, which, blessedly, showed nothing but static.

Closing Clay's door, she went to take a hot shower. As the mud swirled down the drain and she picked leaves out of her hair, the last sensations of Jase's touch rinsed off her as well. When she was dried and dressed again in her work clothes, it was as if nothing had ever happened. She could almost believe it was a story told to her long ago. She sighed. Time to go back into the garden.

The rain had already been sucked up by greedy roots, and she could almost see the tomatoes ripening in the morning sun. She tied back some errant vines with strips of burlap, then collected some basil to make a pesto.

This time Starr heard the approaching car, but it wasn't the old man again. "Customer," she said out loud and wondered who it was. She walked along the wildflower patch where the driveway once had been. A cloud of butterflies hung over her like an umbrella.

"Miranda," she cooed. "What brings you here today?"

A college-aged girl unfolded herself from a sports car she never could've afforded herself. She wore a calico skirt and a peasant blouse cut much too low for her huge breasts. Her hair could use a wash, too. Drug store flip-flops on her feet. *Neo-hippie college freak,* Starr thought behind her cheery greeting. *It's easy to be liberal when daddy's paying.*

"Oh, you would not believe," Miranda huffed. "I'm so glad you're home, sweetie. I have, like, this paper due? Tomorrow? And I need some help real bad."

"I don't write much, Miranda. Maybe you should have started the paper sooner."

"Like, eight pages on fucking Plato's cave? It's hopeless. I need something that'll keep me going, you know, all night? Who knew summer courses were this hard?"

"Come on in. We'll see what we can fix you up with."

Miranda followed her, skirts swishing against the grass, leather purse banging against her hip. They went in the front door, and while Starr clomped her muddy boots in the foyer, Miranda just stepped gingerly inside.

"Clay!" Starr shouted up the stairs. "I got company. Stay in your room!"

"I've never been in your house," Miranda whispered. "Is Clay your husband?"

"Never mind," Starr told her. "It's a long story." They passed the living room, which was overrun by bundles of drying flowers hung from the ceiling, rows of potted plants, and an ancient dining table lost beneath several food processors, knives, and chopping blocks. Heat lamps rose like sunflowers on thin stalks. The air was heavy with the mellow scent of vegetation.

"Looks like a cross between a jungle and an operating room," Miranda said. Starr ignored her. In the kitchen, she gestured to the same chair that had so recently been occupied by a far less timorous visitor. She studied a door-sized rack of glass jars.

"So you need something that will keep you up, but not make you jittery. Why not an energy drink?"

"Those stupid little bottles jocks drink? Bad karma. I want to be all-natural, like you."

"Right. Ok, here's some guarana." She opened a jar of brown powder and scooped some into a ziplock bag.

"Is that heroin?" Miranda's eyebrows lifted halfway up her forehead.

Starr shook her head. "Nothing like it. Totally safe. Mix two teaspoons into some hot water. I don't suppose you have a hot plate?"

"I'll just pop it in the microwave." She still eyed the bag warily.

"Of course. And you might like some of this gingko. It's ok to mix them, might be your best bet." She held out a little plastic bag.

The girl's fingers were weaving a cat's cradle. Her eyes darted around the room. Then she crossed her arms protectively across her chest. "I don't know, maybe I should try some Red Bull."

"That'll get you to half past midnight, then you'll crash and you won't write a page. What's the matter? I've never sold you bad stuff before."

Suddenly Miranda's face changed. Her smile looked genuine, except for the pinprick in her eyes. "You're right, honey. I'll take them both. How much?"

Starr did a quick calculation, based on shipping prices from Brazil, a minimal service charge, and the newness of the car Miranda was driving. Didn't she have a sedan before? "Eighty dollars for the two."

Miranda looked like she'd explode. "What? I could buy an essay for less than that. One that would get at least an A."

"Fine," Starr said with a shrug. "Seventy. Because you're a good customer." She held out the two bags, each labeled with marker. Miranda pulled a credit card. Starr shook her head. "I like paper. It's biodegradable, right?"

The girl grimaced, but then her hand was back in the purse, emerging with a thick roll of twenties. She peeled three off. Finding there were no tens, she reluctantly added a fourth. It didn't seem to change the size of the wad.

Should've made it a hundred, Starr thought. Then added out loud, "Anything else?" Miranda sucked in her lips and shook her head. *This is where I make the money.* "Are you sure?"

The girl burst into tears.

"I'm, like, late? Is there anything you can give me to, you know, get it started again?"

Starr furrowed her brow. "It's not a faucet. Have you seen the doctor?"

Miranda shook her head. "The bills go right to my father. I can't be…if he found out he'd… Don't you have something?"

"Miranda, I don't think that's my place. You really should go to the infirmary…"

The carefully-applied mascara flowed down Miranda's cheek. "Please, Starr. A girl in my dorm said you were the one. I never thought… I can't…" Her breasts bounced ridiculously with her sobs, and Starr found herself wishing she could just be done with the whole thing. What did any of it matter?

Miranda was reaching for the roll of bills, flipping off two, five, ten. Her hands shook and her words were nothing more than the bleats of a sheep.

Then, as if an idea had just come to her, Starr asked, "How late are you?"

A wave of relief washed over the girl's face. "So you'll help?"

"There's something I can try. How late?"

"Two weeks. Maybe three."

Starr nodded sagely. "I've got something here. I don't know if it'll work for you, though. If you had come to me right away…" *Nothing like guilt to up the price.*

"I'll take it."

Starr rummaged in the back of a deep cabinet. She moved boxes and bottles haphazardly. When she thought she'd wound Miranda up as far as she could stand, she held out a bottle of clear liquid. One of a dozen she always kept on hand.

"A tablespoon of this every day."

"What is it?" Miranda's voice had gone dead. But she took the bottle.

"Nothing poisonous. At least not to you. I promise, it's all natural. Now, let's go into the living room."

Miranda's flip-flops slapped on the wooden floor. The sale made, Starr didn't bother to turn the screw any more. She said, casually, "That might work on its own, but I want to give you something else, just in case." A re-purposed soda fridge loomed in the corner. Inside, green tufts grew out of pint glasses. Starr slid back the door and took out a glass. "This isn't for eating," she said, with the stern tone of a nurse. She nipped a few leaves off the wad. *Not much different from what she just showed me in the kitchen*. "Roll these up, like a cigar. Then put it in like a tampon."

"You want me to put *that* in *there*?"

"It's not like you haven't put worse there, or you wouldn't be in this fix. Change it three times a day. Keep this in the fridge in your dorm, and don't let your roommate put it on her salad. I gave you a week's supply. If that doesn't get you flowing again, there's nothing I can do for you." She let the last sentence hang in the air. Miranda nodded, then slunk out silently. Starr recorded the transaction in her log, smiling grimly as she reviewed the list of clients she serviced, and their ailments.

The rest of the afternoon passed quietly. Starr considered that she should probably make a batch of pessaries for herself, as well. Jase seemed like he'd be pretty potent. Meanwhile, some of her regulars came for their doses of sage and St. John's wort and the other herbs *Reader's Digest* said would help them fall asleep or stay awake or remember where they left their keys last night. Only a handful, mostly the wives of professors from Havilah College, gave her any kind of challenge: natural remedies for heart and kidney problems, the kind of thing that bordered on Eastern medicine. She always kept a stock of yew needles and Brazilian *Una de Gato* to treat cysts.

The sun peeked under the lid of clouds to the west. Golden light flowed like liquid down the roof to cling under the eaves. The gumbo was almost done. She went to the soda case and took a few sprigs of Queen Anne's Lace from a bunch identical to the one she'd sold to Miranda. She chopped up a handful and dropped it in the pot. She stirred it in, then took a taste.

Perfect.

Chapter 6

The Hammer and Tongs Cafe had been around so long that the rest of Cuthbert's downtown had grown up around it. Back then, it had been a blacksmith's shop, and the huge brick forge was still used as a grill. It had a lunch counter on one side, and raised, curtained booths on the other. A row of small tables filled the gulf in between. Generations of Cuthbert's elders had gathered here to determine the direction of the town, beyond the inconvenient strictures of Town Meeting, a tradition that drew Winter Wyman here each Friday night without fail, though he made an appearance most other nights as well. He had shaken off the miserable sight of his son's unholy actions that morning. The purification ceremony had helped, but more importantly, he had a duty to perform, and it would be impossible to neglect it.

An alderman's duty, as he saw it, was to be available to his townspeople, even after Town Hall business hours. He took his place at a table in the back, with a reserved booth to his side for more private conversations. A plate of haddock — he ate only fish on Friday — sat in front of him.

It was just six o'clock, and the dinner crowd was trickling in, wholly ignorant and unconcerned that a stranger was at that moment pulling into the Rhode House parking lot. It looked like an unofficial meeting of the Chamber of Commerce. Ron Larsen, the bank president, was there, sitting with Edward Thompson, the real estate agent. Another alderman, Dr. Giles Fuller, who ran the small clinic, was dining with his wife and her sister. A few other merchants, some together gossiping, others alone reading stapled spreadsheet reports, were scattered about the room. The men nursed scotches that were prohibited by their own decree: Cuthbert was a dry town. They did it knowing full well that Chief Bill Butler sat near the door. Somehow he never saw the glasses of booze. Least of all the one in front of himself.

Wyman drank water. He sat alone, though everyone in the place called himself Wint's best friend. They had all come over during the course of the evening to say hello. Thompson had paid respects, as well as Wyman's cut on the rent for a few of his properties. Fuller, too, talked over some town business, and they came to an understanding that left the doctor's face pale, and his eyes hard.

But then that timid little woman approached the table.

Under the table, Wyman clenched his fists. He took a deep breath, and in an instant his public face returned: a fixed smile, a cheerful light in his eye. He checked his heart rate, and by the time she opened her mouth to speak, he was satisfied that it was slow and steady.

"Please excuse me," said the woman. She held her arms in tight, trying to be even smaller than she was. A cheap but neat coat was buttoned up to her fleshy chin. Just above it was the knot of a scarf that hid most of her dyed red hair. "Mr. Wyman, I never thought an alderman would be eating alone."

His smile gleamed bright as a blowtorch. "Even though I'm the *chief* Alderman, Mother Hutchins, I'm a regular person, just like you. I'd be pleased to have your company." He gestured to the empty seat across from him. But Mrs. Hutchins hesitated. "What is it?" he asked.

Her hands fluttered above her trim coat. *Like the butterflies she's got inside*, he thought.

"I…I hardly know, Mr. Wyman. I came to ask for help, but, well, now that I'm here, I hate to bother you. Maybe I should call your secretary."

"My assistant is right over there," he said, pointing to one of the curtained booths. "But why go through a middleman? Please sit down."

Gingerly, she pulled out the chair, but sat on its edge, ready to jump up at the slightest hint of danger.

"Can I offer you something? A glass of water?" He let a wolfish glint sparkle in his eye. "Or something…stronger?"

It had the effect he'd expected: a look of shock, then a careful, nervous titter that broke the ice. "Nothing, thank you, Mr. Wyman. Oh, you're a rogue, aren't you? I don't want to take up any more of your time. I wouldn't even be here if it wasn't for…" Her voice trailed off.

"What is it?" he asked solicitously, leaning closer.

"It's my grandson, Stephen. He's looking for a job, and he can't find anything."

"And you think I might be able to hire him?"

"Oh, no, Mr. Wyman. Not at all. What he wants to do is work at the bank, even if it's just as a teller. He wants to learn the trade."

Wyman chuckled. "Well, it's not like I could just make the bank hire who I want. If I did, it would be the guard, right?" She laughed with him, uneasily, but he cut it short. "But of course, there's always room for a hardworking lad. Ron Larsen is sitting right over there. Would you like me to introduce you?"

Mrs. Hutchins's face went slack, and she fluttered her hand like a fan. "Oh, no, I'd be too embarrassed. Me, talking to a bank president. I'd never."

Wyman gave her his most genial smile. "I'm sure I can strong-arm Mr. Larsen later tonight to find a place for a good boy like Stephen. I've seen him play on Cuthbert High's football team. You have him come see me first thing next week. We'll have a talk, and I'm certain he'll find a good job. How's that?"

Mrs. Hutchins beamed. "Bless you, Mr. Wyman, bless you!"

He stood up abruptly, though his smile remained warm. "Just doing what I can." She stood, too, and he escorted her past the tables to the door. "Run along, now, Mrs. Hutchins. Have him come see me any time." He watched her plod down the sidewalk, waved when she turned as he knew she would. "Bye, now!" he called.

Back at his table, Wint found Mrs. Hutchins's place had been taken. "Hear all that?" he asked his lieutenant, Sam Dyer.

"Got it." Sam was younger than Wint by maybe twenty years. He had a lean face like Wint's, and hungry eyes. But where the older man stalked like Nosferatu, the younger one had a loose-limbed angularity. Every joint—elbows, knees, even fingers—had sharp bends. A ragged hole pierced the top of his right ear.

Wint glared at him. "What else have you got, Sam?"

Sam straightened his legs and reached inside his sport coat. He squinted and read from a sheet torn from a notebook. "Danny McIntyre says thanks for the good word with the liquor board. He said he'd send a case of scotch when the store opens in Havilah."

"Two might be better, don't you think?"

Sam smiled. "That's what I told him. It'll be three."

"Good. What else?"

"I talked to our friend in the state lab. He said he'll make sure that whatever sample crosses his desk won't be reported on until we let him know how it should come out. He's got a nice assistant he caught sampling, too, so she'll be working with us."

"For how long?"

Sam scratched his head. "I'd say we could suck that tit a good couple years. She's young and needs to build her resume. If she tries to leave, our boy's got video of her snorting right at her lab bench."

"Closer to home?"

"Got a shipment of oxy and vikes ready to go, and some bath salts from Mac Fletcher. Just need a delivery boy to bring it all to our campus runner."

Wint laced his fingers behind his head and smiled. "I think I got just the fella for that."

Sam nodded. "One other thing. Some stranger's driving around town in a new Mustang. Looks like a bad hombre."

"So?"

"So, they say he was looking to make friends."

Wyman smiled and waved to someone across the room. Through gritted teeth he said, "So let him make friends. And if we have to deal with him, we will." Wint dropped his arms and leaned forward. "For now, I got another job for you, Sam. I need you to whisper in Bill Butler's ear. Tell him that whore out on Frick's Lane is up to her tricks again."

"Just like that? No excuse?"

Wint nodded thoughtfully. "You're right. Let's do it this way: send Jimmy Cooper out to buy something first. Let her know what happens if she defies me. I'll flay the skin off her bones if I have to."

Sam went pale. "You sure, Wint? That could open up a whole can of worms."

The old man thumped the table sharply. "I know goddamn well what I'm doing. Butler won't arrest her without my say-so, but he'll plow her whole garden under if he thinks she's growing reefer between the rows of parsley."

"Got it, Wint. A shakedown, but no arrest. Show the bitch her place, right?"

"No, Sam. Not like that. It's for her own good to be taught the paths of the righteous, even if it's painful at first. Hebrews 12:11: 'For the moment all discipline seems painful rather than pleasant, but later it yields the peaceful fruit of righteousness to those who have been trained by it.' She knows all about fruit."

Chapter 7

The day after Mrs. Hutchins had led her lamb to the slaughter, Starr sat at the kitchen table wrapping bundles of cilantro with rubber bands. The cooling pot on the counter filled the kitchen with the aromas of the French Quarter. Clay was quiet upstairs, sated after feeding on gumbo and a beer.

The early evening silence was cut by a 1980's beater Ford bucking to a stop in front of the house. Not one of her regulars. She went to the porch to investigate.

"Jimmy," she said to the toadish man who emerged from the car. He wore greasy jeans and a ripped T-shirt with a faded beer logo on it. His patchy beard needed trimming. "Don't you know the government bought back all those clunkers a while ago?"

"This baby?" He patted the hood, careful not to put his hand through a rust spot. "This here's an antique."

"It's destroying the environment. Jesus, I can smell the burning oil halfway across town."

"Well, I didn't come here for car advice."

"I didn't think so." She fixed him with a hard glare. "Been a while."

"Yeah," he said with a grin. "Seems like yesterday, though. Remember the prom?"

"Better than you do, I bet." She folded her arms. "Enough to know I wasn't your date."

"That so? Seems to me that didn't matter to either of us."

She remembered a drunken afterparty in someone's basement. No parents, no lights, and a pounding bass that drowned out the moans of the couple next to them on the sofa. Jimmy's charm had worked a lot better back then, and Starr hadn't liked her own date anyhow, so it was a double win at the time. But when the sun rose the next morning on a rainbow of discarded dresses and red cups, Starr had found herself alone next to a sleeping couple, and Jimmy curled up in the corner with Terry, who now tended bar at the Rhode House. From their tangled limbs, there was no doubt he'd gotten himself a two-fer that night. When she pulled on her dress to sneak home, she'd taken Terry's distinctive orange one as well, hanging it on her family's mailbox so it would be waiting for Terry when she got home.

Clearly Jimmy had forgotten all of that. The man looked genuinely puzzled.

"Cut back on the weed, Jimmy. You're starting to hallucinate."

"Funny you should mention that. Can I come in?"

Starr scowled, but found no reason to say no. Still suspicious, she waved him in. When he saw the living room, he nodded appreciatively.

"I like that smell. Earthy. But don't you ever just sit and watch TV? There's nothing in here but plants."

"Clay watches enough TV for the both of us," she said dryly.

"Oh, uh, yeah. How is old Clay?"

"Pulling through. You should visit him some time. You used to be good friends."

They were in the kitchen now, and she sat him in the same chair that had hosted old man Wint and knocked-up Miranda. What would this loser have to say? She watched him squirm.

"Yeah," he said. "Good friends, but that was a long time ago. Lotta years."

Starr shrugged. "Suit yourself. Now, what do you want?"

Jimmy gave her a gap-toothed smile. "A little pick-me-up. I got a date and want to be at my best."

"Please tell me she's going to drive. If you asked me to get in that heap of yours, you'd be waiting a long time."

"Not a problem," he said, folding his hands like an eager student. "What have you got?"

Starr opened a tall cabinet in the corner. Wire shelves held rows of plastic jars. She scanned the labels, then picked one from near the bottom. "You just want to stay awake, or do you want to impress her with your stamina?"

"Yes, please."

Starr rolled her eyes, then reached in for a second jar. She held one up. "This is for energy. A teaspoon in hot water. Have it before you meet her, so she doesn't see the jitters." She spooned some into a mortar and pounded it into a pulp. She scooped the green mass into a plastic bag, zipped it shut, and wrote the name on it. "This one is if things go right. Better than the blue pills, and no vision problems. If I were you, I'd take it just about the same time you put on the Barry White CD."

"Barry who?"

"Never mind." She turned to fill a second bag. "That's going to be thirty dollars for the two. You want some sage to burn in your bedroom? Gets rid of the bad juju. Plus the stink."

He glanced at the bags in front of him, then looked up with puppy dog eyes. "I was hoping for a little something else. You know, the stash you keep just for old friends."

"Jimmy, I don't sell that stuff. You can stand in line at the pot shop just like everyone else. Even pick your own custom blend."

Now he fixed her with a hard stare. "Don't get all coy, Starr. Everyone knows you sell premium shit. All that organic gardening."

"Says who? Name me one person—I'll call them a liar."

Jimmy bobbed his head, as if trying to decide which name to drop.

"One person," she repeated.

"Aw, you got me. But why grow all the rest of this shit, except to cover up what you're really doing? You don't really believe in all this herbal crap?"

Starr put her hands on the table and leaned forward. "I. Don't. Do. That. Now get out of my house. Take that shit with you. I pity the poor skank you're going to use it with, but you can have it for free. For old time's fucking sake."

Before she finished, he was bolting around the table faster than she could react. In a second, he stood behind her, so close she could feel the sick heat rolling off him. He wrapped his arms around her waist, bending her against the counter, reaching for the button of her jeans. She struggled, but he was almost twice her weight. He pinned her arms against her sides. "I remember prom night, you cock tease. You know what they say about you? They say you haven't had a good fuck in years. Isn't a guy in town claims he's warmed that cold cunt of yours. They're starting to think maybe you're getting it on with old Clay there. Come on, Starr, you know you want it."

"Jimmy, you asshole, stop!" She twisted and pushed against the counter, but it only drove his groin tighter against the small of her back. His breath reeked of stale gum. Vaguely she noted that the bell tower was striking ten.

Is this what it had all come to? Had she surrendered her life to a bunch of pathetic invalids? Mental or physical, they were all fucked up, the people who came to this house. *I should just burn it to the godforsaken ground.* She worked her arm free and launched her elbow into his chin. His teeth clapped shut, and the minty stench mixed with the coppery smell of blood.

The shock staggered him, but he clung to her with one hand, clutching his cheek with the other. She used her momentum to pivot him towards the counter. The mortar was still there, and she was just able to get her fingers on it. She feared the heavy stone bowl would slip, but she caught it tight, and swung it up over her head. It crashed into his face, and his nose exploded. Another blow clipped his temple, and he slumped to the floor, a crimson halo spreading out from the crown of his skull.

All those years ago, in that basement stinking of beer and weed and cheap perfume, she and Jimmy had fumbled at each other in the dark. But as the critical moment approached, she thought of something her mother had once told her. Even then, it had been years since Starr had seen her, but the lesson stuck.

"Men will use women to get what they want," she'd told young Starr. "And they'll take the credit for everything women accomplish. But never forget that you, Starr, are stronger and smarter than any man you'll ever meet, and if you learn to wield that power, you will never be sorry a day in your life."

The lessons had begun that day, and lasted until her mother disappeared. And as Jimmy's panting in her ear increased in urgency, as he reached for that last barrier, she deftly headed him off the way her mother had shown her, breaking the spell on her own terms.

His charming smile cracked in despair, while Starr cooed sweetly that it was all right. It would always be all right. Soon after, he had gone to get a drink, and never came back. She must have fallen asleep soon after, because the next thing she knew he was wrapped in Terry's arms.

Now she looked at his slumped body. They had both failed to escape the clutches of Cuthbert's dead-end roads. But she had never entirely ceded control, not even to Winter Wyman.

Jase Patton, she allowed, might be an exception.

"You better not have bled into my gumbo," she snarled. Jimmy shifted painfully, but he didn't seem to hear her. He was still pitching a tent in his crotch, though, so she stepped on it. His eyes flew open. "Serves you right," she said.

"You're a sick bitch," he grunted.

"You have no idea."

Another noise caught her attention. She looked up to see Clay standing dumbly in the doorway. He wore only his boxers, and his fists clenched at his sides. His babyish cheeks belied the menace in his eyes. Six feet and still muscular, despite the years of inaction, there was no doubt he could do some damage.

Starr nudged the prone man's leg. With a motherly voice, she crooned, "Well, look who it is, Jimmy. Clay, why don't you two go down to the rec room and get reacquainted."

Without a word, Clay shuffled into the kitchen, and lifted the whimpering Jimmy onto his shoulder. They disappeared down the basement stairs.

She called down after them, "You two play nice, now!"

Alone in the kitchen, she gripped the counter and willed her legs still. Her vision had narrowed to pinpricks and rode the wave of black spots, desperate not to pass out. When the spots had dissipated and she thought she could move, she took a mop off its hook, and faced the mess in the kitchen.

Two chairs had fallen over. The mortar, solid as ever, sat in the middle of a scarlet puddle. She'd have to soak it for days, then bury it in hot coals. Streaks of blood laced the floor, the counter, the open jar of eleuthero root she'd given to Jimmy. That alone was worth more than thirty bucks.

But the gumbo was safe. The lid was still on the pot, and none of the spray had come in this direction. "Fuck it," she said, filling a pail with hot water. The hard work brought her focus and strength back. She scrubbed while Clay worked downstairs to repay her years of caring for him.

When she was done mopping, she went back to the cellar door. Over the sound of inhuman thumps, she called, "Clay, make sure to put your toys away when you're finished. I'm going out. Mama needs a margarita."

Chapter 8

The Mustang, black and cold, hid in the shadow of a stand of oak. Jase sat within, eying the flickering window. The house looked precisely as the woman had told him.

"He lives down Rivers Farm Road," she'd said before she had finally left the bell tower and allowed him a moment of peace. "The farm land was sold off to developers for McMansions, but Talis lives in the old farmhouse right next to the road."

"Anyone live with him?" he asked.

She stood in the doorway, adjusting the lock. Not that it would deter even a child who wanted to get inside. But he let her have her illusion. "I can't imagine who'd want to," she said. "He's not a trusting guy, so be careful."

The house squatted next to an iron arch that led to massive new houses, each as dark as a grave. It had four additions that shrank to the size of a shed, as if the whole thing could shut up on itself. The clapboards had once been white, but now even the darkness of night couldn't hide the swaths of dirt that smeared the structure from the eaves to the foundation. The only sign of life was in Talis's back room, where a television's ghostly presence illuminated the rippled panes.

He considered what he'd learned during the previous night. First, the woman was clearly desperate to leave. Why else would she be dressed like that for the locals? It reminded him of those desert seeds that sprouted only after the first rain in years. She probably showed up every week, looking for some stray college professor, maybe even a grad student, who would whisk her away from this backwater. He could use that misery to his advantage.

He was satisfied she knew nothing about the ivory panel. He watched her closely while he told his story, and nothing registered on that open face of hers. No one could hide a reaction to such a surprise. She didn't seem to know about anything else, either. Yes, she'd be very useful during his operation. It might make things harder later, but not for him.

Jase picked up a roll of duct tape and a pink rubber ball from the passenger seat. God love mom and pop hardware stores. Where else could you find tape, toys, and replacement pots for discontinued coffee makers? He swung the tape around his finger like a hula-hoop, and put the ball in his coat pocket. He didn't bother with the night vision goggles.

The crickets of late summer had yet to materialize, and only the distant rumbles of semis on the highway broke the silence. Jase sidled up against the house, remembering the training he'd received as a new recruit. Those had been hard months, but now they were paying off. No one could have detected his approach, let alone an unsuspecting junkie. In seconds, he was in position. He inspected the various means of entry. The back door was open, but the screen door, an old-fashioned wooden frame with a length of mesh held on by a couple of flimsy slats, was latched on the inside.

Jase crouched by the porch step and looked through the corner of the screen. Talis snored in an armchair that leaked stuffing like fungus on a tree. Behind him, a doorway like a dark maw led to the main sections of the house. Just as he'd been taught, surprise would be the key to success. He had every advantage: when Jase burst through the door, the television would be like a spotlight in Talis's eyes, and Jase would be nothing more than an indistinct shadow. He undid an inch of duct tape, ready to immobilize his target.

Jase calculated the distance from the door to the chair at a single stride. He took a step back, then lunged at the door, using the roll of duct tape to tear through the screen. When he landed. he was already pulling out a long strip to wrap around Talis's chest. The unzipping adhesive yowled like a dog in pain.

But as he hit the floor, the armchair flipped backwards, and the TV went dark. There was a skittering across the floor of the next room, then silence.

"Fuck." Jase tore the strip of tape off the roll and shook it from his fingers. He heard footsteps creeping up the stairs and smiled. *Why do they always go up?* Already Jase's eyes were adjusting to the dimness, and he pressed deeper into the house, searching for the staircase that Talis had taken to his doom.

In the second room, he barked his shin against a barber's chair. Retreating, he backed into a standing rack laden with winter coats. They fell on him like nets and he felt one rip under his stabbing hands. *I had to come after the next guest on* Hoarders, he thought. Standing up, he avoided a tower of televisions stacked higher than his head. But he couldn't fend off a wall of magazines that fluttered into him like bats. When they hit the ground, they became slippery as ice. He sloshed through the debris, shelves of glass cascading around him. Thank God there were no neighbors, but how did he get caught in this pigsty?

Then Jase was crashing through the doorway into the next room. A bank of powerful LEDs blazed in his eyes and snuffed out before he could focus on anything but a gap in the floor before him. The lights had blinded him again, but he was determined to push on. Another brilliant flash, this time so close he nearly stumbled into the hole.

"You can slow me down, Talis!" he shouted into the darkness. "But sure as I'm standing here, I'll have you before I'm done!"

No answer. Now was the time he could have used those goggles, though the LEDs might have fried them. Lacking a rope, he wound the end of the tape on the door knobs, and slipped his wrist through the roll. None of the scenarios he had practiced in training had envisioned such crude but effective traps. Everything had been straightforward: proper formation, avoid obvious targeting, get the hostile. And Jase now realized that in every case, the commanders who had designed the practice missions made sure that the missions were always accomplished.

He stepped gingerly, heading towards the wall, away from the hole. It stood to reason that Talis would place the trap close enough into the room for intruders to hit it headlong, but he'd need it far enough in to avoid it himself, and there'd be a path to get around it. Jase dropped to his knees, probing with his hands until he found the lip of the chasm, about a yard and a half from the wall. Two steps, and he would have been swallowed like a rabbit in a wolf's jaw. "Gotcha," he muttered, standing up. He slid with his back to the wall, through the corner, the tape still feeding out from his wrist with a crackle like heat lightning.

Then his foot tapped something, no heavier than a book. A damn pressure plate. Suddenly, the floor pivoted away from the wall, and pitched him toward the abyss. Instinctively, he gripped the tape and climbed it as he plunged down and slammed against the wall. Thankfully, the makeshift line held. He kicked his legs uselessly, hoping the edge of the floor wouldn't cut through the tape. When he stopped swaying, he hauled himself up to the rough-hewn edge by the door. "Guess I'll go the other way," he panted.

The tape roll still dangling on his wrist and feeding out sticky slack, Jase made his way to the left, wary this time of more hidden levers. When his foot met some resistance, he tensed for another fall, but none came, and he shuffled forward another inch. From what he'd seen from outside, he judged that he'd now be into the original house, maybe the pantry. He hit a wall, and followed it into a narrow corridor. The tape was now too long to do him any good, so he ripped off the end and let it drop.

Clear of traps or not, the kitchen was a hazard, stinking with filth and rot. Piles of dirty dishes spread from the sink across the counter. Fast food containers shared table space with syringes and candles and tiny bits of cellophane that twinkled in the ambient light. The doorless cabinets yawned empty, except for an odd cereal box or coffee can.

Then Jase heard a scrape immediately above him. Second floor, middle bedroom. He slid along the central hall toward the stairs. His toes found the lip of another hole, but it was small. Easy for Talis to leap over, but enough to snap an intruder's femur. Beyond it, he found himself at the foot of a staircase.

He'd been in booby-trapped buildings before. He'd trained to search for pressure plates and tripwires. But the camp's urban warfare trainers hadn't told him what to do about an old farmer riding the white pony. He had to consider a man who was both clever and nearly incapacitated. Would Talis trust himself to get past a rigged tread on the stairs? Have some dangling menace above? No, the stairs would be safe. He plunged into the darkness, careful as he rounded the landing, already imagining second-level traps.

The surprise was that there were more steps than he expected to get to the second floor. In fact, he'd have sworn he had made it straight to the attic. The small square window that greeted him confirmed his suspicion. Somehow he missed a doorway to the second floor. *Who designed this house?*

Beneath him, scuttling footsteps told him Talis was on the move again. Jase took the stairs headlong in the dark, in time to see his target erupting from a hidden entrance in the kitchen.

He bounded down the hallway, counting his steps to time his vault over the smaller hole. In another three paces he was back in the passageway that led to pit he'd fallen in. But now he had Talis within his sights. As the wasted man leapt through the doorway, Jase launched himself across what he hoped was the entirety of the gulf, somersaulting through the doorway inches behind Talis. Jase landed on him, slamming his chin to the floor with an echoing knock. While Talis squirmed, Jase reached and ripped a length off the roll of tape that hung from the door. He wrestled it around Talis's hands and knees. Then he took the rubber ball from his pocket, jammed it into Talis's mouth, and wound a double layer of tape over that, too.

Beneath him, Talis shuddered and shook, then went limp, like an old car stalling out.

"Good boy," Jase told him. He grabbed Talis's collar and marched him with hampered steps through the labyrinth. Jase's feet crunched on the broken glass, and he almost lost hold of Talis as the puddle of magazines shifted beneath him. Soon enough they were back in the TV room. Jase righted the overturned chair and dropped the old junkie into it.

"You wasted a lot of my time," Jase said. "Why all the traps?" Talis's eyes swirled madly. He chewed at the rubber ball, but the tape held it firmly. Jase didn't bother turning on a light, but he could still make out the shrunken cheeks and papery skin that clung to Talis like flypaper. His neck was covered in sores, and his hair, tufts of feathery white, stuck out at odd angles.

Jase sighed and tried again. "Let's get serious. You got a package a month or so back. Remember it?"

Talis shook his head and squirmed until he was perched on the edge of the seat, ready to bolt despite his taped knees. Jase shoved him back. He didn't do it gently.

"The package. It came a month ago. About the size of a big book. Now do you remember?" Talis shrugged. Jase took a knife from a sheath on his belt and regarded the blade curiously. Talis nodded warily.

"Now we're getting somewhere. You understood the instructions, did you?" The prisoner nodded.

"They told you to say it came from the Network. Did you do that?" While Talis was still nodding, Jase added, "And did Wyman take it?" More vigorous nodding.

"Good. You'd better hope that he kept it himself. You told him the Network had decided he'd keep it as collateral for a deal in Atlanta?" Desperate agreement.

"Well, Spyro, you seem to have earned a big fat reward, but I doubt you'd want to make the trip to collect. I advise you to keep your mouth shut, even after I take that ball out. I don't want to come back to this rat hole, but if I have to, I know all your tricks."

Talis raised his eyebrows pleadingly. His nose was stuffed with snot and his chest rose in jerking convulsions. Jase wrenched off the tape and pried out the rubber ball. Talis spit a gob of muck to the floor, then snarled, "I didn't do nothin' to you."

Jase flicked the ball into Talis's lap. He brandished the naked blade. "You cost me time and energy." Talis cringed, but instead of hitting him, Jase cut halfway through the tape that bound the man's knees.

"You should be able to fight your way out of that. Keep the ball. I'm done playing and I'm going home."

Outside, a few bold crickets had begun their chorus, but Talis's screams drowned them out. Jase could still hear him as he revved the engine of the Mustang. Then some old Stones on the radio blocked it all out.

He was thirsty, and headed for the Rhode House. With any luck, the woman would be there, and he'd satisfy his hunger, too.

Chapter 9

Across town, Winter Wyman sat at his accustomed place at the Hammer and Tongs. The room was nearly empty, but he wanted to make sure any petitioner had an opportunity to bring him a morsel. There had been a short conversation with Chief Butler when he first arrived, but that had been merely a check-in, not anything approaching business. He'd wait for Jimmy Cooper's report before saying anything important. Wyman had been able to eat his spartan meal of boiled chicken and rice in peace.

As he contemplated whether he should order coffee for dessert, Sam burst through the door, then stood flushed and panting at the table.

"Well?" Wyman said, guessing he'd have to skip the coffee.

Sam tilted his head toward Bill Butler. Wyman caught the signal, and moved toward the curtained booth. Sam followed reluctantly.

"I don't like it in here," Sam said. "I always feel like I'm at confession."

"You've never seen the inside of a confessional," Wyman growled. "Now, what do you want?"

Sam took a pained breath before he spoke. "It's Jimmy," he said.

Wyman's face lit up. "What did he say? Did he make the buy? What the hell is Butler waiting for? He should be at her house right now." He fought the urge to rub his hands together. But it did feel good to have that shameless harlot in his sights.

Sam chewed his bottom lip.

"Well, spit it out," Wyman snapped.

"It's…it's Clay. You don't want Butler anywhere near the place."

Wyman's jaw went slack and his feet tingled. "What happened to Clay? Quick. Tell me."

Sam's head lolled as if he was about to faint. Wyman gripped his lapels. "Quit stalling. What happened to my son?" He shook Sam until the words fell out of his mouth.

"Nothing happened to Clay. You better come. Now."

Wyman saw that he wouldn't get another word out of Sam, not here. He pushed back the curtain and stalked out of the restaurant, not pausing to even throw his usual fifty on the table. They got enough of his business, anyhow. He ignored the curious gaze of Bill Butler, who was very interested indeed that the chief alderman appeared less than sublimely placid. Wyman ripped his Stetson off the rack by the door and plunged into the night. Sam ran ahead to open the door of the Lincoln he'd parked by the hydrant. A moment later the Lincoln swung in a huge arc towards Frick's Lane. Neither man said a word until Starr's house lit up in the glare of the headlights.

"The windows are dark," Wyman said. "Where is everyone?"

"Clay's in his room. Least he was when I left. I don't know where Sta…"

"You don't need to say her name. Where the hell was she? Did she hurt him?"

"You better go in and see for yourself."

They pulled to a stop, but Wint was already opening the door, forcing himself not to shout out his beloved son's name. Instead, he checked his speed, kept his strides even. No one would see him angry.

The front door yawned open. Wyman was dimly aware that Sam, every inch the craven servant, hung back, but he himself stepped into the house without hesitation. Once inside, he let his voice ring out. "Clay? Where are you, son? It's your Poppa. Clay!"

Furniture shifted upstairs. Wyman climbed into the darkness. He stood at his son's door, listening. He expected to hear that obscene filth *she* let him watch, *encouraged* him to watch, against the poor boy's better nature, but the television was silent. "Clay? You in there, boy?" He turned the knob and pushed, but the door held fast. Not locked, maybe the weight of the dresser against it. He banged again. "Clay, let me in. It's Poppa. What's the matter? What did she do to you?"

Sam had gathered the courage to enter the house and was moving around on the first floor. Wyman heard the click of a switch. "Turn it out, you idiot," he hissed. He turned back to the door. "Clay, I'll be back. Don't worry, everything is going to be fine, son. Whatever it is, I'll make sure she gets what she deserves."

But it bothered him that she hadn't started hectoring him in her usual fashion. She never missed an opportunity to tell him how unwelcome he was to check on his own son. But now the house stood dead silent. Why wouldn't Clay answer him? What had she done?

He turned back to the stairs, placing his feet carefully. He stood uncertainly in the hallway.

"In here," Sam said from the kitchen. Wyman walked down the hall, the smell of gumbo mixing with…what? Something metallic.

The kitchen was spotless, and the sting of bleach clung to the air. Dishes dried in a rack, and the pot of gumbo stood covered on the stove. If she were here, he'd ask her for some of that licorice tea, but the unnatural stillness was like a mouthful of dust that no tea could wash away.

"Downstairs," Sam said, opening the basement door with his elbow. He turned on the light with the knuckle of his pinkie, and Wyman tried to peer past him into the cellar, but it was too dark. The two started down the old wooden steps. Sam avoided leaving his prints on even the railing, but Wyman knew the only danger was too many splinters. He came here often enough to inspect her work that his prints could be anywhere. Their footsteps echoed against the cold dirt floor.

The jagged rock walls of the foundation sucked up the light of the bare bulb. Cobwebs hung thick from the rafters and heating ducts. That same metallic stench mixed with the dank mold, stinging his nostrils. They scanned the area, finding nothing.

"In the corner," Sam said quietly. "Near the furnace."

Wyman forced his leaden legs to move. His head was pounding. Then he saw the filthy shoes poking out of the gloom. He braved another step and peeked behind the furnace. Above the shoes, as he expected, were the twisted limbs of the former Jimmy Cooper. His limbs sagged where they shouldn't have, like the rotted gutter on an abandoned house. The stench of blood—he couldn't pretend the metallic smell was anything else—made him gag. "What hast thou done?" he whispered. "The voice of thy brother's blood crieth unto me from the ground."

From far away, Sam was muttering something about what to do with the body. Should they dig right here?

Wyman shook himself awake. "Here? Are you serious? This floor hasn't been dug up in fifty years. You think even an imbecile like Butler wouldn't notice?" He turned back to the battered remains. The bitch was strong, but, Jesus! As his eyes adjusted, he saw more details. Jimmy's body was bent—no, folded—around the furnace, his face hidden. Wyman risked a glance and saw swollen purpled hands whose fingers stuck out at odd angles. Jimmy had been dumped like a broken doll, forgotten and unmourned.

"He musta scared St…her away," Sam breathed.

"What's that?" Wyman said, glancing up in annoyance.

"Clay. Whatever got him so angry must've scared the shit out of her. But why didn't she come to you?"

He pointed at the mess behind the furnace. "You think Clay did this? My son? Do you really think my flesh and blood would be capable of such perversity?"

Sam shrunk back from his fury, but he didn't shy away from the truth. It's what he got paid for, even if it came with a ration of ridicule. "She's a big girl, Wint. But there's no way she played this number. Not on Jimmy."

"He was a strung-out scumbag," Wyman argued. But only half-heartedly.

"Still bigger than her."

"You don't know her like I do," Wyman said, crouching near the body. "Right now, it doesn't matter."

"So what do we do?" Sam asked. "We can't leave him here. Where are we gonna bury him?"

It was rare for Winter Wyman to be stumped, but for once he had trouble focusing. "First thing," he managed to say, "we get Clay safe. I'll go try to talk to him. Stay here."

"With him?" He pointed to the stiffening body.

"He won't rise up and slay you, you coward. But if you want, sit in the kitchen. Just don't turn on any damned lights."

They climbed back upstairs, heels echoing against the steps like drums. Sam groped his way to a chair at the kitchen table, while Wyman continued on up to Clay's door. He tapped lightly and said, "Clay, why don't you open up? Tell me why she slew your old friend. You know I'm not mad, not at you. Clay, open up."

He waited five, ten, twenty minutes. He thought he heard his son's mattress squeak, but no matter what he said, he couldn't coax him to open the door, and no matter how hard he pushed, he couldn't force his way in. Reluctantly, he joined Sam downstairs.

"Well?" Sam asked.

"I don't know." Wyman gave in and cracked the refrigerator open enough to find the pitcher of licorice tea. He found a glass in the drainer and filled it.

"You think that stuff is safe?" Sam asked.

"She makes it specially for me," Wyman replied.

"You ever wonder why someone like her would make a drink that you enjoyed so much? I don't think it's out of the kindness of her heart."

"Even a witch has a soft spot, Sam."

Sam slumped in his chair. "If you say, so. But I wouldn't trust it. Probably some hoodoo potion."

Wyman shook his head. He put the pitcher away, not bothering to offer any to Sam. He sat at the table and looked at his watch. Nearly midnight. Where had she gone? If she'd fled, he might never find her, and good riddance. but then he'd need to make new arrangements for Clay, and he couldn't imagine what they might be.

The cold tea went down smoothly. He hadn't realized how dry he'd been. The sweet anise-like bite revived him, and he found himself thinking more clearly. He stood abruptly and turned on the light.

"What are you doing?" Sam said, surprised. "I thought you said not to."

"Who's up this time of night? Look around, see if you can find any clue where she went."

Nothing seemed amiss in the kitchen. The pot of gumbo still sat on the stove, cold to the touch. He found nothing else on the first floor, nothing but her ridiculous array of so-called medicines and herbal remedies. He moved upstairs, resisting the temptation to try Clay again. He walked boldly into her bedroom and switched on the light.

He was struck by the familiarity. He recognized the striped wallpaper, decades out of date. The bed was neatly made, with a couple of skirts laid out on it, and two or three blouses and sweaters, as if she had casually dressed before she ran. The top of her dresser was bare except for a framed picture, face down, and a jewelry box that held only a few rings and bracelets. Nothing seemed to be missing. The clothes left in the closet hung primly. He pushed them aside, and was almost disappointed to find an old blue plastic suitcase. He grimaced. She must have fled, but where were the signs of panic? And after all that blood.

Of course. She had to have washed it off herself, but there'd always be a drop to be found. He rushed to the second floor bathroom, exultant over what he would surely discover clinging to the faucet and bowl.

Nothing.

Fear gnawed at his gut. He emptied the wastebasket, but still found no hint of blood. He pounded downstairs, flooding the place with light, overturning chairs and buckets of dried stems. Sam cowered against the stove, watching Wyman's frantic search with a stunned expression.

Finally, Wyman found it. The one clue. The mop had left a small puddle on the first cellar step. So she had done some clean up. He scoured the kitchen again, and found one ruby drop on the edge of the counter. He also found the heavy stone mortar soaking in the sink under a thin skin of soap bubbles. Cold-blooded strumpet.

But if she'd been so careful to clean up, why had she left Jimmy to be found so easily?

Panic burned through his mind like a torch. He had to admit it. He raised his eyes to the ceiling. *Sin lieth at the door.*

"Sam, she didn't kill Jimmy. Something happened, but she didn't do it. She must be at the Rhode House. Go get her. I'll wait here."

Chapter 10

Starr lay next to Jase on the twisted sheets of the futon. One of her hands played with the corded necklace around her neck, the other stroked his lean chest. It was crazy, the way she'd fallen for him. When had she ever done something like that? As much as she hated that asshole Jimmy, he had been right about one thing: she hadn't enjoyed anyone's sexual favors in much too long. It was about time that she was making up for it.

The night had been a journey of one discovery after another. Jase had arrived at the Rhode House not long after she'd downed her second margarita. As usual, Terry poured it expertly, but in sullen silence. Starr recognized it as Terry chalking up another loss in their rivalry. Starr got the handsome stranger, and Terry was stuck behind the counter. When Jase walked in, Starr's body flushed, then immediately went cold. He was covered in dust, his shirt ripped along the top of his chest. Behind her, Terry let out a short whistle, though Starr couldn't tell if it was a warning or glee.

Despite the obvious bruises from whatever mishap he'd experienced, Jase swaggered to the bar, ordered a Maker's Mark, and winked at Starr. "Let's go," he said, knocking back the drink. Flashing a victorious smile at Terry, she followed. Minutes later, they were back at the Church in the Woods, and though Starr tried to assert herself, he took control like a man possessed. She gave in, not caring what he did, so long as it was with her.

The bell mechanism chimed a quarter to twelve. When it finished, Jase climbed off her and said, "What is this place anyhow?"

Her eyes played along the rafters and walls of this, her secret refuge. An old wooden structure, dark and warm, its beams were shaped by hand a century ago. The futon sat near the base of the winding staircase to the belfry. Wrought iron framework held the huge brass drum that ticked through its rounds like a giant's music box. One of its brass screws was about to strike the cable to sound the hour. Beyond the mechanism, the carillon keyboard waited patiently to be used once again.

"I first came here in ninth grade," she told him placidly. "Our music teacher took us on a field trip to see the carillon player's last performance. This tiny old lady who looked too frail to handle the batons."

"Batons?"

"Those big levers. They work like piano keys, except she played them with her fists. If you tried it now, they'd splinter. Anyhow, she played the noon chimes, then *Ode to Joy*. You'd never think a little old lady like that could muster up the strength to play the way she did, but she looked like a demon and never missed a note. She was actually sweating when it was over, and most of my classmates, I think, were put off by that. But I was mesmerized. She seemed to be in this state of sublime peace.

"She told us she'd been playing the carillon since she was seventeen. Over fifty years. Then, while we all watched, the workers came in and started setting up her electronic replacement. Her stool was still warm when one of the workers kicked it over to reach the guts beneath the keyboard."

"That's the way it is," Jase said. "Time marches on."

Starr fought to ignore his callousness. "The bells were silent three days while they worked. The town was never so quiet from the day it was founded. Then the automated system started. That's the day she hung herself. She tied bells to her hands and ankles so the last thing she heard was her own playing."

Jase shifted uncomfortably. He asked, "Who comes up here nowadays?"

She understood the signal, so she pushed her memories back into their mental box. She edged close and gave him a Cheshire Cat smile. "No one. We're completely alone."

"No one else ever?" He sat up, searching for his clothes. She sat back, instinctively drawing the sheet around herself.

"No one."

"Electricians? Bell tuners?" He was pulling on his briefs, then his pants.

"I'm telling you, it's only me."

"Good. I'll make this my base."

Starr shrugged, letting the sheet fall a bit. "You can't live here. There's no bathroom, no stove, just this bed. I like to take naps here in the afternoon. You're my first guest."

"All I need is a roof. I can always piss against a tree. I won't be in this backwater long." He tugged at the sheet for a better view of her and asked, "What keeps you from becoming that bell lady?"

She clasped her hands and stretched luxuriously. "Well, there's my garden. Plenty to do there all the time. And Clay, or course."

"What's important about clay?"

"It's a name. Clay. He got pretty messed up after the war. I take care of him. I suppose I'm more his keeper."

He sat next to her, but suddenly the distance between them seemed to be miles, not inches. "I'm sure you could find someone to take your place if you wanted to."

He said it tonelessly, as if he were making reluctant conversation. But it was as close to an invitation as anyone had ever given her, and she resolved to take it. No matter the cost. She decided to tell him so, but the words caught in her throat.

"What's the matter?" he asked, more annoyed than concerned.

"Nothing," she said. "I just feel like I'm losing bits of myself." *More like everything she'd ever known about herself.* She got up on her knees, looked him in the eye. "Now you."

"Me what?"

"All I know is your name. Tell me something. Where did you grow up? How did you end up chasing after stolen artwork? Are you a dog or a cat person?"

He leaned back from the barrage, then his face split into a grin. "For a second there I thought you were serious. The only dogs I ever met were guard dogs."

"Come on, I mean it. At least tell me where you grew up. What are your parents like?"

He regarded her with both fascination and dread, the way you might size up a hornet's nest you suddenly noticed in the corner of your bedroom window. When she raised her eyebrows expectantly, titling her head in a way that said she wouldn't be put off, he sighed.

"I didn't grow up anywhere. We moved a lot. My father died before I was born, and my mother couldn't hold a job to save her life."

"Was she nice to you?"

He stood up, ran his hands through his hair. "I don't even know what that means. She fed me, made sure I could take care of myself. When she thought I was old enough, she took me to the barracks outside whatever town we were squatting in at that time, and signed me up. I started training before I got my diploma."

"I bet you looked good in uniform."

He shrugged, and as if it reminded him, he swept his shirt off the floor and put it on. "I never had time to think about that."

She pressed on. "So if you didn't grow up in any particular place, what was your favorite?"

"Jesus, I don't know. One place looked pretty much like another. Some places were colder, other places dustier. But the people were all the same: dull, suspicious of strangers, judgmental. I hated every school I went to, got in a lot of fights. I guess I must've driven my mother about as crazy as she drove me.

"Where is she now?"

"My mother?"

Starr rolled her eyes, pulled the sheet up again. "Of course your mother. Do you call her every week, no matter where you are?"

He stood at the window, peering into the night. "Honestly, I have no idea where she is. When she signed me up, we were living in a motel. I went to visit her when I got leave, and she'd been gone, checked out the day I went in."

His frankness took the wind out of her sails. She wanted to go up to him, to show him the tenderness she felt, but his voice had gone cold, worse than the bored tone he'd tried on her earlier. She decided she knew enough, at least for now. It was time to turn to business.

"You didn't tell me what happened with Spyro Talis. He didn't have the ivory?"

Jase didn't seem fazed by the sudden topic switch, except his voice become a notch lighter. "No, but I didn't expect he would. He gave me some intel, though. I might need your help."

"Sure," she said. The moment was over, so she started reaching for her clothes. She hoped she sounded as uninterested as he did. "What do you need?"

"Maybe an introduction, if you can swing it."

She had pulled on her underwear, and picked up her skirt. "Who to?"

His answer caught her breath and she slumped back to the bed, tangled in her skirt. *Fool,* she told herself. *Is that worth the price, to help a man you don't know, except carnally?* A couple of drinks and some pillow talk. Was that enough to start a new life on? Maybe Clay had it right, whacking off in his bedroom like a teenager. "Say that again?" she stuttered.

"I'm looking for Winter Wyman," he said causally. But his eyes bored into hers. "Know him?"

"Of course I do," she said. A sudden chill gave her goosebumps. She stood up to hide her reaction, turning from his gaze and putting on her bra. "He's one of the most important men in town."

"What, like the mayor?" he said, reaching around her from behind.

She twisted in his grasp, unsure of how to counter his gambit. "Sort of. Alderman, actually."

"I hear he follows some non-governmental business as well." His voice was muffled against the back of her neck. His tongue flicked like a snake's.

"More than you know." She stroked his hand absently.

"Like what?"

"Well, for starters," she said, "He's my father."

Chapter 11

Wyman stood alone in Starr's kitchen, frozen between two hellish scenes. Upstairs, his son was most likely engaged in onanism, the only thing his once-perfect body knew how to do anymore. Downstairs, a ravaged corpse was stiffening behind the furnace. All around him hung the stench of pagan offerings like brimstone and sulfur. And he could be rid of none of them.

Disgusted by Clay's self-abuse, and sickened by the humid, musty air, he chose to return to the basement. The dead can defile your touch, but they can't hurt you.

Everything was as he'd left it, of course. The cloying scent of blood permeated the air, but it was nothing compared to what *she* lived with upstairs. Careful not to contaminate his hands, he examined the corpse of Jimmy Cooper.

The body was crumpled in the corner, forced into the narrow space behind the furnace. His legs were broken in multiple places, as if he had extra knees. His mangled arms still shielded his face. As far as Wyman could tell, every finger had been broken. Reluctantly, Wyman aimed the light at what was left of Jimmy's head. Congealing blood clots stuck to the lumpy skull like glaze on a ham. It took him a while, moving the flashlight in many angles, to figure out which side his face was even on. When he found it, Wyman realized that the nose had been bashed in until it was flush with his shattered cheeks, overshadowed by the swelling of his eyes.

Wyman muttered to the body, "Thy bruise is incurable, and thy wound is grievous…thy lovers…seek thee not."

He hoped it was true. Had Jimmy told anyone about his errand? Would anyone know to come looking here? Best thing to do would be to put the body in the car and drive it away to…where? Not any of the usual places. The risk of tracing Jimmy Cooper back to Clay was too great. And if that happened, no bribe would be large enough to keep Bill Butler from taking them all in.

It was past one in the morning when Sam returned, reluctantly descending into the basement. His hesitant steps echoed off the stone walls. Wyman backed away from the body, looking expectantly up into the shadows. Hearing only one set of footsteps set his heart pounding.

"Where is she?" he demanded, before Sam's face came into the dim light.

Sam looked stricken. "I went to the Rhode House. Her car was there, but no one inside had seen her, not in a couple of hours."

"Well, who did see her?"

"That bar lady, whassername."

"I have no idea." *Terry. Her name is Terry. Ed Thompson's girl. He knew more about that girl than Sam would ever suspect.* "When have you known me to set foot in that foul den?"

"Well, never, Wint. But I thought you knew…"

Wyman shook his head miserably. "Never mind. What did you find out?"

Sam stole a glance at the feet sticking out from behind the furnace. He licked the bead of sweat that formed on his upper lip. "Well, she was talkin' to that Mac Fletcher a couple nights ago."

"The pansy who thinks he's Sinatra. She wouldn't rut with him. It's against her organic way of life."

Sam nodded. "When he left, some other guy moved in on her."

"Who?"

"The bar lady said he was a stranger. Good looking. Maybe he was the guy in the Mustang?"

Wyman scowled. "Probably was. Did you go looking for it?"

"Yeah. I asked around, but nobody remembered hardly anything. So I took a drive around town. Went up past the motel but…"

Wyman clenched his fists. "You didn't ask for her by name there, did you?"

Sam shrank into the gloom. "Of course not, Wint. I just drove by. Nothin' but a couple of old sedans in the lot. I doubt she'd have gone off in one of them."

"So where is she?" Wyman barked. Sam shrugged.

Wyman stalked around the room as if he might find her there. He said, "We can't wait for her. Let's get him upstairs."

"What for?"

"What do you think?" Wyman shouted. "We'll put him in his car, park it, and burn it."

Sam shook his head. "That ain't no good," he said. "One of us will have to drive the Lincoln, and we're sure to be seen even this time of night. Some old biddy is always lookin' out the window."

"So we'll arrange to meet somewhere. How about the rest stop halfway up to Havilah?"

Sam's shoulders fell in resignation. "Sure, I guess."

"That's the spirit. Drag him out from there, and I'll find something to wrap him in."

Sam tugged at the body, but it had stiffened to the point that it was wedged firmly behind the furnace. "I'll pull on his legs," Wyman said, giving up on his own search. "You push."

Sam paled, but Wyman slapped him in the face. "It's just a piece of meat," Wyman said. "Think of it like that, and you'll be fine." *But later, I'll need to purify myself for touching a corpse. An offering at the altar.*

"Don't think I'll eat a steak again," Sam groaned, but he took his position.

"Tell me when you're ready," Wyman said, crouching to get a grip on Jimmy's worn-out sneakers.

"Lookin' for a place to get a hold," Sam wailed.

They were both pushing and pulling like lumberjacks. But Jimmy, in a last act of defiance, refused to budge. "I think I broke something," Sam said, panting.

"You or him?" Wyman said.

Sam whined, " 'It,' Wint. Say 'it.' "

Wyman wrapped both hands around one ankle and said, "Fine. You or *it*?"

"I think I broke its collarbone."

Wyman dropped the ankle, but it didn't move. "Enough. We'll need to find another way."

Sam took a seat on the cellar stairs, wiping his hands on his pant legs. "If we wait long enough, it'll loosen up again."

"We can't wait. It'll be daylight soon." He checked his watch. "Already four o'clock. And on the Sabbath, no less." He looked around the basement and his eyes lighted on a toolbox. "What's in there?" he muttered. He lifted the metal lid. He found only a few rusty screwdrivers and a hammer. Still, it gave him an idea. "Find me a saw."

Sam sighed and rubbed his sharp elbows. "Do we really need to? I mean, that's desecrating a corpse."

"And burning it in a rest stop isn't? Hurry up."

Once again Wyman was left alone with the body. He glanced up through the window and gray light told of the approaching dawn. Where the hell was she? Just wait until he found out what she'd been doing instead of protecting his son from this vileness. "I will judge thee according to thy ways," he whispered, "and recompense upon thee all thine abominations." But first, regrettably, he needed her help. And he needed it now.

Sam's footsteps clattered down the stairs. He had a rip saw and a fold-up pruning saw. And Wyman was glad to see he'd thought to bring a muddy blue tarp as well. "Found them in her shed."

"Let's get to work," Wyman said grimly. "I'll take the pruner."

The space was too small for comfortable work, and as it turned out, the ripsaw was just too big for the close quarters. Wyman handed the pruner to Sam, who recoiled from it. "I'm an old man," Wyman said with a sneer. "How would you like it if I had a heart attack and fell dead right on top of Jimmy?"

Sam swallowed hard and edged in to take the legs off. The first few passes with the saw went fairly easily, but as he got deeper, the muscles grew tougher, and dark blood oozed out in thick globs. Wyman worked the tarp under the legs as best he could, and it caught most of the spillage. Sam closed his eyes when the saw teeth bit into the bone, and even Wyman muttered verses to himself to drown out the sound. When the leg came loose, Sam passed it to Wyman, who put it on a corner of the tarp. But there was still the second leg.

This time, the gouts of blood were darker and heavier. Everything had flowed to the lower parts of the body. "Please don't say I have to do the arms, too," Sam begged.

"Enough with the simpering. It's nothing but blood and bone," Wyman said. "Besides, once the legs are off, we should be able to move the torso." Sam gulped, cringed when a gelatinous red mass landed on his shoes, and bent back to work.

When both legs were off, Wyman stood near Jimmy's head. "You take the other end," he said. "Try not to tip it, and we'll put the whole mess on the tarp. After that, we can get it upstairs somehow."

Sam groaned. Wyman snapped, "I pay you plenty, friend. Now earn it. Remember, 'Keep my judgments, and do them; and ye shall dwell therein in safety.' " But he felt the tension of the task as well, and wiped his forehead with his sleeve.

Then a voice echoed from the top of the stairs. "What the fuck are you up to in my basement, old man?"

Chapter 12

Starr left Jase in the bell tower. Already it seemed to be more his space than hers, and for a moment she understood how the old carillon player had felt when she had been displaced. She turned for one last look at the bell tower and Jase in the growing light of dawn, then made her way home. For the second day in a row, her car was waiting back at the Rhode House. So she hiked the familiar paths through the woods. This time, she stopped to cut the chicken of the woods off the oak tree. All she had was the two-inch blade on the jackknife attached to her keys, so it took more work than if she had been fully prepared, but anyhow, it left enough of the fungus on the tree that it would grow back later. She hefted the salvaged ripply thing, guessing it weighed about five pounds. Plenty to eat over a few days. It occurred to her that the only way to get such a tasty treat was to have a rotting tree. So much in nature worked the same way.

When she emerged from the trees with the chicken under her arm, she passed the compost dump that marked the far corner of her property. It swarmed with black flies, but she never noticed them anymore. Her house loomed over the garden. The porch railings resembled the bars of a jail cell; she'd be locked in once she crossed the garden. She feared her dreams of escape would evaporate when she started cleaning up after Clay's night, so she lingered, picking mint for her morning tea. Everything was still.

She noted with some worry that Jimmy's car was still parked out front. He must be sleeping off a hell of a headache, she thought. But as she climbed the back steps, Starr heard voices, and they weren't friendly. She put the mint and mushrooms on the counter, then looked into the dark cellar. Wyman stood with his back to her, dragging his sleeve across his face. Another step down revealed the edge of her blue tarp with something like a log in it.

Then she saw the blood. Her bowels turned to water and she fought to keep from soiling herself. Her mind reeled with panicked thoughts, one cascading over the other. When she saw that look on Clay's face, she thought he would bat Jimmy around a bit, just some brotherly protectiveness. She never imagined anything this serious. Then to make matters worse, Wyman had to show up and stir more shit into the pot. Somehow that reminded her Jase had asked Starr to make introductions. As if she could bring that up now. "And by the way," she'd tell him. "This guy showed up and wants something he thinks you stole. Wanna meet him?" That would go over well. Then again, maybe, finally, Wyman would get what was coming to him.

This last idea steeled her soul, and with more confidence in her voice than she felt, she shouted, "What the fuck are you up to in my basement, old man?"

Sam muttered, "Aw, shit," and leaned against the wall. His face was splattered with dark grime, and both men looked like they'd been working in a slag pit.

She said again, "What the fuck are you doing? You're filthy."

He stood crookedly. His doleful eyes seemed to perch ready to fall from his deeply lined face. But despite his obvious exhaustion, none of Wyman's ferocity had leeched away. "Look to yourself. You stink of whoredom: 'For though thou wash thee with nitre, and take thee much soap, yet thine iniquity is marked before me.' "

Starr looked at the jumbled body parts scattered on the blue tarp. "Quoting scripture at me? You nasty hypocrite, you killed Jimmy Cooper. Talk about a fucking beam in your eye."

Wyman ran a fouled hand through his hair, leaving clots of brown and black like berries in bramble. His voice took on a matter-of-fact tone. "Still, I'm going to need your help. You'll have to clean up after us."

She rolled her eyes. "The least you could do is ask how your daughter is. Look at me, I might've been hurt."

"No daughter of mine," Wyman growled. "Putrid filth is more like it."

She stalked toward him, her finger lancing the space between them. "Well, this piece of filth is the only one who can help you. So what'll it be?"

His face twitching, Wyman waved a hand over the dismembered corpse.

She stood over the remains, shaking her head. "He was an asshole, no doubt, but you didn't have to kill him."

Sam found his voice. "Wasn't us," he said. "Like you said, you look terrible. It coulda been you done it."

"Watch it, Sam," she said. "Just because you're his flunky doesn't mean you can talk to me like he does. Last I saw Jimmy, he was fine, though he tried to fuck me." She turned to Wyman. "For your information, old man, I kept my honor."

Wyman chewed his lip but said nothing. Starr filled the silence. "What's done is done. I'm not even going to ask how you came to be in my cellar if you didn't do it, but I have a pretty good idea. I'm guessing you sent old Jim here to do me wrong, and when he didn't report back, you came looking for him. Well, what's your next move? You can't just hide this mess."

"Wint says we're gonna burn him in the rest stop."

Starr laughed. "That's a fine fucking idea. Half the town is awake by now."

"I know," Wyman said, shaking his head. "But I think you and your pagan magic can do something about it."

Starr raised her eyebrow. "Magic? There's nothing particularly magical about gardening. Despite what you'd say, it's the oldest profession: The Bible says that God created man to till the earth." Before he could respond, she added, "Yeah, that's me, the Whore of Babylon quoting scripture for my own purposes."

"Nevertheless, I need you to do it."

"Need? Well, well, well. What'll you do for me? If I just called Chief Butler, I'd be rid of your insults, and I'd be doing the town a good deed. I might even get a reward and blow this shithole."

"Do it for my son, you conniving witch."

"Who's that again?"

"Don't make me say it," Wyman said through gritted teeth. But she was going to have her way. Broken, he agreed and said, "Do it for your brother."

Starr smiled. "Why not? I've cleaned up more of his little accidents than you can imagine. But there'll be a price, and I'll make sure you pay it."

His shoulders slumped. "Just tell us what to do," Wyman said, his voice as broken as his spirit.

She knelt down next to the body, careful not to touch it. The stink of blood and shit washed over her. *How different from the way she'd spent the night.* "Ok, let me think." She tried to imagine the mangled body as nothing more than bone-in meat. She gauged the size of his limbs, estimated what was beneath his rib cage. It was a lot of flesh, for sure. Still, she could figure only one way of getting rid of it.

She stood up, ready to give orders. "Ok. You'll need to break him down into smaller parts. Take off the head, the feet, the hands, and cut the limbs at least in half, smaller if you can. Nothing more than a foot or so long. There's not much to be done with the chest. Strip off the clothes and burn them."

"You'll do that," Wyman told Sam. But Starr shook her head.

"Sam needs to go to the lumber yard," she said. "They'd ask too many questions if you went."

"What's at the lumber yard?" Sam asked.

"Sawdust. As much as they have. Barrels of it, if you can. Even on a Sunday, they should be open by the time you get there."

"What for?"

"Just get it. I'll change into my gardening clothes."

"Now's not the time…" Wyman started, but Starr held up her hands.

"I've got more to do than just help you with this," she said. "I'm not wasting any time. Sam will need to take care of the car, too. So everyone get to work. I'll be ready for the next step in less than an hour. Go!"

The men jumped into action, and Starr was pleased to watch the old man screw up his courage just to slide the pant legs off the severed limbs. She wished she could stay to watch him do the rest, but she did have her own chores to attend to. She went upstairs, noting that she'd have to clean up her muddy footprints later as well. She'd need to get rid of the bloodied mop, and do a more careful cleaning of the kitchen.

In her bedroom, she stripped off her jeans and sweater and looked at herself in the full-length mirror. A twig was caught in her untidy black curls, and her breasts had ugly bruises, especially around her nipples, where Jase had bit and pawed her. Her legs were scratched and bleeding, her feet muddy black. Despite the horror of the moment, she felt a thrill to remember how she'd gotten in such a state. But now she had work to do. She dressed in worn overalls, covered her hair with a kerchief. Outside, she stepped into rubber boots.

Starr kept the larger tools in the shed. She found the lock broken, and figuring that Sam had done it looking for tools, she made a mental note to have him fix it. She selected an iron rake, a pitchfork, and a shovel. She trudged to the back of the garden, where she had stood in peace just a few minutes before.

Three compost bins stood in a row, built from fenceposts and rails. The first, piled almost to the top of the four-foot fence, had her most recent garden clippings, still a vibrant green. A lower pile was cooking in the next bin. Instead of green, these sticks and cuttings were a dead brown, but still mostly whole. In the last bin, dirt-like compost was almost ready to use. The bins were small for the purpose, but they'd have to do. She judged that if the pieces were sized right, they'd fit in a single layer near the center, hopefully deep enough not to attract animals. She had a decent amount of clippings and waste, and the sawdust, if Sam did his job, would cover it. And if all else failed, she'd collect more greens from the woods to get "the fire" going.

She leaned the tools against the second bin, and lifted the boards from the front of the first. With the pitchfork, she emptied it all onto the ground at her feet. The deeper she got, the less recognizable the decomposing elements became. All the better. The damp musty aroma cleansed her sense of smell, and she breathed deeply to take it in.

Figures it would be Jimmy Cooper who caused all the trouble. Even growing up, he'd always been the one to lead the charge into one scrape or another. Pulling pranks on substitute teachers in elementary school, lighting fires in trash cans in middle school. Once they got to high school, Jimmy had found a connection that could get weed and pills from Havilah students. He was a master at pulling the "Hey, mister" scheme outside of the packie.

Starr separated the compost into piles of "brown and crunchy" and green stuff that added nitrogen, so it could go back relatively intact. She knew she'd never get it all back in without leaving some evidence on the ground. All the dirt never fit back in the hole, either. But she trusted that no one else but a gardener would notice the difference.

But Jimmy had his good side, too. No one shoveled more neighbor's walks and driveways come winter, and when he had a stash of anything, he was insistent on sharing it. Jimmy was the one who started inviting Clay to parties, who truly showed an interest in bringing the boy out of his shell. When the other kids thought Clay was a silent troll, Jimmy got him to laugh and even take part in some of their less transgressive hijinks. But then again, it was Jimmy, for once reading an assignment in English class, got the idea from a poem that Clay would be the perfect star in a game he called "Balder Dead." On balance, she thought, Jimmy had probably gotten exactly what he deserved.

The bell tower had chimed the hour twice before she got the pile cleared out to below ground level, she switched to the iron rake. Stones had forced their way up from the depths, and she pushed them aside. At last, she picked up the shovel and dug yet another pit and dumped the stones in with a clatter. She went inside to see what Wyman had accomplished.

The basement stank. She'd need some serious fumigation down here. Burning sage wouldn't be enough. But the old man had indeed got a lot done. The tattered clothes were in a pile on one corner of the tarp, and Jimmy's naked remains were hardly recognizable as human.

In a fit of bizarre organization, Wyman had neatly lined up the feet and hands on one side. Next were pieces of limbs, each almost exactly a foot long. The head lay on its side, eyes thankfully averted.

That left only the torso, a bloody mass with ugly holes where everything had been attached. Sinews and veins stuck out like the wires of a shattered robot. Welts and giant bruises showed where most of the ribs had been broken.

"Are you sure this is going to work?" Wyman panted. "I don't need you ruining what I've built."

"That *you* built? Well, fine, if you want to play it that way. As for this, I can't promise anything, but it's the best I can think of. Just remember who saved your sorry ass. Again. Not that you'll care once the crisis is over. But there will be a price. You can say Amen to that." She pointed to a clear spot on the floor. "Leave the clothes over there. Sam should be on his way, and I don't want any of my customers happening upon us while we're playing Sweeney Todd."

Mutely, Wyman did as he was told, and together they folded up the tarp. When it was secure, they made their way up the stairs, Starr walking backwards and bent down to level out the bloody package. Once, a piece of leg threatened to escape, and Wyman had to flap his elbow like a chicken to coax it back in place.

Outside, Wyman gratefully lowered his end, but Starr snapped, "Don't leave drag marks. Seriously, have you forgotten everything?" With a shuddering breath, he lifted his arms, and they shuffled around raised beds of tomatoes and peppers hanging like shrunken heads, and all manner of herbs that only Starr knew the use of.

"Ok, here," she said. They lowered the tarp to the ground, and Wyman waved his hands to dispel the black flies.

"Nothing good can come of them," he said. "They feed on offal and rot."

"They cause the rot," she countered. "And right now, they're your best friends. They like meat, and meat they're going to get."

Just then, Sam reversed the Lincoln onto the grass next to Jimmy's car. Inside the open trunk were two cardboard barrels. Starr shook her head. There was nothing she could do in sending him to get the barrels in the first place, but to parade them like that? Everyone would have seen it.

"I told them I had an oil spill in my garage," he said, trotting over to them. "They said it musta been a gusher to need so much."

"You did good, Sam," Starr said, swallowing her disdain. "Ok, you two, get the pieces in there. I'll bring over the barrels."

"Us men can carry them," Wyman said, his loathing for her losing out to his need to be the strong one. "You put the pieces in and Sam and me will bring the barrels."

But Starr folded her arms and stared him down. "I'll help, but I'm not lugging that body. Put the biggest piece in the middle, and the smaller parts around it. Leave space between everything, a couple inches if you can, and don't let anything get closer than nine inches from the edge." Her tone left no room for an argument.

"How do we tell nine inches without a ruler?" Sam whined.

Wyman held up his hand, with his thumb and pinky stretched out. "This is a span, like in the Bible. Like a cubit is from your finger tip to your elbow."

"Oh. I always wondered. What's a bushel?"

But Wyman ignored him. Together they placed the torso in the middle as Starr had said, and she shifted the barrels out of the trunk, rolling first one then the other to the bins. By the time she'd finished, what was left of Jimmy Cooper was arranged in an obscene starburst. At least they'd had the decency to put his head face down. Lying there by itself, it looked the size and shape of the chicken she'd harvested that morning. She thought that now she might have to throw the fungus away.

"Now what?" Wyman said.

"Now I cover it with all this sawdust. You two gather green leaves and mold from the woods. That'll get the bacteria eating fast. Everything should be gone by Thanksgiving. The bones will take longer."

"How much longer?" Sam said.

"Don't know," she answered. "But they'll be under enough mulch that, with any luck, no one will ever find them."

"I can't depend on luck," Wyman said, his voice gaining its old confidence.

"You're going to have to," she answered. She added sweetly, "Just think of me as your lucky Starr." Then she shoveled a thick layer of sawdust into the bin, and put down wet greens to hide the edges. "When you're done, get yourself some of that licorice tea you like so much."

She piled on clippings, then kitchen waste, more sawdust, and so on. The leaves and mold Wyman and Sam brought back from the woods made it all look as though it hadn't been disturbed in weeks.

Chapter 13

J ase found it a relief when the woman finally left him in peace. He didn't mind her being so willing in bed, but her incessant questions made it clear that all she wanted out of him was a ride out of town. Where did she think he would take her?

He unloaded his gear and set it up in the bell tower. The stories she'd coaxed out of him, though not quite the truth, rattled him anyhow. He wasn't used to looking back on the days when his mother had dragged him from one crappy job to another, always blaming her failure on a boss who had grabby hands, or a jealous co-worker who thought she was a climber. How many times did he come home from school only to find the station wagon loaded up, his mother swearing about getting screwed over by an ungrateful boss?

He wondered if he could disable the bell mechanism, but decided against it. The sudden quiet would be like an alarm itself, like that old Sherlock Holmes story about the dogs that didn't bark. Someone would come and investigate, and while his location wasn't exactly impregnable, the longer he went undetected, the better.

He needed a way to announce himself. Something that would nail Wyman's attention. He imagined Talis would have freed himself by now. Would he have delivered the message? The woman told him the best time to introduce himself to Wyman. How would that go? If he didn't have the right sort of build-up, he wouldn't be able to bring Wyman down as he'd been instructed.

He flung the sweaty sheets off the futon and sat down with his laptop. Turning on the wi-fi hotspot, he reviewed the files. So far, everything had gone exactly as planned. He could get the panel any time he wanted, but that was only part the job, and the rest required more leg work.

Using the bell tower as a base of operations, Jase planned to spend the next few days doing recon around town, making a few side trips back to Havilah and beyond. The job turned out to be bigger than he'd been led to believe, but then, the rewards were worth the efforts. If he pulled it off, he wouldn't have to worry about landing another gig for a long time. Maybe never. And the woman was a nice perk, too, while it lasted.

He discovered that the crowd at the Rhode House was only slightly smaller than on weekends. Not much to do in Cuthbert, Jase noted, except to get drunk or stoned. He didn't recognize the song on the jukebox, but it had a grinding garage sound that he liked. The surly bar lady gave him his Maker's Mark. He winked at her, but she turned away. He'd missed his chance, so instead he raised his glass to her back.

He turned to face the room, leaning his elbows on the bar, and surveyed the crowd. He was already starting to recognize faces. There was the Sinatra wannabe chemist, the old couple in the corner, the bikers. A neon-ringed clock said it was a quarter to nine. His ears filtered random bits of conversation. The bikers debated tire size. A trio of girls giggled and lamented over their boyfriends. A knot of men and women squeezed around a table built for two. They looked to be professional types, leaning in to examine a laptop while one of them pointed to the screen. They could have chosen a more conducive space for a meeting, so why gather here? Jase let his eyes wander, but he kept his ears on their table.

The one pointing to the screen was clearly the leader. He was going on about a survey, ordinances, contributions. When Jase heard him mention "public nuisance" and "foolish traditions," he snapped his eyes back to them, stealth be damned. They must have been talking about the bell tower. He remembered the woman talking about a faction who wanted it shut down. This must be the crew.

The man giving the presentation grew heated as he spoke. "Most of the people living in Cuthbert are too young to know this is a tradition older than the town. If they don't know or care, what's to stop us from changing it?"

A woman with a pursed mouth and sensibly short hair added, "It should be cinch to gather signatures. All you have to do is hang out here for a while, and at the market. Target the younger folks, the ones who'll be as annoyed as we are."

"And the new arrivals, like the adjunct professors from Havilah College," a second woman chimed in. "I bet they hate those damned bells."

"Except the Poe scholars, I suppose," said a man with a goatee who might have been a Poe scholar himself.

"I'll take care of the college faculty," the leader said. "I know a fair few of them."

"What about opposition?" asked the first woman.

The leader looked up from his laptop. "Besides Mr. Tradition himself?" He shrugged. "A bunch of old-timers. You know, the crowd that's been here for generations, blah, blah, blah. I'm sure someone's great uncle thrice-removed built the damn thing, but time marches on. Am I right?"

Thrice? They wouldn't get far talking like that, Jase thought. Meanwhile, they turned to writing a petition, arguing about whether to use the word "decibels" and deciding not to, in case the people they wanted to sign got confused about types of bells. Jase sniggered and concluded that he didn't have to worry about them. By the time they finished inching their way through town bureaucracy, he'd be long gone, his job done and the ivory panel back in its rightful place.

He turned around and ordered another shot. In the same breath, he added, "What's your name?" She couldn't pretend not to hear.

"Terry, not that it'll do you any good," she said. Still, she showed off, pouring the shot from a foot above the glass. "I don't mix with customers. You want conversation, talk to him. He'll gab your ear off." She pointed to the hipster who had sidled up next to Jase. "Don't tell me," Terry said. "A martini." She mixed it, tossed in the olive, and slid it to him.

"Terry, you're platinum, baby," he said. She gave him the finger. He turned to Jase instead, saying, "Hey, Charley, dig her clyde?"

Jase scowled at him. He remembered this Rat Packer doing some kind of deal with the woman the night he arrived. "You talk like that all the time, someone's going to take you 'round back."

"Hardboiled," the man said, appreciatively. His porkpie dipped up and down. "I only meant she's got a bad attitude. She always has, to be honest, especially since Patty…" He stopped short, glanced to see if she'd heard him utter what must be some taboo. He adjusted his hat and added, "But the dame pours 18-karat gasoline." He held out his hand. "Mac Fletcher."

"Jase."

"Just the one moniker? That's a gas." Jase rolled his eyes. "Ok, ok. I'll cool it. What's your bag?"

Jase took a gamble. "Acquisitions."

"High-roller! I get it. Me, you'll never guess. Go ahead, try."

Jase studied him for effect, then said, "I'll bet you're a black market chemist."

Mac actually stumbled, and clamped his hat on tight. "Whoa! You some kind of witch doctor?"

"A keen observer of the human condition," Jase murmured. "What's on tap now? I might like to invest in a scheme."

"Always looking to get some wampum," Mac said. "But no use talking here. Let's cash out." He threw back his drink. Jase left a bill on the bar, and followed his new friend to the parking lot.

In the dark, Jase wondered if he was on the right track, but didn't have a better move to make. Mac walked towards a Japanese compact he'd tricked out with too much chrome. "Fly with me, Charley, or follow?"

Jase pretended to consider, then said, "I'll follow." He revved the Mustang while Mac idled at the exit, blinker flashing dutifully. On the road, Jase had to stay in second gear to avoid grinding Mac's car into the pavement. For all his hipster prattle, he was an aggressively polite driver, keeping exactly a mile an hour below the limit, and signaling at least a hundred yards in advance of every turn. Jase found his blood pressure rising every time he had to deny himself the satisfaction of shifting into third.

Mac led him on a winding uphill course that cut through farmland and forest. They finished at a two-story house with gingerbread details that hadn't seen paint in many years. Jase doubted Mac ever closed the deal and brought a dame back here. He figured Mac to be the local crank: all talk, but harmless.

Having a visitor got Mac so nervous he forgot his own persona. "Hey, it occurred to me that, uh, you might not be all you say. How do I know you're not gonna bust me?"

"Is that why you drove like an old lady?" Jase drawled.

"No," Mac said too quickly. "Uh, maybe. Anyhow, ok, my, uh, lab is in the basement." He opened a bulkhead door and descended into the dark. "Watch your head. I don't have a light out here."

But Jase waited at the top of the steps until Mac had unlocked and unbarred the door and light spilled into the night. He followed into a bright room with warped plywood floors and amateurish plasterboard walls. Rows of fluorescent tubes and cords looping from fixture to fixture gave off an industrial glow. A freezer chest huddled against the far wall, by the stairs. Next to it was a glass-doored refrigerator with racks of Petri dishes. Counters ran along two walls. The first had a line of gooseneck desk lamps shining directly above plastic bowls filled with water. The second held three fish tanks, empty but for colored gravel. The last wall was dominated by a pair of locked metal cabinets.

In the center of the room, a stainless-steel workbench held a chunky-looking microscope, racks of test tubes, and instruments Jase couldn't identify. Dank mold fragranced everything, but beneath it, Jase sensed another, sharper scent he couldn't place.

"What do you do here?" he asked.

"Biohacking," Mac said.

"Doesn't sound like something The Chairman or Dino would approve of."

"You can't live entirely in the past," Mac said, his annoyance obvious. "What do you think I am, some kind of crank?"

Jase let the question hang in the air. "Why the spotlights?" he asked.

"Oh, you'll love this. It's going to make me a millionaire." He scooped a handful of gravel from the nearest tank and scattered it on the center table. He handed Jase a magnifying glass. "What do you see?"

Jase leaned over the counter. The blue gravel looked like boulders beneath the glass. Then, amid the pebbles, he found a smattering of pink balls. "Eggs?"

"Huzzah! My ticket out of this Endsville. I've got a backer, and it's all locked up."

Jase didn't see where this was going to help him. He'd expected a hydroponic pot farm, or a coca processing operation. The woman said he made bath salts, but he didn't see any signs of chemicals or plastic bags. Maybe in the cabinets. Jase needed something to use as leverage with Wyman. What good was homemade penicillin and fish eggs? "I don't get it," he said.

Mac looked like he'd burst, he was so excited to tell his story. "This is going to blow the dimmers right out of your head, baby! Those eggs will solve the food shortage. See, they're triops eggs. Get it? Like little shrimp. Except, you know, *better*."

"Forget it," Jase said. "I've had enough."

But Mac had a full head of steam, and while he talked he blocked the door. Not that Jase couldn't drop him without the least effort, but the hipster's passion checked him. "It's a hack, baby. Look, no water, right? Those eggs won't hatch until you add water. You can store them indefinitely, but if there's a famine, all you need is a pond and a day, and poof! Food! It's like a micro-garden, except it's meat. Can you imagine how much I could produce in a single warehouse? And almost no carbon footprint."

"It's just Sea Monkeys. Stop reading comic books, Mac. There's a real world out there."

Mac waved his arms crazily. "Sea Monkeys are just brine shrimp! See, regular triops are bigger, but still no good for eating. That's where the hack comes in. I've crossed them with a little of this, a little of that, and my triops are as big and meaty as jumbo shrimp, minus the deep-sea fishing. Look, look, look! These are normal triops."

He dragged Jase by the wrist to the row of spotlights. Each plastic bowl had clear water with bits of sand and brown stuff floating in them. When he looked closer, Jase saw something wriggling in each of them, nearly imperceptible flickers in some, others the size of fleas. In two bowls, though, a dozen critters the size of nickels nosed at the plastic. Their bifurcated tails stuck out from beneath carapaces shaped like shields. Periodically, they turned on each other in short, sudden battles that sent up bursts of dust in the water.

"Like a cross between cockroaches and horseshoe crabs," Jase said distastefully.

"Not bad. The Greeks called crossbreeds *chimaera*. Same thing. But over here is a full-grown Mac Fletcher special." In a tank all by itself, a creature half the size of a banana nudged at the bottom. Its carapace looked like the hood of an old car. It had two dark eyes like pinpricks.

"Are all those legs?"

"No, gills. They got just a few real legs closer in, see?"

Jase's lips curled in disgust. "Why is it called triops? It has only two eyes."

"No, no, it has a third eye, really. See that splotch on top? It's a light sensor, so, technically a third eye. Even so, the damn things are practically blind. Imagine if it really could see you?"

Yes, imagine. What would it see with a third eye?

"Ok, Mac, I'll admit I'm impressed. But it's no good. I was looking for something more… traditional. I wanted to dazzle an old man who thinks he can't be dazzled."

But Mac was taking a box out of one of the metal cabinets, along with a jug of water. He shook the water, saying, "Like mixing a cocktail, except it's only purified H_2O." He poured some into an empty bowl and checked the temperature. Satisfied, he took the lid off the box and shook the contents into the bowl. White sand cascaded into the water, and Mac swirled it with a metal spoon. Bits of dried leaves spun around the sand, and Jase thought he glimpsed some of the pink eggs.

"They hatch that quick?"

Mac shook his head. "I wish. It's like a day or two. But if the temp's right and they have enough food to start—that's the chunks in there—it's practically magic."

Jase knelt down to watch the whirlpool slowing down. "I saw you talking to that woman the other night. About this?"

Suddenly Mac lost his tongue. He pretended to busy himself by adjusting the microscope, though he had nothing under the lens. Jase stood up. "You said you'd have something for her soon. You meant some triops?"

"Woman? Oh, you mean Starr. Yeah, she wanted to taste a batch. She's good with the gardening, but comes to me for the meat, dig?" But his patter was more hollow than usual, and Jase wondered what Starr had done to cause such a reaction.

He clapped Mac on the shoulder, who didn't look too happy to be taken into Jase's confidence. "I'm starting to think you might come in handy, Mac. You have a pretty good handle on playing God here."

Mac ducked out from under the embrace. In response, Jase stood up to his full height, and gave his hardest look. Mac shrunk from him, reluctant to agree or disagree. After a beat he said, "Sure. You're the big-leaguer. Any idea of yours is sure to be a gas."

Jase smiled. He had the makings of one crazy way to announce himself. That prize was in his grasp.

Chapter 14

Winter Wyman sat at his desk, eying the man who stood across from him with brazen distaste. It didn't help that he himself still felt unclean from his recent encounter with Jimmy Cooper, though he had done all the requisite purification ceremonies after touching the corpse, and had still been able to take his customary pew at High Mass. It had been several days since they laid that ghost to rest, but now here came another miserable creature to take his place. Wyman wondered if perhaps he should clean house entirely and reorganize his employment rolls.

While Spyro Talis rambled on about some dude from the city invading his house and tying him up, Wyman played affectionately with the razor-sharp letter opener. Periodically, he glanced over at Sam, who stood in a corner by the door, pretending not to be surprised by Talis's ludicrous story.

"And so you let him wander all over your house like a wolf among the fold?" Wyman said when he found an opening.

"I didn't have no choice," Talis whined. "He come prepared, like he knew about the traps I set up to keep from getting my stash robbed."

"Well, it's not exactly *your* stash, is it?" He noticed the bits of tape adhesive that still clung to Talis's hair, and something pink clung to his teeth like moss. He tried to ignore the unclean junkie stench that emanated from him. "But that's neither here nor there. The important thing is that this stranger got the best of you, and that's bad business for me."

"He didn't find the stash though. Just wanted me to give you a message."

"A message for me? Why'd he go through you? I hear he's been hanging around the Rhode House lately. If he wants a word, he can come see me anytime." He leaned closer, though to be anywhere near Talis revolted him. "Or maybe there's something in it for you, too?"

Talis waved his hands frantically, as if to ward off a blow. "No, no. Nothing like that. He just wanted to make sure you got that package I give you a few weeks back. And of course I did. Wasn't any business of mine. I don't even know what was in it."

"No," Wyman said, fingering the letter opener's rapier point. "An honest gentleman like you would never deign to open a package that wasn't addressed to you. Not for a million dollars."

Talis simply stood, weathering the onslaught.

"You just do whatever you're told, a good citizen, right? Never get mixed up in anything dirty. Nothing except that poison you inject into yourself. Am I right?"

Talis still said nothing.

Wyman signaled Sam, who stepped forward and clamped his hand on Talis's arm and shoulder. He stood up, still holding the letter opener, and came around from the desk while Talis squirmed in terror.

"I very much appreciate your delivering the message, friend Spyro. But I say your usefulness in my ventures has come to an end. I have an appointment in a few minutes. Let's head downstairs and discuss your retirement options, shall we?"

He opened the corner door, the one that led to the back hall, and led the two men down the waiting stairs.

After being let in the house by that panting, creepy assistant of Mr. Wyman's, Stephen Hutchins sat on the edge of the leather sofa, afraid to put even a dimple in the cushion. He wiped his hands on his thighs. The air was heavy with the smell of leather and sandalwood, though underneath it was something acrid, like urine. What the hell had his grandmother been thinking, asking Wint Wyman to get him a job? He felt damp patches growing under his arms, and hoped they didn't show.

His gaze darted around the room like those iridescent green flies. Everything in here said "Power." All that dark wood paneling and heavy brass fixtures, those crystal tumblers and bottles: Stephen bet they held scotch older than Moses. He pictured men sitting here with watch chains hung across their vests smoking cigars, making deals that would change the course of history. Usually, such men made decisions about boys his age. Those decisions were never good.

At least his grandmother had told Wyman he wanted to work at the bank. She was very clear about that, she'd told Stephen. Still, he couldn't help yelling at her when she'd come into his room, all smiles. He was laying on his bed Saturday morning, watching football videos, and as usual she just opened the door. He could have been doing anything, but the old lady knew nothing about privacy or boundaries. He put the tablet down and stared when she made her announcement.

Didn't she know what everyone in town knew? Didn't she know where all the drugs in town came from?

She crossed her arms, and he had to admit that, standing in his doorway, she was every bit as imposing as a linebacker. "He's an alderman, dear, not a drug dealer."

"Gramma, he's the biggest drug lord around."

She shook her head. "No, that's Spyro Talis. He's the one that got his hooks into your parents."

Old lady or linebacker didn't matter anymore. Stephen clenched his fists. "Don't mention them."

The old lady smell wafted off her like smoke. Stephen leaned back as she said sternly, "Then don't talk like that about the finest man in town. He's the one that stands between devils like Talis and decent folk. It's a shame that Mr. Wyman couldn't save your parents, but they made their own decisions."

"Don't talk about them like that," he growled with simmering hatred. "It wasn't a choice. They were set up."

His grandmother sighed. "Of course, Mr. Wyman does bend rules once in a while. All great men do. But without him, we'd be back in the old days, when folks had to lock their doors at night. Besides, you're not going to work for him. He's putting a word in for you at the bank, nothing more. Now put that foolish screen away and get yourself cleaned up. I washed your best shirt. Dress up like a gentleman and get over there. He wants to meet you today." Her attitude left room for no argument.

And so here he was, dressed in a too-big suit with a too-short tie, his shoes so stiff they gave him cramps. Had Wyman—Mr. Wyman—forgotten him? Vague noises emanated from somewhere deep in the house. The muffled voices reminded him of the anxiety of kneeling in the confessional while Fr. Vitalis counseled some other sinner. Come to think of it, the air, too, had the same heavy feeling, threatening to stifle him behind a velvet curtain.

And then, just like the confessional screen sliding at St. Tryphon's, a door opened behind him, and Stephen leaped to his feet.

Winter Wyman himself entered. Stephen had never been this close to him, though of course he'd often seen him around town. The man appeared to float over the carpet. His skin had the waxy pallor that Stephen had noticed at his grandfather's wake. Papa had looked almost fake, but Winter Wyman was certainly real. He flashed a smile that, despite Stephen's fear, seemed genuine, and he stuck out his hand.

Stephen's hand shot out, too, almost missing his target. Wyman's grip was cold and dry. He held Stephen's eye with his own icy blues.

"N…nice to meet you, Mr. Wyman," Stephen spat out.

Wyman's grin widened. "No, Stephen, it's nice to meet you. I told your grandmother I'd seen you play for Cuthbert. You did the town proud, son."

"Thank you, sir. I'm already missing those days."

Wyman slapped him on the back. It hurt like a blow. "I bet you are," Wyman laughed. "Have a seat. Can I get you something?"

Stephen's eyes darted to the bar, more out of curiosity than thirst. Wyman caught the glance, and without a word poured a measure into one of the crystal tumblers. Then he was pouring a second one, and there was nothing Stephen could do but accept it.

The glass was heavy, the pour more than generous. The peaty smell of the whiskey stung his eyes. "Go ahead," Wyman said, so he took a sip.

A searing heat flowed down his throat, and up into his sinuses. He couldn't help coughing, but Wyman was saying, "The best thing is to wash that sip down with another. Don't tell me a buck like you never had a snort."

Stephen steadied himself, and took a smaller, slower sip. Wyman was right, and as it trickled down the back of his tongue, it almost evaporated before it hit his throat. A gentler heat reached his toes and his fingers. Wyman gestured to the sofa, and Stephen let the cushions embrace him. Wyman sat in a leather-covered chair across from him. Its brass tacks shined like gold.

"Well, now," Wyman said. "Let's get to business. Your grandmother says you'd like to get in the banking game."

"Yes, sir," Stephen said, hoping Wyman couldn't hear the thickening of his *s*'s.

"Not exactly the safest line these days. Banks eating up banks, executives sent to Danbury in handcuffs. Sure you want to join the likes of them?"

"Oh, I wouldn't do anything like that, Mr. Wyman. I'm going to business school come the fall, and I wanted to get some experience."

"Business school, you say? Didn't think they could teach stuff like that in a classroom, on chalkboards and writing tablets."

"Well, they've got computers to do that now," Stephen said weakly.

Wyman's eyes bore into Stephen's. "Of course they do. Computer-controlled boards and wireless tablets."

"I'm sorry, Mr. Wyman, I didn't mean—"

But the old man's voice grew gentle again. "Relax, Stephen. I'm just pointing out that the more things change, the more they stay the same. You've heard that before, haven't you?"

"Yes, sir."

"Good. Now, I'm good friends with Ron Larsen. I suppose you know him?"

"He's president of Cuthbert Savings."

"That's right. Well, it so happens he's got an opening. I already put a word in, and he's expecting you in his office at nine sharp Monday morning. Can you be there?"

Stephen almost spilled his drink. "Yes, sir, Mr. Wyman. Thank you."

"Don't mention it," Wyman said. "Can you get there yourself, or do you need a ride? I'd be happy to—"

"Oh, no, that won't be necessary," Stephen said quickly. "I have my own car. Bought it myself and everything."

Wyman nodded, as if he'd known it but had forgotten. "Don't forget your drink," he said, and Stephen automatically took a sip. It went down smoothly, and he found himself taking a longer gulp. A happy warmth filled his belly. He wanted to sink into the leather, but he heard his grandmother's voice telling him to sit up straight. He took another pull at his drink.

"I'm glad you've got your own car," Wyman was saying from a distance. "It might be that I need some help, too. You see, one of my assistants suddenly left my employ, and I'm looking for his successor. Would you mind running an errand for me? Not far, just to Havilah College. My niece and her friend are taking summer courses there and they're supposed to join me for dinner tonight. Bad luck, though, her car broke down. Could you pick them up, say around six o'clock? That way I can concentrate on cooking for them."

"Sure. I'd be glad to," Stephen said. But he wondered if he'd be able to walk out of the house in a straight line, never mind drive all the way to Havilah and back.

Wyman added, "And if you wouldn't mind bringing this package to the gentleman in the guard house at the main entrance, that would be a huge help."

It was a brown shopping bag, the top rolled tight. A warning light flashed somewhere deep in Stephen's brain. Wasn't this how unsuspecting kids got roped into the drug trade? But his grandmother had promised. Besides, he realized now that Winter Wyman wasn't the devil people made him out to be. He said, "Sure." Already his tongue felt heavy, and he worried that he might be slurring his words.

"Splendid, Stephen. Splendid." Through blurred eyes, Stephen watched him go to his desk and scribble an address on a slip of paper. "Here," he said. "They'll be waiting for you. And don't worry about bringing them back tonight. I'll do it tomorrow after morning mass."

Stephen shook his head clear. "Yes sir," he said, emphasizing the clarity of his voice.

"Fine," Wyman said. "I knew I could depend on you."

The guard sat in a booth at the entrance to Havilah College, and when Stephen offered him the paper bag, he smoothly stowed it in a cooler at his feet. The guard just said, "thanks," and raised the barrier. Stephen drove through, perhaps a little too fast, afraid the guard might call him back and arrest him.

The campus road curved right, and Stephen followed it along a downward slope, past basketball courts teeming with middle school kids, a summer-occupied dormitory, then to the center of campus. A few sunbathers stretched out in the middle of the wide lawn that skirted the Student Union, while others read in the shade of an oak tree.

Stephen parked and walked back to the field. He tried not to look at the girl sunning her back with her bikini top undone. Instead, he leaned against the third light pole to the left of the entrance, and waited, just as Mr. Wyman had told him to do. A few minutes later, a pair of girls — women, he told himself. College students were women — came laughing down a staircase carved into the hill. The taller one had dark hair that flowed in waves past her shoulders. She wore Daisy Dukes with half the pockets visible below the hem. Her checked shirt was unbuttoned dangerously low. He had a harder time looking in the eyes of the shorter girl, a redhead. Her cut-off T-shirt barely covered the top of her sharp breasts, and her tan legs slid out from a very short skirt. How could she sit down? Both girls carried large purses.

The redhead approached him. "Are you the guy my Uncle Wint sent?" Stephen could only nod. Was she really Wyman's niece? Were they even students here?

"Great. I'm starved," she said. "Where's the car?"

"Over here," he managed to say. Sorry to turn his back on them, he led them to the lot.

As they walked, the girls—women—ignored him, dishing on a party the tall one had gone to the night before. The main draw had been a keg and a bowl of assorted pills. Listening, Stephen wondered what the redhead's uncle would think about how they were dressed. Despite his drug connections, Mr. Wyman seemed pretty strait-laced about sex stuff, but who was he to say?

He unlocked the passenger-side door and the back, expecting one of them would want to sit up front, but they both climbed in behind him. "Ok, driver, take us to the dinner *pahty*." They laughed hysterically while Stephen fumbled for his keys, then missed the ignition twice, before he finally got the motor running. He shook off the last dullness of the scotch and managed to say, "What are your names?"

Wyman's niece spoke first, in a rapid stream that hit his ears like water from a firehose. "My name's Amber. This is my friend, Crystal."

"You're kidding, right?"

"Serious," said the girl who called herself Crystal. "We wouldn't lie about that, would we, Amber?" They giggled again, and Stephen, realizing they were laughing at him, gave up. He sped off campus, glad to hit the highway back toward Cuthbert. The sun was setting. It would be dark by the time they got back.

The rest of the drive was a dizzying cascade of gossip, rumor, and speculation about people Stephen had never heard of. He concentrated on the road, reminded himself he was doing a favor for a man who had done a favor for him. And as stupid as these two girls were —they were definitely girls, he decided—he realized the red flags he'd seen when Wyman had asked him to do this were even more stupid. How could he have thought he was delivering drugs, when all he had gotten in return was a pair of middle-school brains in grown-up bodies?

He stole a few glances in the mirror. He told himself he was looking for family resemblances with Mr. Wyman, but he knew that was a lie. Amber's face lit up while she gushed about some total loser who had the nerve to ask her to blow him. Crystal told a similar story about a guy who was all hands and tongue. They were clearly doing it for his benefit, and Stephen wondered what would happen if he got a hard-on listening to them. Geez, he couldn't let that happen. She was Wyman's niece—or worse.

He pulled up in front of Wyman's house and walked with the girls up the porch steps. The old man himself opened the door. Had he been watching through the little square windows? Stephen worried he'd somehow failed a test.

But Wyman just hugged both girls, as if they were equally loved. His smile, awkward though it was, made him ten years younger. He handed Stephen a folded bill. "Good lad. And by the way, best to keep this quiet. I don't want my friends to think I'm throwing a party. Just a nice family dinner, right?"

"Yes, sir," Stephen said. Wyman led the girls inside, holding them, well, a bit close, even for a doting uncle. But Stephen shrugged, made sure the door was closed before he checked out the bill in his sweating hand, and found Ben Franklin leering back at him.

Chapter 15

The best thing for Starr, after disposing of a body and meticulously cleaning both an unfinished dirt floor basement and a kitchen to the point of forensic perfection, was to be back in her garden. While her father made his hypocritical obeisance at St. Tryphon's, she knelt, placid if not serene, calmly breaking up clods, deadheading flowers, weeding. Digging her fingers into the damp soil was a meditative act, feeling the press of dirt under her fingernails forced everything else from her mind—Jase's arrival, their wild nights, the gruesome reality of Jimmy's murder and its aftermath. The pieces swirled together while she tried to connect them in a pattern, one she could work to her advantage.

She had saved up a good amount of money. There was no mortgage on the house, and despite their mutual hatred, Wyman paid her well to care for Clay. She had no illusions about who the golden child was in their family, especially after her mother had left that awful night. But he hated even more than women the thought that he was in anyone's debt. It galled him to be reminded that the very position he held in Cuthbert had been attained through someone else's work, and so he kept what was left of his family tied together with loathing and exorbitant amounts of money.

If need be, she had access to Clay's monthly checks from the VA. "Guilt offerings" Wyman called them. "Traveling expenses," was more like it. She sighed. What was the use? She couldn't imagine a world beyond this backwoods corner of the state. Every time she imagined herself packed and driving away, she came to a black emptiness beyond the ramp onto the highway. Her entire existence smothered by a velvet curtain.

But Jase had driven right through that curtain, trailing a scent of exotic spices that could never grow here. Especially now that Jimmy Cooper was slowly poisoning the very earth beneath her.

Still, there were arrangements she'd need to make. Clay, most of all. She'd have to find him a bed in a home somewhere. Who would take a man his size with such a raft of syndromes, not to mention an unhealthy interest in porn? Starr had found one residential program that was willing to take him on, and even took her brother for a tour. But when Wyman learned that it would cost a quarter mil a year, with no guarantee, not even an expectation, that there would ever be a cure, he balked. Besides, Clay was otherwise healthy, and could live decades. "No point in even getting started," he told her. "Paying you is good enough."

But those weren't insurmountable problems. Once she was gone, Wyman would have to make real life decisions like anybody else. What would he have done without her in the first place? What should he have done when a grateful nation returned his son, battered and broken? But Starr had done her time. Five years of unbroken babysitting, cleaning, and administering meds both prescribed and her own. And had any worked? She could hardly tell.

The pile of cuttings grew by her side as if by magic. She had cleaned out three beds without realizing it, and even the half dozen or so customers who stopped by failed to disrupt the flow of her thoughts. She smiled and made small talk and listened to their intestinal and skin care complaints without muddying the clear stream of images of a life far beyond here, of exploration alongside Jase, and maybe on her own as well.

But every once in a while, Starr's eyes did flit involuntarily to the compost bins, the way a tongue seeks out the empty spot of a lost tooth. There was no denying that boulder in the stream. Well, she might as well get to it. She raked the wilting weeds into a bundle and carried them to the back corner of the yard. She was careful to mix them with the remnants of the weekend's work. Her eyes scanned the ground for anything seriously amiss, but she found nothing.

The bin's contents looked inert, but she knew the real work was already starting deep inside. In a few days, the heat would start to build, but that wouldn't be a problem, at least until winter. Then, she knew, the snow would melt as it hit the compost, leaving a black spot in a field of white: the dark heat of rot. But who would notice? She threw a few more scraps on top and went inside. No sense dwelling on it. Besides, there was dinner to serve. Her outdoor work completed, she traded her rubber boots for bare feet.

The leftover gumbo sat in the heavy pot in the fridge. She hefted it onto the stove. As it warmed, its aroma pushed against the sickly-sweet odors that drifted in from her workroom. Had it always smelled like that? She looked around her, assessing the room as if it weren't her own. How much could she get for the place? The ceiling could use a coat of paint. There was the crack in the plaster by the door, where she and Clay had tumbled once as children. Their mother had covered for them, though, before Wyman came home. Otherwise they both would have gotten beatings. Not that beating Clay ever achieved a thing.

The gumbo bubbled, and she saw in the swirling steam the time their mother hid them in the cabinet below the sink, when their father had come home furious about some deal gone bad, and blamed her for it. At ten, Starr couldn't imagine what her mother had to do with her father's work, when he was always out and she was always home, but the sound of the slaps, the mysterious *thunks* that seemed to move around the room separate from their mother's cries, kept Starr and Clay still and silent. Wyman hollered about fornication and she clearly remembered him saying, "If you remain hostile toward me and refuse to listen to me, I will multiply your afflictions seven times over, as your sins deserve." It was creepy and mysterious enough to have attached itself to her memory, where she could take it down at odd times and examine it like a mutant vegetable. But their mother had never said a word in response, and the children clutched each other, arms awkwardly kinked around the sink drain, their eyes blinking messages of encouragement in the gloom. Long after quiet had fallen in the house, after the door slammed, sending a picture to crash on the floor, their mother dared to open the cabinet and send the children to their rooms. Clay never questioned the bruises on his mother's bare shoulders, or the scratches on her palms, but Starr memorized every one as if each were her own wound.

The gumbo was ready. She scooped it into bowls, then made two plates of lettuce greens, tossing them with oil, vinegar, and her own herbs. She put it all on a tray with a couple of beers and carried it upstairs.

She listened at the door before calling out. It was quiet, no television. "Open up, Clay," she said in as neutral a voice as she could muster. "It's dinner time."

She heard him shuffling to the door. It opened a crack and let out a wave of foul must. "Come on," she said, ignoring the stench. "Food's getting cold, beer's getting warm."

He stepped back, giving her room to get by. She put the tray on a side table, then put up the window shades. She studied the state of his room. The floor in front of the TV was clean, the bed sat on but not slept in.

"Rough night?" she asked the mute figure. He guarded the door like a sentry. She noted the scabbed knuckles on both his hands. When she got closer, she saw what appeared to be freckles on his forearms where no freckles had been before.

"We better wash you up before we eat," she said. "I'll be right back."

She returned with a basin and cloth. Clay still stood at attention. "At ease," she told him. "Sit."

Silently, he took two long steps, squared off, and sat on the bed. Starr moved the dinner tray to the top of television, and put the basin on the table in front of him.

The stains were stubborn, and she rubbed his skin raw to loosen them up. Eventually, the dried blood began to seep off, and the water turned pink. All the while, Clay stared at nothing in front of him, and he allowed her to manipulate his arms and hands like a doll. The scabs on his knuckles were too new to come off. When she was done with his arms, she examined his face, under his chin, on his neck.

"I know you wanted to protect me," she said to him lightly. "But I wasn't hurt, you know. Maybe a little scared. Next time, just give the guy enough that he learns from his mistakes, ok? No need to give a temporary problem a permanent solution."

A cloud passed over Clay's face, the closest he had to showing emotions. Starr nodded. "Don't feel too bad. We took care of it. Jimmy's helping out in the garden now. Poppa's friend Sam drove the car into the quarry. It's like it never happened. But listen, honey, can you do something for me, please?" She toweled him dry, and put the basin near the door. "Can you please try to get a little better? You know, speak up once in a while? It would make everyone so much happier. You, especially. And then maybe you could go out, see things, not need me quite so much." Another cloud shaded his eyes, and she quickly changed the subject.

She tried another tack. "Remember what it was like when we were kids? We used to go to parties. You laughed, sometimes even made jokes. And when we were old enough to drive, someone always had a car to see movies at the Havilah Theater. Remember that, Clay? Popcorn and candy and once I think a girl kissed you in the dark. You didn't tell me about it, but I saw the smudge on the side of your mouth. I think it was Patty, wasn't it?"

But except for a twitch at the mention of the girl's name, Clay remained impassive. Maybe it was best to keep Patty's memory locked in the past. But something needed to jolt him back to life.

"It would be so much fun if we talk about those days. No need to do it now. Just think about it, ok? Hey, let's eat." She brought the warm bowls of gumbo back to the little table and opened the beers. She clinked hers against his, and they ate silently. Clay gripped the spoon in his fist like a child, but not a drip spilled between the bowl and his mouth, which was more than Starr could claim. She hid the shaking of her hand by holding her beer too tight. As it warmed in her hand, she felt calmer, and again, tentatively, started to eat again.

She barely made it through the meal before the tension of the last forty-eight hours overwhelmed her, forcing her to bed, though she wanted nothing more than to cut through the woods and lie by Jase's side. How could it be that just when she was ready to leave, she had been pulled back in, having to hide yet another of her brother's "accidents"?

Would she ever be free?

Chapter 16

Despite the clanging bells at the Church in the Woods, Jase checked his watch. Nearly six on Wednesday evening. He'd had a restful night, even slept through most of the hourly tolling, though he was constantly on guard for the woman to come knocking at his door. When it became clear she wouldn't, he let himself drift off without worry. He got an early start, heading to the Havilah College library to do more research before he needed to be back here for his debut. The woman said Wyman would be holding court at his usual table at the Hammer and Tongs by then, his sidekick nearby, dispensing and demanding favors from the stream of petitioners.

He kept the Mustang on a tight rein, eyeing the neighborhood, registering landmarks in his head. The entire downtown could fit on half a city block: a drug store, a grocery, storefront post office, real estate broker. So much for commercial interests. Not far off was a "professional" building, really just a three-story, turreted Victorian pile where a doctor, dentist, and lawyer shared space. He must have found the sleepiest town in the east.

The Hammer and Tongs stood alone across a tiny common, its windows casting orange shadows onto the empty street. The tiny lot behind the restaurant was full, so Jase simply stopped in the middle of the street by the entrance. He put on the hazards and climbed out, not bothering to shut the door. A somber smoker watched him and dragged on the last of his butt.

"Watch that for me, will you?" Jase said to him. Up close the guy was a wreck: pop eyes, the tendons in his neck taut against paper-thin skin. His clothes — checked shirt, white belt and shoes — were a parody. But the guy winked and answered, "You betcha, Chief."

Jase strode through the door and surveyed the room. Low lights, quiet. Nothing like the Rhode House. The police chief, a dour man with a scared look, sat with his wife in a corner, where he could watch everyone who came in. There was a scattering of suits and skirts; probably the entire population of the Cuthbert professional building was in attendance.

He had no trouble recognizing Winter Wyman at the far end of the room. The man sat straight as a rod, his white hair flowing to the shoulders of his dark suit. He smiled patiently at a man who was talking excitedly, his hands making great sweeps in the air. Wyman, though, hardly moved, except to raise and lower his fork as he ate. His eyes never rested, but constantly scanned the room. For a moment they lingered on Jase, but only long enough to register his presence. Then they went back to their patrol, as if Wyman were a prison guard.

Behind Wyman, another man, obviously the sidekick Sam, sat in a booth with the green curtain open, staring hard at Jase. His sharp elbow strained against a ratty checked coat, and he played nervously with a spoon, occasionally dropping it with a clatter. *Not very tight security*, he thought. *But why does he look so scared?*

Jase moved past the other diners, mostly respectable looking middle-aged couples, until he approached Wyman's table. He stood over the gesticulating man, whose hands froze in mid-arc.

The old man fixed his gaze on Jase. "Can I help you, young man?"

Jase took an empty chair from the next table. "My daughter's sitting there," a woman protested, but Jase ignored her and sat at Wyman's side. The other man still had his hands in the air. "Finished?" Jase said to him. The man nodded and scurried away, whatever thought he'd been uttering left unspoken.

The two men locked eyes, and it seemed the whole dinner crowd held its breath to see what would happen. Wyman broke the silence. "You could learn something about manners," he said. His fork still moved: down, up, down, up. He was eating plain boiled chicken. *Of course*, thought Jase. *The man thinks he's a wolf in a henhouse.*

"Where I come from, manners are a sign of weakness," Jase answered, his gaze firmly on Wyman's pallid face.

For half a beat, the fork paused, but Wyman quickly regained control. He slid the food off the tines with brittle lips. "And where is that?"

"That," Jase said heartily, "is not your problem." Before Wyman could say anything, Jase drew something out of his back pocket and slapped it on top of the half-eaten chicken, knocking rice onto the table. A color photo showed a piece of ivory on an anonymous Oriental rug. "This is."

Wyman curled his lips in disgust, but he studied the picture. "Well?" he said after a few seconds.

"That was taken in Istanbul, in the back room of a little rug factory." Jase slapped another picture on top of it. "That one is the basement of a biergarten in East Berlin." One more. "That's the office of a cell phone store in Monrovia."

"I've never been to Russia," Wyman said. Jase couldn't tell if he was serious or mocking him.

"No, but this piece of ivory has visited a few hot spots, before landing here in Cuthbert."

Wyman shrugged. "So?"

"The name's Jase Patton." He stuck out a hand, but Wyman ignored it. "I'm with the Network, same as you." A glimmer of fear rippled across Wyman's face, as if he wished he had chosen to shake the proffered hand. "I talked to a very angry man in Atlanta a few days ago. It seems the collateral he was going to put up on a deal involving some very nasty guns and a few pills has been slow to arrive."

Wyman leaned back, and dropped his fork on top of the pile of pictures scattered on his plate. "That's why I always pay in cash," he said easily. "As Ezekiel says, he who 'hath given forth upon usury, and hath taken increase: shall he then live? He shall not live: he hath done all these abominations; he shall surely die; his blood shall be upon him.' "

"The Bible says something about stealing, too. Isn't it in that Top 10 List?"

"Young man." Wyman's eyes grew steely, and he leaned forward. "I've had enough bantering. I got your message from Talis. The last one he'll deliver, by the way. You want the ivory panel? So ask nicely. Anyhow, I'll tell you no, and you can get your blasphemous carcass out of this restaurant and thence out of town. You were not invited, and so are not welcome. If you linger, you'll find your situation bloody, painful, and terminal. Let the gunrunner and his customer work it out. If you'll excuse me, I'm awaiting guests at home. Sodom was destroyed for a lack of hospitality, and I won't allow myself to suffer the same."

Jase grinned, but made no sign of leaving. The soiled photos soaked up the grease from the chicken and rice. Wyman gestured to the sharp-elbowed guard, and the two of them vanished into the night. The rest of the diners studied their plates, afraid to eat, afraid to look.

Jase sat back in his chair. He collected the pictures and wiped them on the tablecloth, leaving an obscene smear. He took a satisfying gulp of Wyman's drink, and looked around the room, giving a friendly smile to anyone who dared or accidentally met his eye.

When he was sure that Wyman had made his getaway, Jase shoved the ruined photos into his pocket, then strolled back to his car. It waited where he had left it, the door still open.

"No one so much as breathed on it, Chief," growled the smoker, who had just lit up a new one. "Considered taking her for a wash, but thought you might be leaving soon."

"Good man," Jase said. "I owe you a drink." The smoker made an elaborate bow.

Jase got in the car and did a lap of the town common, then followed a meandering route to a spot about half a mile from Wyman's house. He'd make the rest of the way on foot.

Jase knew that art thieves didn't keep their hot acquisitions behind curtains to be opened at midnight, gawked at like porn. Steve McQueen's Thomas Crown was a Hollywood fantasy. In a world where bills were numbered and even Swiss accounts got hacked, innocuous decorations like paintings, sculptures, even furniture, could move unnoticed. No one would recognize an Old Master in a suburban living room, and if they did, who would guess it was real and not a cheap repro? Still, he had an idea that Wyman thought there were such people, and so would set out to be one himself. Jase hated that kind of a fool. But understanding him brought Jase one step closer to completing his mission. That would please his employer, but it would also please Jase, both in the pocket and the soul.

It took about twenty minutes of slipping through backyards for him to make his approach at Wyman's house. He crouched behind a tool shed and saw a broken swing dangling from a tree. He tried to imagine the woman as a child using it, but failed. He turned his attention to the house instead.

It had once been a stately mansion with a mansard roof and huge wraparound porch. Light blazed through the entire first floor, but only a single second floor window threw light onto another porch, probably outside the bedroom. He guessed that would be where the panel was hidden, and he hoped that he'd spooked Wyman enough to go check on it. Jase imagined Wyman kneeling before the relic like a miser worshipping his treasure.

He checked for motion-detector lights. The arrogant bastard didn't have any, so Jase sprinted across the yard, and shimmied up a pillar to the second floor. Before he could slip through the window, though, a car pulled up in front. He heard several voices, high pitched and giggling. Girls? *You old devil, Wyman.* He watched a worried teen drive off, and he heard the front door close like a trap.

Jase lowered himself into the shadows behind the porch railing. The girls' voices grew closer. Probing with his toes to avoid loose boards, he crept along the porch and around the corner toward the bedroom window. It was lit, but he chanced a glimpse anyhow.

Bingo.

A massive four-poster bed dominated the far wall. A blonde and a redhead, college age, he guessed, kneeled on the bed, naked. Wyman lay between them, also naked. He was fondling both of the girls, his withered chest heaving with effort. But his eyes were cast to the sky, and his lips moved as in prayer.

Jase stifled a laugh. The final piece of his plan fell into place. He never thought that he could appeal to Wyman's wallet, but now he knew he could exploit his weakness for superstition, and he had a pretty good idea how to do it.

No matter what the girls did, the old man hung limp.

Chapter 17

The next day, Jase decided to eat his lunch at the Hammer and Tongs. It was time to get his face a little better known in the area. Besides, he needed new sights to drive last night's visions of Wyman's perversity out of his consciousness. He never did bother to see if Wyman had ever gotten it up. By the time Sam ferried the girls away an hour later, Jase had retreated to the woods and kept up surveillance from there. The girls left the house subdued and silent. A minute later, Jase did, too.

By day, the Hammer and Tongs had none of the previous night's Puritan formalism. The sun streamed through open curtains. The weekday lunch crowd was younger and livelier, probably clerks and cashiers from the few shops and offices. He sat at the counter and ate his pastrami quietly, letting the other diners flow around him while he kept an ear on their conversations. Nothing of interest.

The door opened and he glanced up. He recognized Terry, the Rhode House barmaid as she slouched in. She wore a flowing pink dress that swirled just above her ankles, revealing a tattooed snake around her calf. Another coiled on her bare shoulders, its mouth angled up as if it were about to slide into the black hair lacquered on her skull. She took a seat around the corner of the counter, far enough away for privacy, close enough to talk, if things worked out.

"Hey there, girl," the waitress said. "What can I get you?"

Terry sighed. "Whatever." She looked at Jase's sandwich. "That looks good."

"Pastrami, then," the waitress said. "Be right out." She stuck the order above the kitchen window. She leaned in close and said to Terry, "You hear about Jimmy Cooper?"

"That loser? What about him?"

"Did a runner, they say. Someone told Sharon he got a job in Denver, but he never told me anything about it."

"Never told me anything about working, period," Terry said. "Why the fuck did he go across the whole continent? Maybe everyone around here already knew he was a useless dick." She dropped her chin onto her fist.

"Asshole left a tab here. What about the Rhode House?"

Terry shook her head. "If he doesn't pay, it comes out of my paycheck. I work too hard to let him get drunk for free." Then her tone grew forceful. "You're too nice, Jules. Give a leech like that a free sandwich, he'll never feel the need to earn it. Jesus, he must have paid for a bus ticket with the money he didn't pay you. And what good did he ever do you?"

The barrage was enough to push Jules away from the counter. She covered her humiliation by filling a glass from the fountain and putting it in front of Terry. "Anyhow," she said, without much conviction, "just thought you'd want to know."

The gesture must have worked. Suddenly Terry said, in a friendlier voice, "Speaking of free sandwiches, you going to the picnic next Saturday?"

Jules perked up again, the storm past. "Winter in July? Never miss it."

Terry nodded. "Yeah, I guess I'll be there, too. Course, I'll be working. As if slinging beers six nights a week isn't enough."

Jules was sympathetic. "We're donating the pasta and potato salads. I'll need to make it all after closing that Friday, so I guess I won't get much rest either. But hell if I'm not going to have a good time. Old man Wyman sure knows what makes people happy." A bell rang, and Jules turned to get Terry's order.

Jase listened to their talk, sussing out the dynamics between them. He had finished his sandwich and made a show of mopping up the mustard with his fries. The dill spear would be dessert. He wondered who Jimmy Cooper was.

"Don't I know you?" Terry said, leaning over.

"No reason you should," Jase answered. He flashed a smile, the one he used to make friends. "Unless you remember every freeloader you sling a beer at."

She waved a recognizing finger at him. "And a Maker's Mark. I got you. What brings you to Cuthbert? It sure isn't the scintillating adventure."

"You can find adventure anywhere, if you look hard enough. I had some business, thought I'd stay a little while. What's this Winter in July?" Better to start with town wide events before moving into sore topics.

Terry rolled her eyes. "Winter Wyman's scheme to buy off his loyal subjects."

"Subjects?"

"He's kind of the big man around here, though he's an alderman same as the others."

"You don't sound like a loyal subject."

She shrugged. "It is what it is. He pretty much owns the town, and I need to work. I can play nice, at least until it's time to make my move. Too bad for him his family couldn't figure out how to do it."

"What's that mean?"

Instead of answering, she bit into her sandwich, and stretched it out by licking her fingers, too. She said, "He may be the big man in town, leading businessman and all that. Maybe a bit more, if you know what I mean. But Christ if his family isn't fucked up. His wife up and left him one night, no reason, just split. And his hippie bitch of a daughter's selling herbal remedies. She thinks anything must be good if it comes out of the dirt. Poison ivy is natural, too, but you don't see me wiping my cunt with it."

He raised his eyebrows but said nothing. He guessed Terry and the woman were about the same age. He wondered what kind of soap opera they'd acted out in high school. Wondered if they'd fought over a guy. More likely, from what he'd seen, they'd been vying for the title of Toughest Chick in the yearbook. His ears pricked up as she went on.

"It looked for a while like the son was going to be the normal one. Strong silent type. But he went to Iraq and boy, did that fuck him up. More than Wyman could have done on his own."

"Wounded? PTSD?" The forgotten pickle oozed into the remains of his slaw.

She shook her head. "No, nothing like that. Clay was always quiet. But he knew how to have fun, I guess. Played football, wrestled, that kind of stuff. He could handle pain like nobody's business. Always cutting himself or breaking a bone, but he didn't give a shit. He'd hang with us out in the woods. Sometimes we'd get drunk enough to play a game to see who could get him to admit something hurt him. It got fucking weird, though. We'd cut him with broken bottles and all he did was laugh." She shrugged. "That's it. He dated my friend a while, then he went to the desert."

"No serious injuries there?"

"Well, he's still got all his parts. Least, the ones you can see. I've heard he never leaves his room. Wyman's got the hippie taking care of him, but I doubt floral arrangements are what he needs. They say he's practically a vegetable himself. Should probably be in some hospital, but the old man won't admit it."

"Where was he?"

"I just told you, Iraq. Or Afghanistan? One of those places."

"No," Jase insisted. "What city? Mosul? Basra? Baghdad?"

Another bite, another shrug. With a full mouth she mumbled, "How the fuck should I know? Those places all sound the same. It's the fucking desert: sand, palm trees, cactus. What difference does it make?"

Jase pushed his plate away. "Might be a big difference. Maybe this old girlfriend knows. Where can I find her?" *There were a lot of units, so no need to think he was at al-Ahrar Bridge, but why take chances?*

She put the sandwich down and carefully wiped her hands. Then she looked him straight in the eye and said, "You can't. Some prick at a party bashed her fucking brains in and washed them down the drain."

He frowned. "I'm sorry," he said, letting the sympathy flow through his lips like cool water. "They ever catch him?"

She didn't answer. Instead, she pushed the lump of slaw around her plate with a fork.

"Terry, did they find him?"

"Look," she said quietly. "I don't know. I… I talked to Wyman about it. He's got long arms, right? Turns out it was a guy who showed up at the party, no one knew him. But Wyman tracked him down, and no one ever saw the guy again. And no one ever mentioned Patty again, get it? Wyman has a way of making people disappear, and I don't ask questions, not that kind. But I'll tell you this much, I would have liked to have seen what happened to him myself. Patty was my best friend. I'd kill the bastard myself if I knew he was still alive."

Chapter 18

Starr aimed the rain barrel hose on the flower boxes hanging from the front porch. As the first drops landed, Jase pulled up in the Mustang. It had been days since she'd seen him, and she was proud of her resolve not to run to the Church in the Woods to see him. But now he turned up at her own house, and the resolve leeched away.

What's he doing here *of all places*? She smiled, hoping it masked the twitching of her mouth.

She said with feigned casualness, "I never told you where I lived."

He climbed out and leaned against the fender. Starr realized Jase was posing exactly as Jimmy had only a few days before. She hoped their stories didn't have the same endings.

"I figured you were in easy walking distance from the bell tower," he told her. "Plus I asked down at the Hammer and Tongs."

"Of course." She turned back to watering. "Jules has a mouth the size of Cape Cod."

"I thought you'd be happy to see me. It's been quiet up the hill."

"I hardly think 'quiet' is the word." She flashed him an inviting grin but it felt fake even to her.

"You know what I mean."

"Maybe I can come tonight," she suggested, warming to the idea.

"I'd like to spend some time with you now."

Her pulse sped up, but then she glanced up at the second floor corner window. "Now's not a good time. I have clients."

He crossed his arms. "Homeopathic remedies, herbal teas, St. John's wort and all that?"

He'd done his homework, and she started to worry. "That's right."

"Unlike the pharmaceuticals your dear old dad sells? You two compete for market share?"

"Don't call him that." Another look at the window. "What do you want?"

Jase laughed. "What's up there? Got a madman in the attic or something?"

She dropped the hose and charged him. "That's not funny. If you came to make jokes, you can just clear the hell out."

She stood defiantly before him, nostrils flaring, fists at her sides. He unfolded his arms and pulled her in. He kissed her hard. She twisted, unsure whether she wanted him to leave or take her there and then. "Not here," she said, despite herself. "Later."

But he held her anyhow and whispered, "Afraid your brother will see? I'd like to meet him."

That gave her the strength to pull away, but her face was still flushed. "Is that why you're here? To gawk at Clay? Well, he doesn't take visitors."

"He always been like that? Or just since your mother left?"

She cocked her head. "You doing recon on my family now?"

He turned up his hands. "I just wondered if that's why she split."

She eyed him warily, noting that her questions made no impression on him at all. "No," she said carefully. "It happened to him later. In the war."

"Iraq? What unit? I bet we could swap some good stories."

Starr shook her head. "He won't. He doesn't talk to me, so I doubt he'd have anything to say to you."

"Then you tell me — was he in Baghdad? During the invasion. The time I told you about?"

She looked at him with suspicion. "Maybe. He never wrote about it, except that it was always sunny. He saw a lot of firefights, but just said they were fun."

"I never heard anyone call that fun." He looked off in the distance, and Starr wondered what painful memories he was reliving himself.

"Maybe he was trying to keep us from worrying."

"Was he always that considerate?" She didn't answer. "Fine. I told you, I just need to get that panel. I thought maybe he could help."

"I said I would help." She moved closer, but the moment had passed. Jase was all business again.

"Tell me about the Winter in July picnic," he said.

She turned back to the house, picked up the hose and sprayed a basil plant. "It's a party he sponsors every year. Hamburgers and hot dogs, that kind of thing."

"You going?"

"Of course," she said, still keeping her back to him. "I always enter the cooking contest. It's the only way I can get *him* to eat my food."

"What's your entry?"

She was too proud of her cooking not to look at him as she said, "Gumbo."

His face cracked with an involuntary smile. "Oh, really?"

The appearance of another car cut off her answer. Her gorge rose when she recognized Wyman's Lincoln. It parked behind the Mustang, blocking it in. How would she explain this? She looked to Jase for help, but he remained immobile against the car like a mushroom on a log. He didn't even turn his head, just kept smiling like an idiot as Sam angled the car to keep him from driving off.

Wyman emerged from the back seat. He looked at Jase but spoke to her.

"What's he looking for?"

Jase said, "Gardening tips."

Wyman pointed at Starr. "Beware of what she says. Only trouble will spring from the earth with this one."

"What do you want, Wyman?" she said, dropping the hose again.

He turned to her. "I want to see my boy. Is he cleaned up?"

"No, I left him in wallowing in his own filth. What do you think?"

He sneered, and said, "I will break the pride of your power; and I will make your heaven as iron, and your earth as brass."

She looked up at the blue sky and spread her arms to the greenery around them. "If you could do that, I wouldn't be in this little patch of Eden. You'll find your darling boy where he always is, probably doing what he's always doing." She hoped Jase hadn't heard the wavering in her voice. He had to believe she was strong enough to go off with him.

Wyman grunted but said nothing.

Jase watched smugly as she tried to move things along. "Your tea's in the fridge. Does that make you happy?"

But Wyman wouldn't cooperate. "Never mind my happiness," he said viciously. "Has he had his ablutions for the day?"

"I'm sure he'll be glad to join you in your prayers," she said wearily.

"Don't disturb us," he warned, waving a finger at both of them.

"Don't worry," Jase said. "I'll keep her entertained downstairs." Starr's breath caught in her throat as Wyman turned and approached him.

"You had better not be talking about what I think you are. Her mother, to my shame, was a whore, and so is she. 'All they that seek her will not weary themselves; in her month they shall find her.' Watch out, you don't know what kind of viper that one is."

"I'll take my chances."

Starr turned away, focused on yanking out some weeds with one hand while she drove her nails into the palm of the other. The pounding in her ears drowned out what they said. A minute later, Wyman stormed past her and disappeared into her house.

"If I were you, I'd drive a stake through the heart of that old vampire," Jase muttered.

"The garlic didn't work," she said, still not facing him. She blinked a tear out of her eye and it soaked into the dirt. "I don't think a stake would, either."

"He likes young girls, you know," Jase said quietly.

"You think that's news? At least he can't do anything about it."

"He told you?"

She stabbed the ground with a garden scoop. "In town they call me a witch. Maybe they're right. Anyhow, I know things I shouldn't." She composed herself, stood up, saw that Sam was safely ensconced in the air-conditioned Lincoln.

"Well," Jase said. "Maybe we can come up with a way of getting you out from under his thumb while I get what I want. You game?"

"Anything," she said. They talked it out in whispered sentences while she worked.

They would never pull it off, she thought. It all came down to a house plant? Anyone would think they were insane to try. But the number of sane people in her life could fit in a window planter.

When they were through outlining a plan, Jase angled his car out from behind the Lincoln. Sam scowled and gave him the finger. Starr went to work in the kitchen, using her mortar and pestle until

Wyman stomped into the kitchen scowling. "What is that foul stench?"

"I'm crushing valerian root for Mrs. Carmody's insomnia."

"That smell would keep any right-thinking person awake," he said. But he braved the odor and helped himself to some licorice tea in the fridge. "Did you check his temperature?" he said after he tasted the drink.

"Twice," she said. "As always."

"Clay can't risk a fever."

"You say that as if I wasn't the one who's done all the research and training. You want to catch me in a mistake, you'll have to try harder."

Wyman tried a different approach. "Where's that stranger? What's he want, sniffing around here?"

She slammed the pestle on the counter. "Did it ever occur to you I might make some friends? That I might have a life of my own?"

"You're not here to make a life of your own. Your job is to see that no harm comes to my son. Same as always."

"Not always," she said quietly. "There was a time before."

"We won't discuss those sinful times, woman. They're dead and forgotten."

"Not for me. I remember everything. Like the time when you drove over—"

Wyman's glass shattered against the wall, leaving a syrupy black stain. The medicine smell of licorice overpowered the valerian. "I'm warning you!" he shouted, raising his fist. But she stood her ground.

"Go ahead," she said. "You know what happens when someone hurts me. Or do you need to dig through the compost pile for a reminder? You think he'd choose you over me?"

"He wouldn't harm his father."

"Don't be so sure."

Wyman glanced at the ceiling, as if he could see through to Clay's room. He grimaced, and said, more calmly. "You should know not to anger me."

They were at a standoff. Starr took a deep breath, willing herself calm. She nodded. "You're right. There's no point in fighting." She cast about the room until something caught her eye. "Here, take this." She handed him a potted lavender. "Keep it in your office. It's good for staying calm."

He took the plant gingerly, afraid to dirty his hands.

She laughed. "Go on, there's nothing sinful about it. They put lavender in baby shampoo."

"Thank you," he said. The words left his mouth reluctantly. "Now, fetch me another glass of tea."

"That's going too far," she said, her attempt at peace shattered like the glass. Instead of pouring him another glass, she took the pitcher from the fridge and sloshed it down the drain. As she did, she noticed two or three lines of blood where flying glass had sliced her. The valerian was ruined, too, she realized. "That's the last batch I make for you, old man."

"We'll see about that." His fury smothered whatever power the lavender might have had, and he went out of his way to crunch the shards of glass beneath his heavy shoes as he left the house.

But, she noted, he did take the plant with him.

Chapter 19

The sheep and goats at Nephele Farms had been evicted from their pasture. Their angry bleats echoed in the great red barn, but no one heard them over the amped-up bluegrass music. The mucked-out field had been converted to a parking lot, and Cuthbert High students waved orange flags directing cars into irregular rows. The aroma of grilling burgers, hot dogs, and fried dough overwhelmed the rank farm odors.

Huge tents covered the lawn between the barn and the apple orchards. Inside the largest one, hundreds of Cuthbert's citizens sat at folding tables and paid homage to the great alderman Winter Wyman.

Jase stood in line in the smaller food tent with men in hiked-up shorts and sandals, shouting wives, and bored kids who nevertheless knew better than to skip this. His black pants and shirt contrasted with everyone else's neon and patriotic stripes.

Strolling along the buffet line, he served himself a pair of burgers, some of Jules's pasta salad, and chips. Hoping to avoid the hot air inflating the central tent, he wandered outside looking for a table. He skipped the beer tent, saving Terry's baleful eye for later, and took instead bottled water from an ice-filled galvanized tub. He cut through the makeshift midway, dodging knots of gabbing neighbors and high schoolers who were making balloon animals in stalls made from cardboard boxes. He arrived at a sea of outside tables.

Most were full, or had folded chairs leaning against them to save seats, but one mother, her blond hair as short as Jase's military cut and wearing a track suit zipped to her tiny chin, shooed her youngest away and waved Jase to sit with her.

"Thanks," he said. The kids, a teen-age girl and two round-faced boys, ignored him, concentrating on their food.

The woman beamed, as if she had just performed the kindest act in history. "Well, I could tell you aren't from around here, so I thought I'd show you that we're friendly folk in this town." Her voice had the strained hollowness of a life-long smoker, made worse by hollering after her children. But her smile was sincere.

"It's such a beautiful day," she continued. "We always have good weather for this."

Jase gave her his best down-home grin, all teeth. "How long have you been coming here?"

"Right from the beginning, back when this one was still in her carriage." She gestured to her daughter, whose hair was shaved on one side, the other dyed red.

He barely noticed the piercings under her lower lip, but did recognize the humiliation of being singled out by her mother. How often had he slunk away from his own mother's care and attention? Like the time she had dragged him to a bully's house and demanded the two settle it right there on the front lawn. Or when he'd lost his lunch money and she made him wear a sign the rest of the week that said, "I'M TOO STUPID TO EAT." Maybe this mother would never be so outwardly cruel, but nevertheless, he knew all too well her fervent wish to both rebel and be loved, and the agonized fear of being noticed.

"And Wyman pays for it all?" he asked, all cheer and friendliness.

"Mostly," the woman said. "Some of the businesses, they just donate. Everyone loves him, he does so much for the town."

Jase took a bite of a burger. It was surprisingly good. After he swallowed, he said, "What does he do? Besides parties, I mean."

"Oh, like he finds jobs for the kids. He's always there when you need a helping hand. And he keeps the drugs and crime out." She waved at friends across the field.

"Don't the police take care of that?"

The woman scowled dismissively. "Who do you think runs the police? Fucking Bill Butler?" Jase paused mid-chew, but none of her kids noticed her swearing. "The only reason that loser still has a badge is so Wyman has time to deal with everything else. Believe me, it's Winter Wyman who keeps the bad elements out of Cuthbert. You can't get a pill for love or money in this town, thanks to him."

Jase noticed the daughter staring fixedly at her bag of potato chips during her mother's speech, her hand unnaturally tight around a can of grape soda. He knew she'd tell a very different story, but decided he didn't need to hear it. Her mother continued, "Why, just last week, he drove two of the worst out: Jimmy Cooper, who never worked a day in his life, and Spyro Talis, an old man who should have known better than to be mixed up in drugs."

A second woman with a polyester pant suit and a purse the size of a satchel on her wrist tottered over to the table. Her plate was piled with burgers, salad, rolls, and a stubby corncob. "Sylvia," said the mother. "Sit here." Jase grabbed a chair for her to sit on.

"The man sounds like a saint." Jase said when they were settled again. He'd heard about Cooper yesterday, but this seemed to confirm what Wyman had hinted at and Terry had outright claimed: Wyman could make anyone disappear.

"That's the truth," said the new woman, shaking her head sorrowfully. "The cross he has to bear, what with his simpleton son, and his wife run off. I wouldn't kick him out of my bed, old as he is. Don't know where she thought she'd find better."

They were circling in on what he hoped to get. Jase pressed for more. "And he has a daughter, too, I heard? Takes care of the son?"

"Oh, her," Sylvia said. "Slut's another embarrassment. She's turned that house into some kind of weird voodoo church, always burning incense and shit."

"Herbal remedies, is what I heard," Jase said.

The first woman snorted. Grudgingly, she said, "I'll admit, when my little one was colicky, she made him some peppermint tea, calmed him right down. I'll give her that much. But they don't teach that weird shit in school, you know. She got it some other place."

But the vein seemed to have dried up. Sylvia changed the subject to a complaint about a teacher at the high school who she thought gave too much homework. "Kids don't want to read, so why force them? It's not like I read either."

The first woman jumped on the bandwagon, and they outlined a litany of gripes, effectively icing him out. Jase finished his meal, with no real expectation they would get back to him. When he was sure she'd said her piece, Jase stood up. "Thanks for letting me join you ladies. It was a pleasure." He glanced at the teen, but she was gazing into the orchard, like she was plotting an escape. The two little boys were punching each other in the shoulder.

"Happy to. Hey, you never said what you're doing in Cuthbert."

"Business trip," he said breezily.

Sylvia said, "Do yourself a favor and introduce yourself to Wyman. Can't hurt to have him as a friend."

"I will. Thanks."

He dumped his empty plate and made his way to the tent sporting an ancient sign that declared "Cook-OFF!" The bluegrass band had fallen silent, and an MC reminded folks to check out the farm stand. He still hadn't seen Wyman himself.

When he sauntered into the cook-off tent, the warm fragrance of baked goods mellowed out the sharper scents of barbecue. A dozen cooks ladled samples into small bowls and paper plates. He saw Wyman's daughter smiling to the crowds as she dipped again and again into a huge crock of gumbo. Despite Sylvia's vitriol, hers had the longest line. Jase ignored the offered fried chicken, chili, and bread until he made it to the end of the table. She grinned.

"You made it," she said. "I thought you'd get lost." She heaped rice into his bowl and poured him an extra scoop of gumbo. She shook a bottle of hot sauce at it. "Judging's in fifteen minutes. After that I'm done. Maybe we can take a walk?"

"Sure," he said. He tested the food. The cayenne drained his nasal passages, and the hot sauce bit the back of his throat. "Good stuff. That shrimp in there?"

"Maybe." She winked, and he thought of Mac Fletcher's three-eyed creatures, which he'd had the opportunity to see again earlier that day. His stomach began to turn.

"Actually," she said, "it's slices of a giant mushroom I found the other day, a gorgeous chicken of the woods."

"That's really what it's called?" Glad that it wasn't a mutant species, he bit into a piece. Another wave of heat cascaded down his throat. "Ok, I see why. This is damned good. Any chance of winning?"

"With Wyman himself judging, not very lik—"

A commotion at the edge of the tent cut her off. It rippled through the crowd and a minute later, the tent was empty, as people drained to witness the spectacle. Jase and Starr followed.

It was a parade, but clearly not one that Wyman had planned. At its head, the leader of the Rhode House bell activists banged a gong in no kind of rhythm.

"That damned Rich Sutton." The woman shook her head ruefully. "This will be the end of him."

Sutton's cohorts jangled Christmas chimes or knocked cowbells, and one woman held a sign that read "HOW DO YOU LIKE THESE BELLS?" The crowd booed, and a burger, heavy with ketchup, splattered the sign. But Sutton and his gang kept up the clangor until someone wrestled the gong from him and flung it into the cow pasture. The sign came down, too, and Jase thought he saw the mother who'd been his lunch date just a few minutes earlier at the front of the mob. The protesters might have gotten hurt if Winter Wyman himself didn't rise out of the mass, waving his hands.

"Enough!" he cried. Jase was stunned to see how quickly they complied. Sam's thuggish glare probably helped. Sutton and the others cowered behind Wyman like bullied children. Wyman bellowed, "These people have the right to express themselves, and I for one will listen to their complaints. But we'll do it calmly, and quietly. Over there, in my office."

People laughed as Wyman gestured with exaggerated hospitality to the barn. Sutton and the others marched like whipped dogs up the dirt track and disappeared into the gloom with Wyman and the moaning sheep.

"That's a new reason for me to lose," the woman said to Jase.

But he was already walking away.

Chapter 20

Their attention on the barn, Jase slipped unnoticed towards his car. As he opened the door, the red-headed teen from the food tent appeared in front of him.

"Take me with you," she said. "I don't care where you're going."

"I've got no time, little girl," he said. "Go back to your mother."

"She thinks everything is wonderful in this town. Nothing I say can change her mind."

Jase leaned on the door and studied her. She couldn't have been more than fifteen, maybe younger. "Is there something you want to say to me?"

She folded her arms and looked away. But she stood her ground.

"Listen," Jase said. "If you've got something to tell me, I'll listen. But if you're going to stand there and pout, shove off."

After a quiet moment, she repeated, "You have to take me with you."

"Why?"

"Because if you don't, my mother will make me work for *him*."

That stopped him. "Doing what?"

She rolled her eyes. "You think I shaved my head for attention? He goes for the pretty ones first, but eventually he'll get through the whole freshman class. I swear I'll run away before I set foot in that house."

"I can't take you with me," Jase said slowly. "But I do intend to fix the problem. Good enough?"

She shrugged. "Do what you want; everyone else around here does." Jase watched her wander back toward the crowd surrounding the barn. No doubt about it, Winter Wyman was a hell of a guy.

The girl's resigned shrug rankled him as Jase drove off. How many times had she been dismissed and ignored? Was he just one more adult who had failed to protect her? He could sympathize, to an extent. Who had watched out for him as his mother dragged him from one town to another, state by state, whenever the police started sniffing around at her. What adult had ever filed a complaint about the kid in dirty clothes with obvious bruises sat in the back of the class in sullen silence? It wasn't until he found comrades once he was recruited and trained that he began to come into his own, and even that part of his life was a cesspool of malfeasance on the part of those who should have looked out for him. If he hadn't found his way to his present job, things would have turned out much more miserably.

Leaving the farm behind, Jase drove through the deserted streets of Cuthbert, ruminating on his mission and the girl's predicament. Were those two objectives in line with each other, or in opposition? He'd need more intel before he could make a determination. He arrived at Wyman's house. This time, knowing the corrupt and impotent alderman was otherwise occupied, he parked in the driveway. As before, he climbed up the porch supports, and in a few seconds of fiddling with an ancient lock, he was through the bedroom window.

He pegged Wyman as someone who would want his prize nearby, ready to view at a moment's notice. He checked the walls for a safe, pressed the floorboards for a hidey-hole, rummaged through his drawers, but found nothing of interest except a gilt-edged Bible and a bottle of blue diamond-shaped pills. The hallway rug was held down with a liberal amount of brass tacks. The rest of the second floor was nothing but a pair of Spartan bedrooms and a bathroom that hadn't been updated in half a century. The grimy claw-footed tub was chipped, showing layers of green, pink, and white paint.

The place was larger but had the same general plan as Spyro Talis's rats' nest. Still, he was no less cautious moving from one area to another. Just because he'd come this far didn't mean there wouldn't be a pressure plate or some other alarm.

He made his way down the back staircase to the first floor. The kitchen appliances were vintage, enameled in a hideous Harvest Gold, and dark stains orbited the cabinet handles. A jar of instant coffee was open on the counter, but the sink was empty.

The central passage had another bathroom, only slightly more presentable than the one upstairs: it had clean towels and the striped wallpaper was intact, even in the highest corners. A small utility room displayed an iron sitting obediently on a board. But he didn't bother investigating the room any further: an ivory panel demanded pride of place, even in hiding.

He opened the next door and the heavy fragrance of sandalwood hovered in the air. The drawn shades added weight to the atmosphere. A massive desk in dark wood, leather, and brass squatted like a troll. To the left was a wall of books he doubted Wyman had ever read, and in front of that, a long leather couch. Crystal decanters stood at the ready on a side table. The small houseplant on the desk seemed out of place, but the woman had done her job, and Wyman had unwittingly helped. The plant was pushed far to the corner of the desk, as if to be out of Wyman's line of sight. It had just been watered, and a half inch pool refused to sink into the dirt. Jase took from his pocket an envelope the Mac Fletcher had given him and shook it into the mud.

He searched the rest of the room with expert efficiency. The desk was locked, but Jase's multi-tool treated it like a child's puzzle. He found a Glock on top of a collection of Mass cards, a few wrinkled commendations and "Man of the Year" awards Wyman hadn't bothered to frame. Stashes of pills and bundles of cash in neat rows. But no ivory. He checked the desk for false spaces. Nothing.

He checked the bookcases for scratches and disturbed dust that might suggest heavy traffic. The first two shelves were immaculate. Jase scanned the titles, and realized that black and red and green leather covered volumes were nothing but show copies, the kind decorators sell by the yard. There was no consistency of genre or language, and several titles were repeated. Just another wilting attempt to polish a mealy apple. But Wyman's faux literary pretensions were not at issue. There must be something hidden here. and then, there it was, on the third shelf: tiny grooves beneath a medical reference. He lifted the tome out and peered at the wall behind — solid paneling, no echoes answering his pounding fist.

He examined the book. It smelled of leather and mold, and there was a spot on the edge that had been worn and dirtied from use. *Gotcha.* The spine cracked as he opened it. He flipped through the pages. No book safe, but on the dirtied pages he found a chapter discussing remedies for soft erections. One suggestion was a hand pump. He could just imagine Wyman squeezing a bulb while he tried to get it on with yet another college girl, or worse.

Someone spoke downstairs, and Jase pushed the book back into place. He stood by the door, but the sound wasn't repeated, and no one was on the stairs. He regretted parking so brazenly in the driveway, but there was nothing to be done about that. After two silent minutes, he eased his way out of the study into the foyer, looking for a hiding place. The basement door was shut tight, so whoever was down there likely hadn't come this way. The door was locked, so hopefully they wouldn't come up here, either. On the other side of the hall, he slid open a pair of shuttered pocket doors, then glided them closed again. Everything was quiet.

He investigated his surroundings. The room was empty, but lacked the stale air of an abandoned space. Unlike the old electric sconces that lit the rest of the house, recessed fluorescent fixtures illuminated the bright white paint that covered all four walls, as well as floor and ceiling. The overall effect was blinding and overwhelming. *What happens in here?* He tapped the walls, still looking for the safe that he knew must be nearby. Except for the straight edges and corners, it seemed as though he was in a giant egg, unable to find a weak spot to break through anywhere.

Another step echoed deep in the house. The panel must be in the basement, but that would have to be a visit on another day. He'd been here too long already, and didn't want to tangle with someone when Wyman might be on his way. Jase slipped through the pocket doors and re-latched them. An inconclusive search, he thought, but not without some actionable intel, and at least one tactical advantage. He let himself out the front door.

And stood face to face with Wyman's angular henchman. "In there," he growled.

"Thank you, Jeeves," Jase said as he stepped back into the foyer.

"The name's Sam," the man said. "But there ain't no need to talk."

He pointed, and Jase returned to the study. Sam followed and shut the door. Jase sauntered about the room, pretended to study the titles on the shelves. "Mr. Wyman read all these?" he asked. When Sam scowled, he tried, "You, then?" That got no response either, so he turned to the decanters and removed the stoppers, checking their contents until he found bourbon. He picked up a tumbler the weight of a bowling ball and poured himself a double. "I assume you don't drink on the job," he said. Smiling, Jase took a seat behind the huge desk, sipped his drink, and waited for his host.

He liked this view. The warm power of the room suited his mood. Without turning his head, he could watch both the door behind Sam as well as the one that led to the utility room.

He held the crystal tumbler up to the window, watching the light refract into tiny rainbows that spun across the huge expanse of the desk. Something stirred in the foyer. He took another swallow.

The door flew suddenly open. Jase raised his glass in salute, and Wyman's face fell, an expression Jase recognized as disappointment in a failed entrance. The sandalwood, the deep leather couch, the heaviness of the atmosphere were all meant to lull a visitor into a logy stupor so Wyman could burst in like a pillar of fire. Instead, Jase tipped the tumbler at him and finished the drink in a gulp.

"I helped myself to the drink. Hope you don't mind."

Wyman recovered himself and stretched out a hand. "You need a refill."

Jase let it dangle an uncomfortable second, then surrendered the tumbler. "Bourbon," he said lightly. But when he got it back, he found scotch. *Touché*. He drank it anyhow. Why waste?

"Did you find what you were looking for?" Wyman asked, pouring a double for himself.

Jase made a show of settling into the boss's chair. "No, no I didn't. I also missed the judging. Who won? I'd put my money on that gumbo."

Wyman snorted derisively. "Peasant food, laced with bottom feeders to boot. I'm not a Jew, but I follow the dietary laws. Mrs. Todesca's tuna casserole with peas took the blue ribbon." He jerked his chin toward the plant. "Despite your friend's attempt to curry favor with me."

Wyman folded himself in to the couch, his arms flung across the back: a king in his informal glory. "I'm surprised you came during civilized hours," he said. "Why not just swoop down in the middle of the night and take what you want?"

"I'm not a thief," Jase told him. "And you're still a member of the Network. Think of me as a librarian collecting an overdue book. If you recall, you were only supposed to hold it in escrow, until a certain transaction was completed. That deal's gone down, so it's time for the panel to move on to its next home. A deal in Atlanta is on hold because of you."

Wyman put up a warning hand. "Hold on a moment, son. You seem to think I know what this Holy Grail was in the first place."

Jase put the tumbler down with a thud. His voice lost all of its lightness. "Oh, you know, Mr. Wyman. Don't bear false witness."

Wyman's nostrils flared. "Ignorant people think that means not to lie. The Bible adds, 'against thy neighbor.' It means not to lie *in court*. It means not to lie in court *to implicate someone else*. It has no bearing on this conversation. You're not wearing a robe, Mr. Patton, and there's little chance I'll ever see anyone who is."

"But I am sitting at the big desk." He leaned forward, folded his hands. "Fine. In the interest of clarity, then, I'm here for the ivory tablet. The Nimrod Panel."

Wyman settled back but said nothing. Jase continued, "I know it's here. If not in the house, then somewhere nearby. I was sent to get it, and to make sure there are no lingering hostilities. You're still an important part of the Network, and no one wants you to be unhappy."

It was Wyman's turn to put steel in his voice. " 'Still,' you say? I've got soldiers in every corner of the state, and most of the region. I control every pill and vial that gets sold within a hundred miles of here. There isn't so much as a stolen bicycle that I don't get a taste of. *Still?*"

Jase knew it was a hopeless bluff, but let it go. "Nevertheless, you made an agreement. You know how it works, better than anyone."

"They could have sent you with some cash, then."

"Uh-uh," Jase said, shaking his head. "That sets a bad precedent. What if every kingpin decided to keep the collateral? No, Wyman, make it easy on everyone and let me bring it to its next stop." *Well, second stop. First he'd secure his promotion with his employer. After that, he'd sell this piece of junk to a dealer in Toronto. Let the Network try to figure out what happened to their poker chip.*

"Or?" Wyman said.

"Or, bad things will happen."

Wyman took a long pull at his drink. Jase wondered if it masked fear, or simply displayed arrogance. After a leisurely swallow, he said, "You mean a bullet to the brain? You'd be starting a war, young man. Ever seen a war?"

Jase shrugged. He drained his glass. Then he waited.

Wyman leaned forward, now clearly desperate to cover the signs of worry in his wrinkled brow.

Smiling, Jase said, "That panel comes from a very ancient place. It predates many of those stories you're so fond of quoting. I think you've already seen what it can do. No one person should be allowed to have access to—"

"Do?" Wyman echoed. His tongue showed through his teeth like a greedy wolf's.

"Of course," Jase said smoothly. "We're both grown-ups. The way it restores health and vigor. I bet you're feeling like a horny teen again. But if it grows tired of its surroundings, those benefits might sour."

Jase leaned back comfortably. He could almost see the gears turning in Wyman's mind. What benefits did he think Jase meant? After reading about the bulb inflator, he had a pretty good idea. Just a little bit more to hammer the point home.

"You've been in possession now for almost a month. No one else before you has used it for that long without seeing some reduction in its powers. I'm sure you've noticed something yourself."

"Of course," Wyman said smoothly, as if he had just won the entire pot. "That's why it's not here, not in the house. But there must be some mistake, because I never intended to keep it anyhow. If you're the one who's authorized to retrieve it, then by all means, do so."

"When?"

"I'll have it for you tomorrow."

Chapter 21

Pain fascinated him. Not that he had ever felt it himself, but he had seen it in others. He liked to watch it surge through a body, like the flicker of life. Because he could never know the sweetness of pain, he liked to inflict it on others. If he had to, he would watch it on the television. When everything else failed him, pain kept him company.

When he was small, he had no conception of pain, but he knew that those around him felt it keenly. He watched as they set out to avoid it, though they seemed always to enjoy talking about it, with so many strange words: ouch, boo-boo, charley horse, funny bone. None of it made any sense. When he got bigger, but still before his transformation, he practiced on smaller creatures. The first were things he found deep in the woods, where no one would disturb his experiments. He carefully gauged the level of pain as he systematically progressed through one attempt after another, observing the effect he had on the thrashing furry things.

Later on, he moved up to less furry creatures, the ones he caught not in the woods, but in dark corners and behind buildings, muffling them so they wouldn't cry for their mothers. It thrilled him to watch the dark bruises come out on their pale hides, and then watch them fade day by day, and then set out to create new ones. Some of those little ones tried to get him punished, but he was always protected, always allowed to try again.

Around the time the transformation began, he learned that he had to hide his experiments, but he found other ways to seek the inexpressible sensations. He tried activities where he had license to chase, and hit, and crush, though the fact that his prey wore protective helmets and padding, as he himself did, was less satisfying than the informal versions they did in backyards and streets, where there was no one to tell him he had gone too far.

But it was the men in uniform who taught him how to give pain, and he was pleased, as they were, to discover that his practice had made him good at it. They showed him how to bend, how to break, how to shatter bone. He spent many happy hours practicing how to leave deep bruises and flowing contusions. How to scatter constellations of fingerprints in flesh. While lesser ones cried out, or gave up before he did, the one who wore the crisp uniforms always singled him out for praise. They stuck colored pins on his chest, told him the colors meant something, but he never cared what.

It wasn't enough. He taught himself how to spin a blade in his fingers, how to trace the thinnest red lines. He could shave off one thin layer of skin at a time, exposing raw nerve like an archeologist digging level by level. He'd see first the clear fluids ooze through pores, then dig deeper to watch the blood bloom like roses. His subjects knew never to complain.

He could carve a pound of flesh with the edge of knife, pop fingers from their sockets, and untie ligaments at a touch. He liked to watch the bulging eyes, feel the reverberations of screams in his belly. It told him he was alive.

When he had no one to practice on, he turned to himself. But he never felt that ecstatic pleasure, only a slight neutral pressure. He had broken the bones in his hands every quarter-inch like the marks on a ruler. But he'd never ached, never experienced that sharp joy of a barked shin, not like the plant lady talked about.

In a world where he heard nothing, saw nothing, spoke nothing, pain was his only friend. It whispered to him in the dark. It painted elaborate murals in his mind. It encouraged him to indulge in his every desire.

It hadn't always been like that, but then he hadn't always been happy. There was a time, before he'd seen the desert, when he'd been lost, unable to vent his urges, unable even to name them to himself. He had tried to live like the others—rutted in beds and cars like them, felt a brief loss of pressure as he spilled his seed in some whore or another. But the release lasted only seconds, and then built again to an unbearable level.

The others, like the one who first brought him the idea of his transformation, were too small to satisfy him. But the one called Jimmycoopah, he had first delivered the truth. When Cooper made the revelation of the ceremony he called "Balder Dead," then he knew truly what his destiny was, and he began his transformation. As with his earliest experiments, the ceremony was performed in the woods, often with a sacrificial flame. Jimmycoopah demonstrated his invincible nature by inviting the contemptible lesser beings to hurl any manner of object at him. They tried boulders, bottles, branches, anything they could send flying at him. He endured with feigned laughter (for he learned to utter the sounds of pleasure the same as they did, though he knew nothing of their delight) the attacks with tire irons and cement blocks and once even the blade from a snowmobile. Jimmycoopah said it proved he was the avatar of Balder, the great god, and he came to realize that, yes, he must be. The others hurled, strangely, angry words at him, too. Strange accusations about letters and mail. They said something about breaking homes, but didn't puppies need to be housebroken? He was no dog, he was a god. But it was all done in laughter, and so he accepted their offerings both in beer and with whatever tramp would let him take her against a tree. It was his due.

There were times that even he knew he must not inflict the pain he so dearly loved. Times when, in the interest of slipping into the soft-gloved hand of his only friend, he must for a moment refrain. And so he pretended to be like the others. He drank beers, he drove cars too fast, he ate silently while those he had to tolerate prattled on about family, and futures, and favorite movies. He endured the boredom, and the poison slid through his veins like a snake. Then, when it was time, he stalked into the night and reviewed his training.

But when he arrived in the desert, he hid in plain sight. He looked like the others, slept beside them, stood by them in firefights. Once, he had been close enough to one of his "buddies" catching it that at first he didn't know whose blood had splattered in his eyes. When he heard the guy thrashing in the dirt, half his throat gone, his chest gaping wide, he knelt down and put a calming hand on the wound. They locked eyes, and he saw that this man who thought he was a friend now knew exactly what was happening, that he was enjoying the spectacle of watching the life pouring out of that shredded hole. The last thing the buddy saw was his blissful smile.

To anyone watching, he was the great hero, sticking with his brother. But only the two of them would ever know that the soldier's last moments were devoted to the torturous experiments of what it was like to have one's organs crushed by a steely hand, and to look your tormentor in the eye.

There were many others: farmers, civilians, enemies, strays. In the chaos of battle, as a city crumbled into mud on the banks of a bloody river, he satisfied his sweetest urges, was even decorated for them. Those were the happiest days of his life.

Then, one night, when the tracers lit up the sky and the ground heaved with the shock of rocket fire, he'd made a mistake. Surrounded by too many bodies, too many temptations, he'd indulged in one experiment he'd never before dared. He lifted a dying man's hand and put it in his mouth. Not cannibalism—he didn't want to taste flesh. He only wanted to feel finger bones crushed beneath his teeth. How they vibrated through his jaw! But he'd been spotted, and arrested, and court-martialed. They hurled him back into this straitjacket of a town where too many people knew each other, where once again he had to show a simpering, compliant face to his captors: the old one who howled like a maniac and called him son, the witch-like plant lady who smelled of rot but kept him fed.

At first, he had been welcomed. The others bought him beers, the whores offered their bodies. He repaid them as well as he could. When he played too rough, they knew not to complain. He was a hero, by all the gods!

But now the witch kept him under some kind of spell, drained his will with potions, so all he could do was pleasure himself like a monkey. Yes, she had given him that one toy to play with, the one that resembled Jimmycoopah, and he had meant to make it last all night. But it was a cheap, flimsy toy to begin with, and had broken almost immediately. Still, it had been fun while it lasted, and it gave him a taste of what he'd been missing.

Soon, though, soon, he would rise up again, and they would know his power. And that old man would help him do it.

Chapter 22

The sun would be setting soon, but Starr needed to clear her head of the chaos of the past two weeks. It had all been so crazy—Jase's sudden arrival, their passionate nights together, and then his insane plan to get a stupid piece of ivory from her father. And at the same time, she had to cover up the murder of Jimmy Cooper to protect both her brother and the man she loathed more than anyone else in the world. Luckily, she was well practiced in planting stories as well as herbs, and through hints and smatters of gossip with certain clients, had put it out that Jimmy had gone to Colorado. She'd done it so subtly that she doubted the lie would ever be traced to her.

But today's antics were the last straw: that idiot Rich Sutton and his merry band of malcontents parading through the farm. As if ruining the one day when Cuthbert ever had any fun would be the best tactic to get the quiet they wanted. Didn't they understand that those bells made the town unique? Or were their lives so empty that the gentle tolling of the hours merely reminded them of their inevitable path to the grave? She had no illusion that the confab in the farmhouse led to anything except violent threats on Wyman's part, and she knew that he'd follow through on each and every one. The kicker was that for once, she knew she had a winning recipe in her gumbo, but however well-disposed Wyman might have been to granting her the blue ribbon, Sutton and his cronies had spoiled it. Once Wyman had declared the winner—that old harridan Mrs. Todesca—Starr had gathered her things and headed straight home.

Now she was lifting garlic out of the earth. It was a repetitive, meditative chore: she stuck the old tarnished fork beneath each bulb, loosening the thread-like roots, and knocked off the clumps of dirt that clung to them. She'd already dug up about two dozen, with almost a hundred more to go. But it was easy work, and her mind drifted.

Who the hell did the old man think he was, coming into her house and smashing glasses? As if she hadn't saved him, the way he always needed saving, yet could never admit it. He had a lot to answer for. The list went back to the earliest days she could remember. Days of sin, dead and forgotten, he said? Well, that explained a lot. But those days were very much alive in her mind.

Like the time when she was a little girl, and Clay still slept in a crib. Her mother had just put him to bed, and Starr was looking forward to having mommy all to herself. Where was daddy? Working, her mother said. At the time, Starr was too young to recognize the resentment in her mother's voice, but she came to understand it all too well over the next few years. For now, though, it just sounded like mommy was tired.

They were all living in this house then. Starr snuggled against her mother on the living room couch, in front of the console TV watching *Designing Women*. But they hadn't got to the first commercial when her father burst into the house. She heard a ceramic figure explode against the wall—only now did Starr recognize his pattern of grabbing attention. This time it was a little gingerbread house, not one of her mother's best works. Otherwise, it wouldn't have been left in such a handy spot.

"Get behind the couch," her mother whispered, and Starr wriggled into the slanted space by the wall, barely breathing. A second later, the television fell silent and she heard her father stalk into the room.

"I'll kill him," he screamed. "Double-dealing faithless liar. Who does he think he is?"

"Who, dear?" Starr could picture her mother, resting her hands on her father's shoulders, sliding them down to his arms, then his wrists. It always focused him. "Who was it?" she said gently.

But her father's voice hadn't lost any of its heat. "Ron Larsen. Said he'd sell me that lot on Orchard Road, but then he went and signed the deal with Ed Thompson instead. I would have given him twice its value, but just because they played a round of golf in a hailstorm, he decides they're brothers in arms." Then he unleashed an ear-splitting shriek, and Starr knew he'd wrenched his hands free and grabbed fistfuls of his long dark hair.

But Starr's mother kept her calm. She cooed at him as if he were baby Clay. "It'll be all right," she whispered. "Everything will work out."

"It won't," he whimpered. "They already signed the papers. I needed that land. He promised it." He moaned like a wounded animal.

"What's paper?" her mother said. "Listen, I can write on paper, too. And this is what my letter will say."

Starr smiled at the memory. The scent of garlic hovered over her as she finished the harvest. She took out a small brush with stiff bristles and cleaned each bulb one more time and put them into an old picnic basket. By now, it was past dusk, and her knees ached from the prolonged kneeling. She brought the basketful of garlic to the huge table in the living room. Half of the table was already filled with rows of dried, browning stalks. She put down the new additions, lying them side by side. Using her fingers, she rubbed the dirty papery layers off each head until they all shone white, then snipped the gnarled roots into a bag to compost.

The couch where she had hidden was long gone, replaced by a refrigerated case, but her mother's words still echoed off the living room walls.

"What does Ed Thompson know about real estate? He doesn't even know what goes on in his own house. Just last week I took the kids to the playground, and I saw his wife skulking in the Rhode House parking lot, before it was even open. I thought she had the DTs. But then a car pulled up and she leaned in the window."

"She's a whore?" her father said. Young Starr's ears tingled.

"Better than that," her mother answered. "A junkie. The driver of the car sold her a package of brown powder. She practically danced. She was putting it in a pipe before the car pulled away."

Wyman sounded hopeful, like a child who might not have to go to the doctor's office after all. "Would you be willing to tell that story to Thompson? It might get him to back out of the deal."

"Him and anyone else who'll listen," she said. "He can't go about developing your properties when his wife's got a monkey on her back." She said it the way a mother might promise a lollipop.

When the garlic bulbs were ready, Starr scanned the table for three of the biggest ones. Nestling the bulbs together, she crossed the stems, starting a braid. With each bend, she added another head—smaller, larger, smaller—forcing the brittle shoots into tight neat folds.

She didn't remember anything else about that night. It was too much like so many other of her father's outbursts and her mother's rescues to stand out. But she did remember going for a hike with her parents through the woods on Orchard Road to see the site he'd somehow acquired. Her father was exultant, her mother silent. Periodically over the next few weeks, Wyman would take Starr to the lot to watch the brush get torn up, the trees cleared, the stumps drilled and pulled. He'd been so happy he even refrained from slapping Starr, who cried over the roaring machines chewing up defenseless plants while squirrels and rabbits ran for their lives. She had never forgotten that sadness. Even today, as she drove by the sordid little strip mall he'd built there, she felt the loss of the quiet green space.

The bells of the campanile were chiming eight o'clock. She'd made a half dozen garlic braids, each the length of her arm. She washed up, squeezing lemon juice on her hands to cut down on the garlic smell. Time to check on Clay.

She knocked on his door, more out of politeness than anything else, and wasn't surprised that he didn't respond. When she entered the room, she found him lying naked on top of his bed. His fists were clenched by his sides, his eyes fixed on the ceiling. *At least he's not hard*, she thought. Doing her best to act like a nurse, Starr took a blanket from a chair and draped it over him, noting that the scabs on his knuckles were healing, but still vivid against his sun-starved skin. She chatted about making the garlic braids, and the butterflies that had hovered above her head that morning. She told him who she'd seen at the picnic, hoping a name would spark a memory. Clay responded to none of it, and she wondered, not for the first time, if there was any understanding behind those blank eyes. Had he really known what Jimmy Cooper was up to, or had he just been following some atavistic instinct to hurt?

There was nothing else to clean up. Hands on her hips, she said, "I'm going to make dinner now. Why don't you come down and eat at the table with me?" She studied his face for a reaction, but he didn't even blink.

"I know I smell like garlic, but it's not that bad, is it? You like it when I put it in your spaghetti sauce, don't you?" Stepping from his side, she opened a window, letting in the cool evening air, then turned back to him. "Or I could bring dinner up, of course. But it would be nice having you sit at the table, like in the old days."

Still nothing, and now she was worried. What did she have on hand for catatonia? Maybe some peppermint oil mixed with black pepper and fennel?

She moved closer to check his breathing. The blanket rose and fell evenly. "Clay? Clay, honey? Why don't you get up?" She reached for his shoulder, hoping to jostle him into clarity. But before she touched him, his far hand shot out from beneath the blanket and caught her wrist. He had a grip like a vise. His eyes remained staring at the ceiling, but he twisted her arm so sharply she dropped to her knees, her elbow up above her head, her face close to his ear.

"Clay. Clay, stop it. You're hurting me."

As she struggled, he gripped tighter. For the first time, she feared for herself. Would she end up like Jimmy Cooper, beaten like a rag doll? She tried to convince herself that he would never hurt her, not his own sister and caretaker. But she had no idea what had provoked him. Was he jealous of Jase? Did he think she'd given Jimmy to him as a punishment? And then, as her breath grew short and came in heaving gulps, she remembered what had happened to his only girlfriend Patty. Of course, he hadn't done that. Everyone knew it was guy who just popped up one day. But still, no one ever saw him again, and Clay never said where he'd been when *that* happened...

Then, for almost the first time since he'd come home, Clay spoke, and it did nothing to allay her fears.

"Mine."

Chapter 23

After his chat with Wyman, Jase drove back to Winter in July. The crowds had thinned, and he had his choice of parking spots in the sheep pasture. The blue grass band had been replaced by a radio, and most of the high school volunteers had either left or were sitting in the shade with piles of leftover burgers and sodas.

His first stop was the cook-off tent, but the woman and her gumbo were gone. He saw that first prize had gone to a tuna casserole, something, thankfully, even *his* mother had never forced on him. But there was still life in the beer tent. He followed the loud chatter of the die-hard drinkers. Pushing open the flap, he let his eyes adjust to the gloom.

Dank air filled the tent, and the sour smell of spilled beer choked him. The same crowd from at the Rhode House now slumped on folding chairs that teetered on the damp ground. He found Terry rolling empty kegs onto a hand truck.

"You again," she said. The top of her damp sundress clung to her, but the skirt swirled around her strong legs.

He nodded. "Me again. Any suds left?"

"That all you want?" She led him back to the portable bar and filled a clear plastic cup.

"It's a start," he said, blowing off the foam. He drained half the beer before he tasted it. He'd enjoyed Wyman's bourbon, but was happy to wash away the memory of the interview they'd had.

Terry watched him down the beer with the air of someone who couldn't be impressed. "You should've been here earlier. You missed a good show."

"I don't like bluegrass." He held out the cup. "Pour me another."

"Health regulations," she said, tossing the empty on the ground. She got a fresh cup and opened the tap. "I wasn't talking about the band," she added.

"Tell me. Then I'd also like to hear more about Wyman and his family."

Terry's face fell, and the light in her eyes went dim. "Not here," she whispered. "Seriously, I didn't think you were stupid. If you'd seen what he did to Dick Sutton today, you'd know what I mean."

"Then where?"

"I'm off once I clean this up. We can go to my place. Go get something to eat, and I'll be ready when you get back."

An hour later, he was parked at a brick apartment complex that clashed with the style of the rest of the town. They rode the elevator in anxious silence to the third floor, and Terry let him in after throwing back the deadbolt.

She kept a sparse apartment—bare hardwood floors, an Ikea couch, a flat screen TV that overwhelmed the tiny living area. DVDs lay strewn on the floor like ivy. Her taste ran to dark mysteries and revenge fantasies. Frigid air spilled from the a/c and nipped at his skin.

"You want a real drink?" she asked.

Her galley kitchen consisted of a microwave, blender, and boxes of pasta. The counter was a forest of liquor bottles. She plucked the Maker's Mark from the center and filled a juice glass.

He took it and said, "I don't suppose you bought all of these bottles?"

"Fuck no. The owners don't miss them. And for the work I do, they owe me extra every once in a while." She poured herself a pint glass of vodka and sauntered into the living room. She stood by the air conditioner, letting the cold blast dry the sweat on her back.

Terry stretched luxuriously. Her dress tightened in the right places, billowed in others. He had no illusions about what she hoped for. "I can't believe I got you here. I thought Starr Wyman had her claws into you. I feel like I stole her prize."

Jase said nothing. His eyes roamed the bare walls. He settled into the couch and said, "Tell me more about Clay Wyman."

She glared at him, and drained her glass. "What do you care about that piece of shit?" Again he said nothing, holding her eyes. "Fine," she said, relaxing into a slouch. "I asked a couple of people. He was in Baghdad, ok? Right at the beginning. One of the first that went into that secret prison."

"Atta girl," he said with a grin. *If Clay was at Abu Ghraib, he wouldn't have been anywhere near the Museum. There was no reason they would have crossed paths.*

She made a show of unsticking the dress from her skin. Jase said, "What else can you tell me about your friend? Who was the guy?"

Her hands tightened into fists. "For that I need another drink." She stalked past him to the bar and filled it to the top again. Then she fell into the couch beside him. "I don't know who he was," she said quietly. "I'd never seen him before. Military. Someone said he and Clay were in the same unit, but like I said, after that night, after what happened to Patty, he just disappeared."

"Was Clay there that night?"

Terry shook her head. "Starr was, though. At one point she was throwing herself at the guy, but he just ignored her and went for Patty." She took a long slug of her vodka. "For once, I wish that slut had won. Then she'd be dead and Patty would still be here. Stupid shit Patty. She never knew how to pick a man."

She was falling fast into the darkness. He put down his drink and slipped a hand under her dress. She didn't stop him, just said, "You trying to take advantage of me?" Then she put her own glass on the floor and put her arms around his neck.

"Just trying to keep you focused," he answered after a long kiss.

She adjusted herself beneath him to let his hand wander more freely. "Focused on what?"

"How did Wyman find your friend's killer?

Terry pulled away. "Is that all you fucking care about? She's dead, and so is he."

"It's important," he pressed. He reached for her knee, but she pushed him off and lifted her glass.

"I told you. I went to Wyman. You know, at his fucking weekly audience at the Hammer and Tongs. He said he'd find out from Clay who it was. Then I heard I didn't need to worry. The story in the paper was that a Gulf War vet in Havilah had been shot during a drug deal. I recognized his picture."

"I thought you said Clay was a vegetable."

She shrugged, and the glass dropped and shattered. She looked at it forlornly, but didn't move to clean it up. Jase thought she must have gotten started drinking at the tent, she was too far gone for what she'd had here. "How the fuck should I know? I told Wyman about Patty's hook-up and a few days later he was dead. What do I care?" She broke into sobs and he gathered her against him. He carried her into the bedroom, and helped her forget about death for a while. He had to ignore the lockbox on the bedside table, the kind that held a large pistol. He told himself this was outside the parameters of his mission, but he didn't listen. The other woman he needed, but this one he wanted.

She was as lithe as the snake tattooed on her ankle. When he took off her dress, he discovered the vivid eyes of a coiled dragon tattooed on her belly, as if protecting the treasure below. Her entire short and compact body thrummed with energy.

When they were through, it had long been dark. They lay next to each other, the cold air from the a/c unit blowing over them. He noticed that despite the rough sex — he knew he'd be bruised later on — her hair was firmly in place around her skull, like a 1930s gun moll. "So what did happen in the barn?" he asked.

"Well, no one will ever say what happened inside, but we all saw Wyman bring Sutton and his friends inside, and they closed the door. Twenty minutes later, they all left."

"Doesn't sound like much of a show. Didn't anybody look in a window, listen at the wall?"

Terry rolled on her side to face him. "No one listens at doors when it comes to Winter Wyman. No one needs to. The upshot is that they all went in angry, and then they came out looking like whipped dogs. No one tries to upstage Wyman, especially at his own party."

"So what did Wyman tell them, just to knock it off?"

She caressed his arm, while the dragon looked on. "Let's put it this way: each and every one of them was happy to walk out of that barn on their own two feet, and every time that damn bell rings, they'll thank god they're alive to hear it."

Jase suddenly got up. "I need to go," he said.

"Now?"

Jase sat on the edge of the bed, pulling on his pants. "I'll be back, but there's something I've got to do."

"What brought you to this shit-dump town, anyhow?" She sat up and embraced him, kissing his neck. He tried to move her hands off, but she raked her nails against his chest and bit at his shoulder. He gripped her wrist even harder but she just giggled.

He pushed her back and stood up, turned on the light to find his shirt.

"I told you," he said. "I'm here on business, and I've got an appointment."

The dragon seemed to move of its own accord. "It's midnight, and tomorrow's my one Sunday off this month. Cancel it."

"Like I said, I'll come right back." He slipped into his shoes.

"Does it have anything to do with Dick Sutton and his bell chorus?"

"Probably not. I only want to know more about Winter Wyman. You really didn't see what happened in the barn?"

She shook her head. "Old Wyman basically told them he'd cut their fucking throats if they pulled a stunt like that again. Said they'd be run out of town on a rail with their petitions shoved down their throats and the gong shoved up their asses. When Sutton left, he didn't even get in his car. I saw him stagger onto the road in a daze. Those other bitches, I never saw them at all."

He stood over the bed, kept his eyes focused on hers. "Would you ever cross Wyman?"

Terry curled up in a ball, as if to protect herself. "There's no sense reaching into a rattlesnake's den. Not unless you got some thick gloves. You ask me, Sutton and his girlfriends got what they deserved." She rose from the bed. She approached him like a judo fighter stalking her opponent, and he let her close enough to feel the heat rising off her skin. They kissed one last time, and she tried to curl around him like the snake on her ankle.

"See you in an hour," he said, reluctantly pushing her away.

"I'll be ready," she answered.

He rolled down the Mustang's windows to let the smell of sex blow off his skin. In a few minutes he was at the same dark shoulder near Wyman's house. He followed the familiar path through the trees. Soon he had a light to guide him. The second-floor square told him the old man was in his bedroom. Exactly as he expected. Once Jase had planted the seed that the panel had the power to get him hard, he knew Wyman wouldn't waste a minute before trying it out.

He snuck up on the house noiselessly. The climb up the side balcony was an easy scramble. Flattening himself against the wall, he inched toward the window. It was open and he heard moaning voices and grunts. He chanced a look through the corner of the window.

It was the blond girl he'd seen before, naked and bent low between his legs. Wyman seemed to be in a trance. He held the panel aloft, staring at its creamy white figures. The girl's attentions might have been nothing more than a summer breeze for all he seemed to care. Then she sat back and Jase saw why.

Winter Wyman was stiff as a flag pole. The girl was moving to straddle him.

Satisfied the plan was working, Jase climbed back to the ground.

Too late, he heard the rush of footsteps. He felt a crack on his skull, and he was floating into oblivion.

Chapter 24

Starr waited in the dark outside the bell tower, her arm still throbbing from Clay's burst of temper the day before. From where she stood on the lip of the hill, the campanile eclipsed the thinnest fingernail of moonlight. She told herself the reason she stayed outside was that the cool air felt good after the bug-infested walk through the woods. She wouldn't admit, even to herself, that it would feel wrong to enter the den of the jungle's new lion. *It couldn't be that. This is my turf,* she insisted. Yet she remained pacing in the grass overlooking the slumbering streets of Cuthbert.

Where was Jase? She never saw him after yesterday's events at Winter in July. He should have been putting his part of the plan in action by now. The rational part of her mind swore at her for being so childishly lovesick. Gritting her teeth, she entered the bell tower, picked through the gear he left behind. None of it was personal—no clean clothes, no toiletries. So he had left, and the bastard couldn't even be bothered to clean out his mess.

Back outside, she surveyed the town below. Here and there lonely sets of headlights glided silently through the town, but they were all too sleepy and slow to be Jase. She had lost track of how long she'd been here, like a sea captain's wife on a widow's walk. Everything seemed to have been going well in the Cook-Off tent, until that damned Rick Sutton showed up to protest. She never even got to tell him that Wyman had taken the plant from her, just as they'd planned, though she still didn't know what good that would do. *Where was he?*

Starr's shoulders slumped. She had to leave this place. Why didn't he just steal the damned piece of junk and take her away? Of course, if he did, Wyman would pursue them to the ends of the earth. He'd never let another Wyman woman leave him, not without a hell of a fight. And what would he do to her when he caught them? He couldn't let her live, not with Jimmy Cooper so easily found if anyone thought to look. It would be too much of a risk that she'd talk.

The mechanism wound up to strike, and Starr surveyed the streets again. He wasn't coming back any time soon, she admitted. She sighed and returned to the deeper darkness of the woods. She stepped surely through the trees and entered her yard near the compost bins. She forced herself to walk normally. *Nothing's going to claw its way out. Jimmy's never coming back. No one ever does.* But her frightened half disagreed. *The smell would attract rats and worse. Didn't think of that, did you?*

On the second floor, the television illuminated Clay's curtains. The rest of the house lay dark. Exhausted, she climbed the porch steps. All she wanted was to sleep, to forget everything: her father, her brother, and especially Jase Patton, sex and all.

She left her muddy shoes on the mat and drifted into the kitchen like a ghost. The aroma of garlic still hung in the air. She was considering burning some sage when she caught another scent. Licorice. But she'd poured out the last batch of tea. Then a voice sounded in the dark.

"Where have you been, you degenerate?"

She was too tired to jump. "What the hell do you want?" Without turning on the light, she sat at the table. She could barely make out Wyman's outline, a patch of black darker than the black on the wall behind him.

"You've got the mouth of a whore."

She sat up straight as a school girl. "I used to give you kisses with this mouth. Remember that, Daddy?"

His seething rage vibrated through the floor and table. She heard him start to rise, and knew if he did, there'd be another violent explosion.

"Anyhow," she continued, "where I've been is none of your business. I might just as easily ask why you're here instead of entertaining your own little harlot. Did her carriage turn into a pumpkin? Did she get turned off by what you did to Sutton and his crew? Or do you just not fornicate on the Sabbath?"

"A father may do as he pleases." She thought he sounded oddly proud of himself, and wondered if something had changed since she'd last seen him that afternoon.

"I'm pretty sure your book says something about old men lying with young girls," she said, sounding him out.

His fist struck the table, and this time Starr did jump. His eyes glinted with malevolence."I came here to see my son, and I found him unattended. Now, tell me where you've been."

Starr refused to be rattled. Not here, not now when she was so close to her own goals. "I took a walk in the coolness of the evening, dear father. I wasn't gone more than..." How long could he have been waiting? "Fifteen, twenty minutes," she finished.

"I've been here half an hour."

She sighed. "I guess I lost the ability to tell time by the movement of the stars."

Wyman's voice twisted into a combination of fury and fear. "Don't you understand he needs constant care? You can't ever leave him. Nothing takes priority over family."

Now she unleashed her own fury. "Now you care about family? How the hell am I supposed to shop for him? Get him new clothes when he ruins them? Where the hell are you, except to tell me I'm not doing a good enough job?"

"Keep your voice down. He'll hear you," Wyman hissed. "I couldn't care less how you get it done. Just make sure you do."

"Or what? I'll end up next to Jimmy Cooper?"

Wyman's silence told her she hadn't missed the mark. So now she'd been threatened by both her brother and her father. Over what? The fact that she'd saved both of them? That they couldn't stand for her to be so indispensable? Or was it that she knew too much about each of them, and needed to be silenced for good?

Finally, he said, "I need to see him now. Is he clean?"

The insult was as bad as a slap in the face. "How should I know? You're the one that's been here half an hour."

"Don't start with me, you. Go wake him, and make sure he's presentable." Her eyes had adjusted to the dark, and she saw him put his hand protectively on a satchel.

He's got the thing right here, she thought. Her anxiety came rushing back to her. *Where the hell is Jase? They could take it and leave right now.*

Instead, she led Wyman upstairs. With each step, her dread grew. Only an hour or so before, Clay had let her escape, though she had no idea why. Would he still be in the same violent state? In a struggle between son and daughter, which side would Wyman choose? Or would Clay turn on the old man and save all of them?

Heart pounding and head swimming, she knocked on Clay's door. No answer, no sound at all. She entered and found him still stretched atop the sheet, but thankfully asleep. The television mutely projected bondage porn. Hiding her apprehension, she shook him awake.

"Clay. Poppa's here. Wake up. Poppa wants to talk to you."

"Turn that filth off," Wyman growled from the doorway. "Is he cleansed? Has he... has he spilled his seed?"

She checked by the light of the television. "No."

"Then leave us." Wyman held up the satchel. "This is for no enchanter's eyes."

Let him play with his magic toy. If Clay woke up and did decide to hurt Wyman, she wouldn't have to make a choice about whether to help one or the other. She retreated to the kitchen. Taking a seat at the table, she tried to do her breathing exercises. But the disquieting jangle of bedlam kept distracting her. Through the ceiling, she heard the drone of Wyman's prayerful voice winding itself into a howling fury. The stomping of his boots shook the pictures on her wall. Periodically, Clay's confused grunts cut through the din. She couldn't make out any words distinctly, but at one point Wyman bellowed a series of exclamations that could have been commands. Was he performing an exorcism? What had Jase told him about that hunk of ivory?

Too anxious to be still, Starr moved to the living room, redolent with garlic. The hum of the refrigerators and the lush wall of greenery dampened the sounds above. The fragrance of the room soothed her despite the tumult. Uselessly, she watched through the window for the Mustang's headlights. If Jase would just show up now, it could be all over.

Wyman's voice grew shrill. Clay answered in angry barks.

After an hour, the mix of animal cries abruptly ceased. She heard a thud that might have been a punch, followed by a yelp of pain. Wyman came dashing down the stairs, the ivory panel clutched under his arm and blood pouring from his temple. He fumbled at the front door, then flew outside. A moment later, his car screeched into the night.

Through the window, she watched the red lights disappear into the darkness. Upstairs Clay was absolutely silent.

Chapter 25

Jase woke in a fetid room with a pulsing ache in the back of his head. The only light came from feeble moonbeams weaving through the bars of a basement window. He was slumped on the floor across from it. He wondered how sturdy those bars were.

The painful bite of metal on his wrist told him it didn't matter. As his mind cleared, he realized he was cuffed to an iron ring sunk into the concrete foundation. His swollen hand throbbed. He chafed it with his free hand, but it did little to ease the discomfort.

As he woke up, so did his other senses. The stench of shit, piss, and vomit filled the air, making him gag. Someone's labored snoring told him he wasn't alone in this dungeon. He tried to catch a glimpse of his roommate, but the moonlight was too dim. But at least there was the chance it wasn't his own stench he was breathing.

His thoughts swam in an incoherent whirlpool. How long had he been here? His watch was gone, but he judged it had been around one o'clock when he'd been knocked out. Then again, he had no way of knowing if this was even the same night. The need to piss gnawed at his groin. He struggled to break free, until he kicked a metal bucket. It rolled away from him, and he had to stretch search until he could coax it to roll back towards him. It hurt to move. His muscles had tightened while he was out, but soon enough he got himself into an awkward kneeling position and let fly into the pail. The echo stung his ears. Across the room, the snoring stopped a moment, then picked up as loudly as before.

He guessed he had gone through the day into the next night. His mouth felt like cotton and he was starving. He jerked the chain, but all he got for his efforts was a useless jolt of pain.

"Hey!" he called. A spiked ball shot up his spine and he thought his head would explode. Still, he tried again, shouting, "I'm awake! Hey, I need something to drink!"

The answer came from close by. The snorer croaked, "They don't hear you."

Jase still strained to dislodge the iron ring. "Where are we?"

"Winter Wyman's basement hotel."

Then he remembered. The locked door he hadn't had time to investigate.

"Who are you?" Jase asked.

"Spyro Talis. You're the son of a bitch who broke into my house."

"Sorry," Jase said. "It wasn't meant to hurt you, just part of the plan to get to Wyman. What are you doing here?"

"Thanks to your damn plan, Wyman thinks I'm involved in whatever you're up to. When he found out we'd met, he put me down here. Every day him and his goon smack me around, but I got nothing to say. Now maybe I will."

Jase pulled on the cuffs again, more in defiance than anything else. Nothing in his training came to mind about dislodging a bolt embedded in concrete, not without a knife. "I'll figure out a way to get us out, make it up to you."

Talis's laugh was thin and hollow. "I'm not in chains, mister."

"Then why not escape?"

"What for? After they beat me, they shoot me up. I nod off more here than I ever could at home. Yes, sir, I'll stay at this hotel till the manager carries out my pin-pricked corpse."

They lapsed into silence, and Jase used the time to extract a stiff wire out of the paracord of his survival bracelet. When he had the whole six-inch length free, he twisted it into the keyhole. But before he sprung the lock, someone opened the basement door. He crushed the wire and buried it in his pocket just as a light switch clicked and banks of fluorescent bulbs burned his unprepared eyes. Jase squinted against the glare and watched Sam step into the room.

"It's about goddamn time," Jase spit out. It sounded weaker than he'd hoped.

Sam ignored him and strode over to Talis. He lifted the junkie by the collar, and contorted his face in disgust. "You shit your pants again. No damn respect for yourself." He backhanded Talis twice, but got no response.

In the light, Jase saw that Talis had lost half his weight since he'd last seen him. His arms looked like a road map, the veins red against his pallid skin. Here and there, like interstate hubs, angry sores oozed blood and pus. His face was a swollen wreck.

"Leave him alone," Jase said. "You've got me. What's the point of torturing him?"

Sam dropped Talis with a sickening thud. He turned on his heel, and all his angles seemed ready to cut Jase next. "Stay out of what ain't your business. Mr. Wyman decides what gets done 'round here. You'll have your own turn soon enough."

"What do you want to know? I'll tell you if I can. Just let him go."

"I warned you to stay out of it." Sam shoved Talis against the wall and kicked him twice in the ribs. The crunch of breaking bones was loud enough to be heard over Talis's screams.

With Sam's attention on pummeling Talis, Jase drew the wire from his pocket. His hands shook as he tried to pick the lock on the cuffs. Once he lost the wire, and he looked up anxiously to see if Sam had heard it clatter to the floor. But Sam was too intent on abusing Talis to notice. After a minute, Jase was free. He waited another moment, and when he judged his tingling legs and arms were as steady as they were going to be, he lunged and caught Sam in a powerful choke hold and drag him off Talis, who had mercifully fallen unconscious.

Despite being at least a decade and a half older than Jase, Sam put up a vicious fight. Recovering from the initial shock of Jase's escape, he twisted and wrestled Jase to the ground. In his weakened state, Jase could only block some of the pummeling he received. The few punches he did get in Sam ignored as he would a baby's tantrum.

Jase scuttled out from under the onslaught, but Sam stopped him with a nasty kick from a steel-toed shoe. But as he drew back for another, Jase caught his foot and wrenched it. Sam collapsed and Jase was on him in an instant, fueled by utter rage, pistoning his fists into Sam's nose, his teeth, his ribs. Sam blocked the body blows then heaved Jase off him. Both men were on their feet immediately, standing in puddles of puke and shit. Sam plowed in close, his arms flying.

Jase took some of the blows, parried others. When he found his opening to lunge forward, he wrapped his good arm around Sam's head. He hooked a finger in the huge hole in Sam's ear, and the guard screamed. The ear stretched and snapped, gushing blood. Sam threw a lumbering punch that Jase was able to catch like a fly ball. He twisted until Sam sank to his knees, his face screwed up in pain.

"Now," Jase panted. "Where's Wyman?"

"Right here."

Both men turned to see Wyman silhouetted in the powerful lights. His hair stuck out like a demonic halo. He held a gun in his right hand, and a satchel hung from his shoulder.

He intoned, " 'The heart is deceitful above all things, and desperately wicked.' That's what Jeremiah says. 'He that getteth riches, and not by right, shall leave them in the midst of his days, and at his end shall be a fool.' "

But Jase wasn't impressed. "Trying out for a movie with that speech? Who's the fool, Wyman? You've still got the panel. What's the matter? It didn't work for you? Or maybe it did, but quit? It looked to me like you were in good working order with that girl. I hope you treated her right for what she had to endure."

"What would you know about it?"

"I saw your pitiful liaison before this piece of shit" — he pointed at Sam — "clocked me. What was he doing up there anyhow? He like to watch?"

"I could ask the same of you, Patton."'

Jase rubbed the back of his head. "I was checking to see the panel was working as I promised. But let me guess, you asked it do something else and it didn't come through for you. I can explain that."

The gun wavered. "Well?"

"Not here," Jase said. "I need something to eat, and a drink would be good, too. Besides, this place is disgusting. For God's sake, clean up this poor guy and let him go. He needs a doctor."

"I hate to admit, but he's right," Sam said, pressing his hand to the gushing wound. "I can't stop this bleeding in my ear."

"Shut up," Wyman said. "He means Talis. But Talis is beyond redemption, stiff-necked as an ox. Now that I have what I want, he's due to suffer a merciful overdose of the heroin he loves so much."

Jase nodded. "Fair enough. I don't think he'll mind. But for God's sake, let's go upstairs. What time is it? I notice that this is one of the few places in town you can't hear the damn bells."

Wyman's smile was thin and cruel. "Nearly midnight. The Sabbath is well nigh over. You lost a full day thanks to your perverse curiosity."

It was a struggle to stand, but Jase refused to let Wyman see him tremble. It would ruin everything. "I won't quibble over your definition of perversions, but like I said, get me a drink and I'll tell you what you've missed."

Wyman's gun hand wavered uncertainly. Maybe he was feeling the same worry as Jase. He hid it by tucking the revolver in his waistband. "Sam, clean up the mess. We'll let Mr. Talis have a few more minutes before he gets to meet St. Peter."

"But my arm—"

"Is one of two. Don't make me incapacitate you altogether." He waved Jase toward the door. "Don't bother trying to take this from me and make an escape, Patton. Sam's not the only one on the grounds, and your car has been towed away. I'm afraid you've earned a parking ticket."

"No worries, Wyman. Lead on."

They left the room, while Sam whimpered as blood continued to pour down his arm.

Jase groaned inwardly when he saw the steep stairs leading to the first floor. But Wyman had regained his composure, and he had to at least appear to do the same. "I'll be interested to hear your explanation, Mr. Patton," he said, opening the upstairs door. They walked amicably down the hall toward the office. "And how you've come to understand the panel's properties so well."

"I've made a careful study," Jase said. "Of course, I'm sure you have as well, and you must have made the proper sacrifices after your, er, restoration of manhood?"

They passed into the foyer and Wyman stopped with his hand on the doorknob of his office. He let the gibe pass, but cocked his head at Jase with sincere confusion. "Sacrifices? I was led to understand that so long as the panel was in my rightful possession, it would do as I bid it."

Jase shook his head. "Has anything ever worked that way? You need a burnt offering, or a meal offering. I'm surprised at you, Wyman. You should know better than that."

The old man's eyes widened in fear and shame. He opened his mouth to speak but said nothing. It took some effort for Jase to hide his satisfaction at hitting Wyman's twisted understanding of Old Testament practices. Wyman's shaky hand opened the door and switched on the light.

His tall frame blocked Jase's view, but Wyman's sudden collapse into retching revealed the sight soon enough. Ignoring the old man, Jase watched the myriad inch-long triops skitter across the mahogany desk. Most splashed in the pool around the plant the woman had given Wyman, where he'd sprinkled Mac Fletcher's envelope of dormant eggs into the standing water. Some had fallen to the floor and fanned out, exploring every crevice. Their shield-like carapaces knocked against each other, their forked tails flailing. Everywhere their gills and legs and antennae pulsed, vibrated, probed.

"What… what is this?" Wyman choked out.

Jase stepped into the room and reached down to examine one of the creatures. Its fluttering gills tickled his palm, just as they had in Mac Fletcher's lab. "Looks like a plague," he said evenly.

"You knew this would happen, and you didn't warn me." He gripped the door frame with brittle fingers.

Jase barked, "You weren't ready to listen. Are you ready now?"

"Out." Wyman shot an angry finger toward the door. "Get out of here. Leave me in my anguish."

"I can't do that," Jase answered him. He held out his hand. "My wallet and watch?"

Wyman pointed wildly. "On the desk." Jase walked around the desk, sweeping the triops off his things. He put on the watch and slid the wallet into his pocket.

"You may leave," Wyman said weakly.

"No. We have matters to discuss. Now."

"Very well. In the kitchen." He pulled the door shut, then bellowed down the basement stairs, "Sam! Leave that. Get to my office!" He staggered into the kitchen, still clutching the black satchel. He dropped into a chair, so Jase helped himself to a bottle of whiskey he found on the counter, pouring out measures for himself and Wyman. He put the glass in front of his host, and sat with the bottle between them.

"What are the proper ceremonies?" Wyman asked after he'd had a slug of whiskey.

"Look to your scriptures," Jase said. "They lay out the procedures. I'd say this is a sin offering you're looking to do. You've passed the point of merely making a savory smell to please the Lord."

Wyman pushed his hair back with both hands, then poured himself more whiskey. "You seem to know more about scripture than I would have thought. What you say is correct. I'll perform it immediately. Sam can't drive, so you'll need to get the lamb for the slaughter."

Jase laughed, though it hurt. He held a palm to his swollen eye. "I don't think so, Wyman. You can handle providing the livestock on your own. Besides, you'll have to wait until you've cleansed yourself before you can handle the offering. Plan for the day after tomorrow at midnight. Perform the ritual at the Church in the Woods during the darkness of the New Moon."

Wyman nodded. "In the meantime, I suppose you'll just walk off with the panel."

Jase had considered doing just that. It would bring him enough money to live on for a good long time. And he could be shut of this town and its resident perverts. But finishing the job he'd contracted for would bring him a lot more in terms of power and status with his employer, and that would make the headache worthwhile.

"I'm your friend," Jase said. "Maybe the only one you've got."

Sam's shrieks pierced the quiet. He bounded into the kitchen, his broken arm dangling at his side. Blood still flowed from his ripped ear. "That's it, Wyman. I quit."

Wyman pointed to the damaged ear. "You pledged yourself to me for life, Sam. The only way out is through death."

Sam grimaced but stood his ground. "I won't do it. I draw the line at—"

Wyman drew the gun out of his waistband and aimed. "Well?"

"Well," Sam said, deflated. He lurched around and stalked out of the room, taking a broom off a hook on the wall.

Jase watched him go without comment, the way a visitor might watch his friend's rebellious teen acting up. When they were alone again, he finished his whiskey. "I'll be leaving now," he said. "I have errands to attend to. Remember, Tuesday midnight."

He strode out the front door, leaving Wyman shaking in his chair and Sam cursing the plague of triops in the office. His arm had regained feeling, and as he walked the stiffness and bruises from the fight worked themselves out of his legs, too. He couldn't afford to give into the aches. He had a lot to do.

Chapter 26

Starr woke suddenly from a dreamless sleep. She didn't know what had startled her, but it had left her with a flood of adrenaline that caused her to shake uncontrollably. The crickets in the yard were silent, and she teetered to the window and looked out, wondering if a bear had lumbered into the yard. Instead, she saw the figure of a man. He stood there at the edge of the trees, surveying the area. Even in the dark, he looked tattered, unearthly. For a mad moment, Starr thought he was Jimmy Cooper, rising from the soil. "Wait there!" she called, when she recognized Jase.

Finding her balance, she clattered downstairs and then was running across the lawn. She got close enough to embrace him, but Jase waved her off. "I need to sit," he breathed.

Starr scoured the lawn in the darkness for a few broad plantain leaves. To her mind, there was no such thing as a weed, just a plant growing where it shouldn't. She spotted some in the dim light and picked a handful. She chewed them to a pulp, ignoring the asparagus-like taste. There were a lot of vegetables she liked, but she could never abide that.

Meanwhile, she put her arm around his waist and led Jase to the house. Up close, he looked even worse: blood clotted in his hair, fresh scratches all over his face, one eye swollen half shut. A nasty pall of sweat and filth enveloped him.

Inside, she sat him at the table. He let her dab the wet plantain leaves at the worst of the clots, but winced as she scraped off the new scabs. "I need to clean out the wounds," she said. "Then aloe to soothe it. Take off your shirt." She turned to fill a basin with soap and water.

He pulled the shirt stiffly over his head. When the overlapping purple and green bruises were exposed, she forced herself not to gasp.

"Where have you been?" she said, gingerly applying a cloth to the worst cuts.

"Visiting your father, as a matter of fact," he breathed.

Of course he was. As she soaked the scabs and blotted the dried blood, she wondered how often she had been in this same situation because of Winter Wyman. After Clay had thrashed Jimmy Cooper beyond saving and beyond recognition. The times Wyman had lost his temper when they were children, and she had to learn First Aid from an outdated Girl Scouts manual she'd found in a box her mother left behind. How often had little Clay cut and bruised himself just by being a clumsy little boy, and all of it Starr was expected to clean up.

And of course, there was the series of messes to be cleaned up before and after the anonymous tip that led to the discovery of Patty Wilson's body. Why didn't the dead stay dead?

"Doesn't look like you had a productive talk." Her own voice seemed to come from a great distance, cutting through the fog of memories.

"We did, eventually. This was the warm-up, from his loop-eared sidekick."

"Sam?"

"He's faster than he looks. I slowed him down a bit, though." He managed a grin, but it didn't fool Starr. He was hurt more than he'd admit, even to himself.

Rivulets of bloody water flowed down his face and chest. Whatever she cleaned off was replaced by new gore. An oozing wound had opened under his ribs and he shuddered like a foal when she pressed the cloth to it.

"Looks like the woods had a say in it, too," she said, forcing a laugh. She picked twigs and leaves from his scalp and dropped them in his lap. Then she broke off the fat leaf of an aloe plant and handed it to him. "Rub this over the smaller cuts. I'll get some gauze for the big one on your chest."

While she rummaged through the emergency kit she kept for Clay's accidents, she asked him how he'd come to appear in her backyard.

"I saw that you walked from the bell tower, so I figured it couldn't be far. I thought I could follow the same path."

She unwound a roll of gauze and some lengths of tape. "There isn't much of a path. It's more like a series of landmarks. And most of those are personal, like places where I found a wild herb or something."

"Now I know. Anyhow, it's going to be all over tomorrow."

Her eyes sparked. *Tomorrow.* "I want to hear everything. But I need to clean that up." She let him paint his face with the aloe, and lined the gauze and tape along the table. "One more thing. I'll be right back." She ran to the upstairs bathroom for a jar of homemade calendula salve. She heard the scrape of Clay moving restlessly in the next room. Her spirits crashed. Even now, here she was, taking care of one man, getting ready to deal with the other. The noise in the kitchen must have woken Clay, and she'd have to check on him when she'd finished with Jase. But first, she had to hear about tonight.

Back in the kitchen, she found Jase standing at the refrigerator. Despite his mottled back, he still looked powerful. She regretted her anger, now that she knew he'd been hurt. She should have done something to prevent it. Putting the salve alongside the rest of the supplies on the table, Starr reached her arms around him.

His reaction was swift and instinctive, a stinging blow to the face. When she hit the ground, a shock of pain flashed up her spine and she screamed. He spun with the punch and his face was a mask of confusion: wide eyes, flared nostrils, clenched jaw. But then his expression softened, and he held out his hand to help her from the floor. "I'm sorry," he said. "You surprised me, that's all. Are you all right?"

Starr refused his hand and rose unsteadily on her own. He tried to put his arms around her, and she recoiled. She tried to shake off the pain and the fear. She understood the wild reactions to surprise among those who had deployed. She'd seen it plenty of times with Clay. All of her desire had drained when she hit the floor, but even so she still wanted to be near him, needed to be. But what kind of escape would that be? She had to leave as soon as Jase could take her, because if she lost her nerve, she might never regain it. Though wouldn't it be just trading one patient for another, and tie her down with another mess?

As all of this swirled in her mind, Jase leaned down to kiss her, and she made a decision. She wrestled out of his grasp. She would shake it off eventually, but she needed him too much. But not yet.

It must have been the scream that set Clay off. She never heard his approach, didn't realize he had joined the action until she heard his roar. Starr turned in time to see Clay fling the table aside and barrel towards them. Jase stood paralyzed at the sudden appearance of the wordless figure. Before she could speak, Clay had lifted him by the belt buckle and slammed him against the wall. Finally roused, Jase brought both hands down in simultaneous chops to Clay's neck, but they had no effect, as she knew they wouldn't.

"Clay, stop!" she screamed. "Don't hurt him. He's my…" *What was Jase?* It didn't matter. She hung from her brother's arm, trying to release the grip it now had on Jase's throat, but he shook her off. She realized that he'd gone beyond any rational control. There wouldn't be any docile compliance again. Jase was kicking and twisting, but his face grew purple. Only when Jase went limp did Clay let him fall.

But Jase had been playing possum. Back on the ground, he shook his head clear and landed a solid punch to Clay's jaw. But all it did was turn his head a little. Clay answered with three precise punches to the ribs, making sure to hit the open wound. Jase staggered in pain. Clay laughed, then clutched at the ragged skin again. Jase screamed in agony, but that only made things worse.

All the while, Starr was shouting for Clay to stop. She tried to place herself between the two combatants, but Clay batted her away. But it was enough of a distraction for Jase to re-center himself. When he found an opening, Jase tucked his head down and rammed it into his attacker's groin. He pushed the man back, but what should have been a crippling blow did nothing else than gain him some ground. When Starr saw them push past the overturned table, she changed her tack and told Jase to stop.

"Are you serious?" Jase said, crouched in a defensive stance, ducking a roundhouse swing. "This guy's not human."

The insult angered Clay more than any punch, and he lunged forward for another go at Jase. But instead, Starr jumped between them again, shielding Jase.

"Stand down, Clay," she said firmly, though her legs felt like wilted stems. "He wasn't hurting me."

Her brother snarled, but didn't advance. "Sit down," she said, pointing to the one chair that hadn't been knocked over. "Over there. Then I'll see if you're hurt."

Blinking, Clay turned around and slunk to the chair. Behind her, Jase was panting and wheezing. "He should be on the floor in pain," he said hoarsely. "He hasn't even worked up a sweat. He's a monster."

"Not a monster," Starr said, helping Clay take his seat. "It's a condition. He can't feel pain. It almost killed him when he was a baby. It's called Congenital Insensitivity to Pain with Anhidrosis."

"With what?"

"Anhidrosis. It means he can't sweat. It gave him fevers when he was little, but it made him a super-soldier in the desert. He could work all day in that heat. As long as he knew to keep hydrated, nothing bothered him. I've read up on it, of course. There's an entire family in Italy that has it."

Her calm tones had soothed Clay, who still seethed in the corner, but made no more moves to attack. The danger past, Starr let Jase take care of himself and tended to Clay instead.

"Shhh," she said while Clay muttered and snorted. He flinched like a skittish colt, but she kept her hand out invitingly. "Let me see your jaw. Don't move." He let her take his chin in her gentle hand and she probed for any broken bones or bleeding. Clay allowed her to work, but his red-rimmed eyes never left Jase. "Open up," she said. "Did you cut yourself in there?" She reached back and said to Jase, "Get me a flashlight. Left hand drawer." Like a doctor she palpated Clay's neck, feeling for anything out of line.

"Don't worry," she said softly. "I'm here. I'll take care of you, just like always."

As she said it, she realized it was still as true as it had been the night they hid in the closet. If she left, who would take care of him? Wyman? Sam? Clay had no one—no one but her. She was chained to him. Forever. She'd have to make some kind of deal with Butler.

"There's no way he could have got past the army medical with a condition like that," Jase said, handing her the flash.

She shined the light inside Clay's mouth. "You'd be surprised. Clay was smart enough not to mention it. His recruiter was a pretty shady character to begin with. Always worried about his quota. When they were building up the surge of troops in the desert, it was more important to let people in than to keep them out. Do you really think no one over there had asthma, or depression? All the recruiters cared about was covering their own asses. No one was looking for an extremely rare disease."

"But he'd have to submit a medical history, and all those blood tests."

Starr turned and gave him a sympathetic look, as if he were a naive child. "And Winter Wyman couldn't get his hooks into the most respected physician in Cuthbert? Dr. Fuller supplied the letter, and a few revised reports, in exchange for silence about some pretty damaging personal information. It took some finesse to switch the blood samples, but not as much as you might imagine."

"So Clay really can't be hurt?"

"He gets hurt," she explained, handing the light back to him. "He just doesn't know it. He used to get cuts and bruises at school all the time. Once someone closed a door on his finger and broke it in three places. Look." She held up Clay's right hand. The index finger was twisted, so the last two joints were perpendicular to the rest. "He went back to class and no one noticed for three days."

She tapped Clay's chin and his open mouth clapped shut. "Doesn't look bad, honey. Maybe you just scraped your cheek on your teeth."

"That why he doesn't talk?" Jase asked.

She paused, formulating her answer. "No. He was normal before. At least as normal as anyone who can ignore a hot iron on his hand. The war did the rest. People with CIPA are susceptible to depersonalization. So something he saw over there, or did, along with PTSD…" She found herself unable to go on. The truth was, no one knew why Clay had gone mute, and what she did know, she didn't want to share.

"Shouldn't he be at the VA hospital or something? He could get treatment."

There was no way around it. She spoke slowly, afraid to give away too much. "For one thing, my father wouldn't allow 'the shame' of it. For another, Clay was dishonorably discharged. Don't press me on why. He only gets VA checks because the depersonalization happened while he was on duty. So I'm the treatment. I clean him, talk to him, check his temperature five times a day to make sure he doesn't have a fever."

"That's all that can be done?"

"There are treatments, but Wyman thinks he can pray it away. Mac Fletcher did some research, and found a drug called naloxone has had some experimental success." She pressed at Clay's belly and chest, raised his arms and checked for excessive bruising.

Jase raised an eyebrow. "You mean Narcan? That's for OD's."

Starr rolled her eyes. Why did people think it was all one-to-one? The world was filled with multi-use plants and drugs. "And botox can kill you, smooth your wrinkles, or treat your migraines. Nature doesn't have a rule against double-dipping." Starr finished the checkup. "You didn't do any damage," she said, looking at Jase for the first time. "Listen, even I know there's not a lot of homeopathic help for him. Thanks to Mac, the naloxone brings a glimmer of hope. Sometimes I see the gears running behind those eyes."

"You get a prescription?"

She snorted. "You'd think with the OD's we have, there'd be a free dispenser on every street corner, like in some cities. But since it's not approved for CIPA, Mac has to score it for me. Some weeks he gets me syringes. Sometimes it's the nasal spray. We've got the spray now. Next week, who knows?" She smoothed Clay's hair and straightened his collar. "I'm his nurse, his housekeeper, and his only friend."

Clay nodded. "Mine," he whispered.

Chapter 27

Jase absorbed the crazy tale the woman told him. He wondered why his research hadn't turned up such a perverse set of circumstances. Isn't that something his employer would've told him, too? He wondered, not for the first time, if the setup over the ivory panel was to end him, and not Wyman.

There was certainly reason to think so. From the time he'd been recruited, he'd always questioned his decision to join. He wondered if it was really his, or the influence of his mother, who had filled their days with a steady stream of her own brand of idealism. Jase now looked at it as more brainwashing than true belief. His brothers in arms were sincere in dedication to the mission, but in the few moments he had to himself, he never found the inner voices calling him to action.

So when a stranger with a steady eye sidled up to him in the corner of a bar, he was ready to listen. Maybe it was because he'd entered alone, though he was obviously on leave and should have been with some of his buddies. She seemed to know him, sussed out his doubts, painted a picture of what he could do with his skills if he simply never went back. He only had a beer or two, but at the end of it, her words had charmed him beyond the power of alcohol. She made him see that the mission was too short-sighted, was doomed to fail. The more he listened to her, the more sense she made. She had an answer to all of his objections: how he could take off without being pursued, where he would stay, how he'd start a new life. She made it all disappear with a few words, and he was sold. He never went back, and no one ever came after him.

But if you do it for someone, they could do it to you. What did she owe him? His employer was just that—a business person who had to make decisions that benefitted her and her organization before anything else. Had he tipped his hand at some point? Show that he was getting too hungry to remain a soldier? A suicide mission fifteen hundred miles away would be the best way to be rid of him, no questions asked.

On the other hand, in for a penny, in for a pound. He may have left his uniform behind, but he never left a job undone. He toyed with the new bits of information he had, and revised his plan. By the time the woman had brought her freak brother to his room and come back to the kitchen, Jase had a whole new strategy, and it clicked in a way the old one hadn't.

"But this plan is working," she told him, after he laid out the changes.

"Yeah. We just need to goose it up a bit," he answered. "When it's over, we'll both have what we want."

"You'll take me with you?"

"Of course," he grunted. He'd have to keep stringing her along, but that didn't bother him. When the time came, he'd cut that cord as easy as letting a bass swim off downstream.

She pressed on, never doubting him. "You think Clay will be all right? You'll leave Wyman alive?"

"I told you I would." Jase couldn't tell if she believed him or not. Not that it mattered. He laughed to think he'd been worried that freak would blow his story. The beast didn't even talk, would never know, let alone be able to voice, the lies in his story. "But I have to see to a few things. First step, I need my car back."

"First, you need to get some sleep. The rest of this can wait until morning." She led him upstairs to her bed, and he followed her willingly. But when they had shut the door, he was still keenly aware that the monster was only a few feet away. They undressed each other slowly, kissed softly. But when they were in bed, lying next to each other, the violence of the night, and exhaustion of his recent imprisonment overcame both of them. Neither was up for anything except slumber. They fell into still, silent sleep, like carvings atop a grave.

He woke alone, in a room filled with sunlight. He heard something downstairs, and dressing as quickly as his aches would allow, he went to join her. He tossed a worried glance at Clay's closed door, wondering if the giant was there, or waiting for him below. He had no desire to go another round with her brother, not when things were just now coming together.

But she was alone, and she handed him a mug of coffee. "Do you want breakfast?" she asked. He was ravenous, but needed to get moving. Instead, he reminded her of the tasks she needed to take care of. He asked for directions to the impound lot, so he could get the Mustang back. Finishing the coffee, he set out on foot, leaving her in a flurry of preparations. Before he left her yard, he'd forgotten all about her.

It was a half hour walk, which gave Jase time to work out the final hitches. With a chuckle, he had every detail clear by the time he arrived at the public works yard. After a quick, unchallenged recon, he spotted the Mustang. It was parked behind a row of pickup trucks outfitted with snowplows that no one had bothered to remove for the summer. He sauntered around to the front gate. The guard, a twenty-something kid who still had a face full of acne, didn't take much convincing that he'd be doing Mr. Wyman a favor to just let Jase take the car without the usual formalities. He handed over the keys, which had been hanging on a hook beneath the window of the booth at the entrance.

It all seemed too easy, so when he was hidden from view by the battalion of snow plows Jase dropped to the ground and inched beneath the chassis. He inspected it for extra wires or blocks of explosives, even for cut brake lines. But Wyman didn't have that kind of imagination. The Mustang was ready to ride. He got in and started it up. The purr of the engine soothed him in ways the woman's gentle touch couldn't, nor Terry's more animalistic exertions. But he'd enjoyed both while they lasted. He put the car in gear.

"Hey, Mister," the kid said when he opened the gate to let him out. "You don't look so good. You know, Mr. Wyman's daughter might have something for those bruises. She lives—"

But Jase missed the rest when he gunned the engine and aimed the car back towards the center of town. Time to get it on.

His first stop was at the Rhode House. Terry was getting ready to open for lunch, taking chairs down from the tables. When she saw him, she said, "I guess I know why you never came back. You look like what I wanted to do to you for ditching me."

"We need to talk," he said, sitting in the chair she'd just put down.

"Oh, shit, are you going turn into a puddle on me? I thought you were a good fuck, but if you're going to start asking me what it means, and if I still respect you and shit, you can just give yourself a hand job."

Jase didn't smile. He just reached for a chair down and flipped it over in front of him. "Sit," he said.

He spoke so sharply, she dropped as though she were playing musical chairs.

"I don't have a lot of time, so cut the bullshit. You knew the guy who killed your friend, and you're the one who told Wyman where to find him. Tell me everything you know, and no lies this time."

Her eyes widened as if she'd been slapped. He leaned forward to remind her that was a real possibility.

She submitted. "Fine. It doesn't matter anymore. He said his name was Mike Harris. I don't think he was really military. He came around asking questions, just like you. Except he wanted to know about Starr Wyman. He was a good-looking guy, and I thought he was sniffing around for some pussy. I just couldn't figure out why he was interested in her. He seemed to know all about the town, and everyone who lived here. But he didn't go to school around here. I figured he must've lived in one of those mansions that are technically part of Cuthbert, but the people don't ever mix with us. You couldn't even find their houses are if you didn't know to look."

"So how could he have met her?"

Terry shrugged. "She's Wyman's daughter, and besides everyone goes to her for that herbal shit."

"What did he ask you?"

"That's the strange thing. He seemed to know her, and Clay, but it was like he hadn't seen them since they were kids. I thought maybe he'd had a crush on her and wanted to reconnect. He asked if she was still in the same house, if she still was close to her brother, stuff like that. I said she was going to be at this party if he had such a hard-on to meet her."

"How did he end up going home with your friend?"

"Well, I told you I never liked Starr, and I thought, fuck if I'm going to help her hook up with this guy. I had someone to take home that night, so I told Patty to do whatever it took to keep Harris occupied. She wasn't too smart, but she could tease a man as well as anyone. She pulled him into a corner and who knows what she said and did to distract him."

"Don't stop now," Jase warned her.

Terry nodded, like a guilty child coming clean. "I tried to keep her away, but Starr heard that he was looking for her, so when Harris went to get some drinks, she followed him. I signaled Patty, and she jumped in front of Starr and started ripping her up and down talking all kinds of shit. It got pretty loud, and Patty got a fistful of that hippie's dirty hair. That's when Clay swooped in and hit Patty, punched her right in the fucking shoulder. She was wearing a strapless dress, and you could see from a mile away he'd dislocated her arm. The bones stretched out her skin like it was rubber. The animal actually laughed about it."

"So why did you say Clay wasn't at the party?"

"I didn't want to distract you. Clay's so strange, you would've thought he killed Patty."

"You said he dated her."

Terry nodded. "But it was Harris who did it. I know it was. He's the one that took her home, not Clay."

"Go on."

"Well, when Clay hit Patty, that's when Harris came back. He had no clue what happened, except that Patty was crying and her shoulder was out of place, and she was asking could he please get her out of there. She said it would be worth his while. She got him out the door before he even knew Starr was there. I figured he'd take her to the hospital, but she never went. Next day, the police found her in the shower, her head bashed in, water still running. Her arm was still dislocated, and I heard the other one was, too."

He didn't have much time left. He needed the rest of the story, not the minor details. "How did you track Harris down?"

She gulped. "Jimmy Cooper, the guy who took off for Colorado without even saying good-bye." Something in her eyes told him she was still holding back.

"What I heard was, he wasn't much to care about. What's your interest in him?"

She looked away. "Jimmy wasn't all that bad. Sometimes he talked too much, but he could be... sweet."

"You two had a history?"

Her eyes blazed, the way they had when they were in bed. "Jealous? Think you're my first? Or that you were so good I forget anyone else I fucked? As it happens, Jimmy was the guy I went home with that night. And plenty of times since."

Jase took it all in, then made his decision. He spoke urgently, insistently, and stopped only to make sure she understood and agreed to her role in his plan.

"Can you do it?" he asked.

"Of course I can, you moron. Anything to get back at that whole fucking family."

She looked at him with resolve and defiance, but he'd never know that when he left the Rhode House, he left Terry in tears, banging her fist on the table.

Jase's next stop was in a forgotten part of town. The house he was looking for was the only one on the street with a fence, a white plastic stockade that seemed to be keeping the rest of the neighborhood at bay, instead of trying to smarten the place up. The pickets dipped to give a view of the wide porch, complete with swing, but the fence was higher where it enclosed the backyard. Surrounded by dilapidated houses with unkept lawns and broken down cars, it looked like a polished gem among piles of slag.

Jase let himself inside the gate and slalomed through a field of abandoned toys. He heard the screams of fighting toddlers. Making sure to put on his friendliest smile, he rang the bell. Nothing happened. He tried again, leaning on the button, but the noise inside continued unabated.

He banged with his fist. The chaos stilled, and the door opened.

Dick Sutton looked as harried and aggrieved as the children sounded. Jase kept the smile fixed to his face.

"What do you want?" Sutton said, his voice on edge.

Jase held out his hand. "My name is Jase Patton. I thought we could discuss what happened in the barn with Winter Wyman."

Sutton automatically reached for the offered hand, but then eyed it with distaste. He fought the habit of the well-bred and left Jase hanging. "No way. Wyman made it quite clear what would happen if I mentioned anything about that, uh, conversation." He stepped back, nodding in sudden understanding. "He sent you, didn't he? Tell him I got the message." He started to close the door. Jase put out his foot and blocked it.

"He didn't send me."

Sutton's expression changed from anger to confusion. "Then what do you care? So I hate the damn bells. You would, too, if you had to put up with this all day and all night. If it's not them," —he jerked his thumb at his screaming twins— "it's my wife. And always those goddamn bells."

"Well, I can't do anything about them," Jase said smoothly. "And from the barricade you've built around your property, I'm guessing you don't really like your neighbors, either. But maybe we can help each other. What did Wyman tell you in that barn?"

The fear was deep in Sutton's eyes. His mouth twitched and the strength went out of his grip on the door. Without meaning to, Jase pushed it open. It revealed a living room where books and toys fought for dominance. The toys—dolls, trucks, a playhouse with a fire truck's ladder leaning against the window—seemed to be winning.

"No way," Sutton said, his voice shaking.

"Then let me do the talking," Jase said, pushing himself inside.

He made a place for himself on the couch by moving a stuffed bear that had been propped up to read a copy of Plato's *Republic*. "What do you teach, Sutton?"

"Philosophy."

"Not a booming market for philosophers, is there?"

"Well, I've got a job." He said it with the voice of a man who had defended his choice more than a few times.

"What I mean," Jase continued, "is that you probably do a lot of thinking, a lot of writing. But you don't get out much, do you?"

"Do you often barge into people's houses and deride their professions? What did you say your name was again?" He stood with his arms crossed. Jase got the idea he was trying to loom over him, but the effect was pathetic.

"Let me get to the point. You're not the kind who's used to action."

"Fuck you!" The words lurched haltingly out of his mouth, as if his lips weren't used to forming the sounds. "I can act as well as anyone."

Jase shook his head sadly. "Listen, I'm giving you the chance to do something. Hear me out."

Sutton tightened his arms. Looming became self-protection.

"Good," Jase said, leaning back in the couch. "So. What if I gave you a few propositions to chew over? That's what philosophers do, isn't it? Make propositions? What if no one cares about these bells except you? What if no one's listening?"

"Plenty of people agree with me. I collected enough signatures at the—"

"Shut up. I'm trying to give you information that people really would notice, if you knew how to spread it."

"Why me?" Maybe Sutton wasn't as reliable as he'd hoped. The man seemed ready to fold like a sheet of paper. He ran through the options, though, and found none. Sutton would have to do, but it would take coaching, and he didn't have much time for it.

Jase answered, "Because he beat your ass using nothing but his mouth. No man, thinker or doer, likes to live with that."

"Ok," Sutton said slowly. "Now I'm listening."

Old Blue Eyes sang "Witchcraft" through the open window. It was the only sign of life in Mac's house. No lights, no conversation, no finger snapping. Jase walked around to the bulkhead and lifted the inclined door. At the bottom of the concrete steps he banged on the metal door. Nothing. He pounded again, and heard the scuttle of someone trying to sneak out of a room. He shouted, "Mac, it's Jase! I know you're there, and I'm coming in, whether you open the door or not."

"You wouldn't get to first base, not even a big-leaguer like you," Mac shouted through the heavy door. "You try to breach my defenses, and it's Endsville for you, man!"

"What the hell has gotten into you, Mac? Open the damn door."

"Nothing doing! If I'd known you were going to give those triops to Winter Wyman, I would have told you to cash out from the start." Jase heard the clash of metal on concrete. "Hit the road, man. Wyman's gonna send a hurricane right up my keister. Who else could have made those things?"

Jase banged again. "Mac, open the door. Wyman has no idea you're involved. He thinks you're just a phony hipster."

The insult cut through the panic. "I'm no phony! This is my life!"

Jase laughed, despite himself. He let his voice drop from insistent to quiet menace. "Open the door, or I'll make sure Wyman knows it was you. Not that it'll matter for much longer."

There was no answer. Jase listened, but heard nothing. He imagined Mac standing behind two inches of steel wondering if even that would be enough to keep him out. Then a latch snapped, and another, and the door swung open.

Mac stood in the dark, lit only by the glow of digital readouts on the lab equipment. Jase could barely make out the cruel hook of a crowbar in his hand. But his grip was slack, and Jase wondered if he had the strength to lift it, let alone swing it.

"You were going to end me with that?" he smirked.

Mac reddened, but he said, "No, it would have been the hydrogen cyanide. I rigged the canisters out there in case some fink tried to muscle his way in."

Jase shook his head in wonder. "This town has more booby-trapped basements than Baghdad."

"Cuthbert can be a quiet town, or a riot town, as Frank says."

He reached out and relieved Mac of the crowbar. "My advice, Mac, is that you blow this town."

"I like it here," he said. "I've got prospects."

But when Jase explained what he needed, and what was going to happen, Mac's face fell. "I see what you mean. Yeah, I got some of that in my safe storage place. But you're right. As soon as you leave, I'm packing up and starting over. If that crazy chick knew what I was doing, she'd kill me."

"I don't think she'd kill you."

"You only saw her and me at the Rhode House. She's a class-A freak, man. Anyhow, this Rat Pack thing is getting tired. It's been a while since I listened to the Sex Pistols."

Chapter 28

Not long after Jase left and Starr had fed Clay his breakfast, Chief Bill Butler's blue Tahoe grumbled to a halt in front of the house. She left off cleaning the dishes and watched from the living room window while he talked into his radio and checked the time. Then he looked over some papers on a clipboard. What was he stalling for?

She shrugged and went back to putting dishes away. By the time Butler was knocking at the door, the kitchen counter was clear except for the small compost bucket and its cloud of fruit flies. "Come on in!" she called.

Butler's boots clomped on the floor as he made his way to the back of the house. In the seventies he'd been a greaser, known for using Cuthbert's winding farm roads as a testing ground for his chopper. He'd often outrun the very force he now led, and he still affected the look he'd cultivated in his biking days: a thick drooping mustache, pomaded hair, and deeply tanned face and arms. The only concession he'd made to his position was that he'd traded the white T-shirt for a blue button-down and a gold badge. But anyone could still see the blurred outlines of a naked woman tattooed to his forearm.

"Hi, Mr. Butler," Starr said sweetly. "What brings you to this neck of the woods?"

He stood in the doorway, feet firmly planted. "Afternoon, Miss Wyman. Sorry to intrude. And I'm here officially, so that would be 'Chief Butler.' "

She laughed. "Sorry. I still think of you as I did when I was little. Can I offer you a drink?"

He looked around the house skeptically. "Your father often raves about your licorice tea. Have any of that?"

She put her hands on her hips. "Wint Wyman raves about his daughter? That's a new one. But it so happens I'm fresh out. How about some black cohosh?"

He couldn't hide his disgust. "Maybe just water, if it's all the same."

He kept his place in the doorway while she poured some from a pitcher in the fridge. He drank it in one gulp, then put the empty glass on the table. "I wonder if I could ask you a few questions."

"Go ahead. But could we go outside? I have chores to take care of." She waved off some of the fruit flies.

He waved gallantly. "Lead the way."

She took the compost bucket and stepped into her rubber boots. To her back, Butler said, "I'm here about Jimmy Cooper. I understand you know him."

"Chief, you know better than I do that in Cuthbert we don't have any strangers. Jimmy and I were in the same high school class, so of course I know him."

"Since then, I mean."

She shrugged. "When he was younger, he used to do odd jobs for my father, and sometimes I saw him for that reason. He'd drive if Sam was sick or something. Not lately, though."

"He come here a lot?"

"Hardly ever." They'd crossed the yard to the compost bins. Since last week's rains, it had taken on its usual appearance, and she figured there was no one else in town who could recognize the signs of disturbance anyhow. She felt heat coming out of the detritus but told herself it was just her imagination. No one would notice anything, not until the snows came and failed to blanket this one spot in her yard. But even so, she'd already put out the story that he'd gone west. Jimmy Cooper would molder in peace.

"What about last week?"

She shook her head. "I heard he'd left town," she said. "Two or three weeks ago." She lifted the plastic cone that covered the scraps bin and dumped the bucket. "Someone told me he went to Colorado."

"And who would that be?" Butler was examining the three compost heaps. She wondered if he felt the inordinate heat, too, or if he thought it was just the normal process at work.

"I'm not sure. I heard it at the Rhode House. Maybe Terry?"

Butler shook his head. He was idly probing the middle bin with a stick he'd pulled out from the tangle that crowned it. "She told me she'd heard it from you."

Now it was her turn to shake her head. "Maybe someone else then. I get a lot of gossip from folks who stop by for their teas and remedies. It could've been anyone."

Dropping the stick, Butler faced her. "There's a guy been around, drives a black Mustang. Seems to hang out near Bell Hill. Know anything about him?"

She nodded. No sense in lying about that. "I had a couple drinks with him at the Rhode House, but that was more than a week ago."

"Anything else?"

She folded her arms resolutely. "That's none of your business, Chief."

It was his turn to nod. But Starr couldn't be sure if he had scored a hit with that or not. How much did he know about Jase? Had Wyman told him anything?

Butler pressed on. "He talk to you about Jimmy?"

"Nope." Starr made sure to keep her eyes on Butler, and not drift toward Jimmy's final resting place.

Butler pointed to the house. "What about your brother? Maybe he knows something?"

"I'm sorry, Chief Butler, but I think you know Clay is in no condition to socialize. He hasn't said more than a word or two to me since he came home from the war."

"But I remember that Clay and Jimmy hung out in school. I thought maybe Jimmy had come to visit at some point."

"Nope," Starr said again. She started over to the tomato beds, on the other side of the central herb garden. After a reluctant moment, Butler followed.

"How long does it take for that stuff to break down?" he asked, pointing a thumb over his shoulder. His offhand tone suggested he'd finished the official questioning, but Starr wasn't convinced.

"Depends on what's in there. Leaves and grass, a couple weeks. Vegetables, a bit longer."

He stood over her while she kneeled to break off dead leaves and yellow vines from the tomatoes. "What about something like steak?"

And there it was. "You don't put meat in," she said patiently, as if she were giving a tutorial. "It brings rats, and ruins the compost so you can't use it in the garden. Nothing goes in but vegetative matter. Are you thinking of composting at your house? I'd recommend getting one of those closed plastic barrels that you can spin. This kind I use starts to stink after a while."

"They seem to work for you."

He was hinting too close to home. If she wasn't careful, he'd be grabbing a rake from her shed and digging Jimmy up. And that would be the end of the Wyman clan for good. She and the old man would be in prison, and Clay would end up in a locked ward strapped down and sedated for the rest of his days.

"I don't have neighbors to bother."

Butler looked around as if he had just noticed the fact. "You could have quite a party and no one would complain."

"No one would come, Chief. I socialize only a little more than Clay does, and always down at the Rhode House. You can ask anyone who cares to notice."

"So I gather."

She'd had enough. "Is that all?"

He dropped the bucket next to her. She hadn't realized she'd left it behind. "I think so, Miss Wyman. As I said, just looking for Jimmy Cooper."

"You'll have to fly to Denver," she said.

"Maybe. Funny thing is, you never asked why I wanted him."

She shrugged. "None of my business. Jimmy wasn't an angel in high school. I don't think he's an angel now."

He looked up as if he might be able to spy an angelic host. "His kind don't go to heaven, I guess. Thanks for the composting advice. I'll see myself out."

She watched him wade through the field of wildflowers on the side of the house. Only after his car had turned around and headed back to town, did she feel that she could breathe easy. When she felt she had gained control of herself, she surveyed the garden. As always, there was more weeding to do. The tomatoes were more than two feet high, and a number of fruits were already starting to ripen. In the next bed, yellow pitcher-like flowers hid under the umbrella of squash leaves. So did a pair of hungry rabbits that she shooed away. She took up the bucket and got to it.

She reviewed Butler's questions while she worked. It was obvious he suspected her of having a hand in Jimmy's disappearance. The mystery was whether he knew Jimmy was dead. To her mind, the Colorado dodge had started off well, but now seemed a bit thin. She tried to remember if he'd ever shown an interest in packing up. Well, everyone had. Nothing unusual for folks to leave Cuthbert. No matter what Wyman did—picnics, jobs, a thriving criminal enterprise— this was still the sticks. Whenever a person had the means, they pulled up stakes and hit the road. More importantly, had he ever mentioned a destination he'd like to explore? She had to admit she'd never heard him say anything, so Colorado was as good a guess as any place. Maybe she could find a way to bolster the story, maybe send a letter or postcard to someone.

Starr moved to the herb garden, expertly plucking alien shoots from between the sturdier stems. While she worked, butterflies spiraled among the wildflowers. A hummingbird hovered in the stand of wildflowers Butler had lately crossed.

She would have left, too, long ago, if it weren't for Clay. She almost did, while he was still deployed, but in the end, she couldn't bear to leave her garden, and her beloved campanile. And where would she have gone? She couldn't imagine. She'd chosen Colorado for Jimmy Cooper simply because she'd seen a picture on the news the night before.

It was harder making up a destination to explain her mother's absence. But she had to have an answer, or there'd be too much gossip. No one would dare mention it directly to Wyman, so he would never discuss it. But no one had any compunctions in trying to wheedle information out of her. So when they came for their ginseng or their more exotic preparations, she let out little details, slowly building a narrative.

Where would a mother go? New York? Too close. San Francisco? Too big. She considered each of the places she herself would visit, but it was all a blur. In the end, she chose to tell people that her mother had gone on an extended road trip. Every once in a while, she'd picture her in a small town or an anonymous city, wandering place to place like a banished knight, helping villagers or desperate families before being forced by circumstance to move along, never allowed to put down roots. When Starr allowed that she'd heard from her mom, and she was doing well, trying to find herself, people nodded and said they understood, but they never truly did.

Of course, everyone believed the part that she would send letters home. That's what Martha Wyman did. She was notorious for it.

After Starr's mother had sent that letter to Ed Thompson, Wyman had gotten exactly what he wanted: not just the land, but a toe-hold in Cuthbert's power structure. Thompson had retreated back into his office, a humiliated and broken man, which left a void for Wyman to fill. As for Thompson's wife, Starr couldn't remember if she ever saw her lurking in a parking lot or anywhere else again. One wife was destroyed by another. Starr guessed Wyman bridled at the knowledge that he'd made the deal with a woman' help, and that was something he could never tolerate. The downside was that it forced him to look at his wife with grudging respect. He hated to admit it, but he needed her to be more than a trophy if he was going to advance.

And so that letter was only the first. Somehow, Starr's mother knew exactly which scandalous lever to pull for her husband. Affairs, addictions, kinks, she used all of them to maneuver Winter Wyman into the center of Cuthbert politics and commerce. Starr sat next to her while she typed out the supposedly anonymous missives as Clay napped. She didn't understand most of the words, but she did notice the fear in people's eyes as she and her mother pushed Clay in a stroller down Main Street doing errands. Housewives let her step first in line at the deli counter, conversations hushed at the post office. At the playground, no one would sit on the same bench as Martha Wyman, but everyone would line up to say hello to her. As Winter Wyman grew more prominent in town, first becoming Chamber of Commerce president, then Alderman, then Chief Alderman, it was only fitting that his wife received more respect.

At school, Starr sometimes found girls crying in the bathroom. She had heard of "slam books," bullying notebooks passed from one hand to another collecting insults and accusations. But at Cuthbert Junior High, they were known as "Wyman letters." She never took part, and to her knowledge no one ever named her in one—who would dare?—but the title alone was devastating. As she walked the corridors to class, the deferential awe and fear her classmates exuded was a junior version of the honor her mother had earned on the street.

It all ended in a day.

No one could wield that kind of power in a small town for very long without some kind of blowback. Especially if she had secrets of her own. Too many anxious eyes scanned the streets, especially the roads that led out of town. One day, Winter Wyman got a Wyman letter of his own. Starr was in eighth grade, and she had just walked Clay home from kindergarten. She left him to play in the front yard while she did her homework on the living room floor. Her mother was preparing dinner in the kitchen.

Suddenly, Clay's screams and the terrifying sound of screeching brakes blended together. Starr leaped up to watch through the window. Her father's car lurched over the curb and tore up the yard, stopping just short of the house. Wyman's face was unrecognizable as he leaped onto the lawn. Clay stared uncomprehendingly at his arm, which hung at an odd angle. He hadn't been able to get it out of the way of the speeding car.

Ignoring his injured son, Wyman seemed to close the distance between the car and the house in a single step. Before her mother could yell for Starr to hide, Wyman hurled past her and into the kitchen. She heard pans clatter against the ceiling and the floor. Then Starr came the deeper thuds of flesh and bone thrown against plaster. None of Wyman's bestial shrieking made any sense. Starr risked a glance around the corner, and saw that he held his wife by the throat against the stove, while he waved a letter in his other bony fist, wailing about sin and fire and whoredom.

Her mother had trained Starr for this kind of attack, though. She rushed outside and put Clay, arm still dangling, over her shoulder. She'd have to worry about the broken bones another time. He continued his frightened screaming, and she had to cover his mouth to hush him. Listening at the door, Starr judged her parents were still in the kitchen, so she dragged Clay up the stairs to her bedroom. She shut the door and closed the haft of a padlock she had installed herself. Wyman probably didn't even know about it, since he rarely came into her room, even to say good night. She put Clay in the closet, telling him for the love of God to shut up. Then she waited.

The maelstrom continued for hours. It was no use calling the police; Bill Butler was Wyman's friend, or at least was in his pocket. There were no near neighbors, and besides, who would take one step to check Winter Wyman, especially to help the author of all those wicked letters?

So Starr and Clay rode out the storm, the two of them crouched in her closet behind winter coats and dresses. A table fell over. A window crashed. Both of their parents screamed, and for all they knew a chorus of demons joined in the pandemonium.

"No matter what happens," Starr whispered to Clay, "remember that I'm always going to protect you. I'm your best friend, and you'll always be mine."

The boy nodded. "And you'll be mine." They huddled closer.

At some point, the shrieking faded, and Starr ventured to the window overlooking the front yard. Her father's Buick huddled right up against the house in the stone-lined flowerbed, door still open, her bicycle crushed beneath the rear wheel. While she watched, her mother bolted into the street from the driveway, pursued a moment later by her father.

In the time since she'd seen him rush into the house, his hair had gone completely white. It trailed out behind him like the tail of a comet.

Starr's mother staggered around the car, using it as a shield. Wyman launched himself over the hood, but she ducked behind the open door. She battered him in the face with it and he fell, but bounced up almost instantly, both hands clutching rocks. Starr's mother tumbled into the car, pulling the door shut. Wyman slammed the rocks one after another at the window until it crazed and shattered. From above, Starr could see her mother frantically trying to turn the key. One more rock punched through the window, but at the same time, the car leaped forward into the wall, then back as her mother found reverse, dragging Wyman until he freed his bloody arm. He catapulted both of the stones but they fell behind the car as it sped away.

For the rest of the night, Starr guarded Clay in her room while their father alternately cried and raved downstairs. She tried to stabilize his break by making a splint, knotting some bandannas around a couple of rulers along his arm. When it was time for little Clay to use the bathroom, she helped him use the metal wastepaper basket that sat by her bed. Some time after dark, a car came and left.

Then it was quiet, and Starr wondered if Wyman had gone out, or abandoned them entirely. But she didn't dare leave the safety of her room, and as the hours wore on, they both fell asleep bunched up in the closet, heads nestled into each other's shoulders.

Starr shook herself from her reverie to find she had weeded the entire ten-by-ten bed without realizing it. But there was still more to do, and still more to remember.

Like how she and Clay had awoken the next morning, hungry and scared. How she'd looked out the window and saw the Buick, shattered windows magically replaced, sitting in the driveway. At first she thought it had all been a terrible nightmare, but then she saw the mangled bike half-buried in the lawn, the tire tracks that had eaten up the grass, and the pieces of bloody glass shining in the morning light like rubies. Still, the car's return must mean that her mother had come back, too. She left Clay, unlocked her door, and crept downstairs. She expected to see, as so often happened after parental battles, a quiet domestic scene, as if nothing had happened. But Starr found only her father, drinking weak-looking coffee from a juice glass. The mess from the day before had hardly been touched, except for the table being righted. His hair was still wild and white.

"You're the woman of the house now," he said, without so much as an acknowledgement of what his children might have witnessed the night before. "I've made my own breakfast for today, but from now on, that's your job. You're to get Clay dressed and fed and to school. By the time I come home tonight, I want all of this cleaned up."

"I think his arm is broken again," she said.

"I'll take him to Dr. Fuller, then. I want this house cleaned up in the meantime."

"But I have school, too."

"That's of no concern to me. Go or don't. As far as I'm concerned, you're to make sure that the house is run the way it should be, and that you take care of Clay. What you do otherwise is your own business."

He never told Starr where her mother had gone. Nor had she ever found out how the car had been returned, window fixed, in the middle of the night. For months Starr watched the mailbox, hoping to hear from her mother, but nothing ever came. By the time the next school year started, she began to accept that Wyman had probably killed her, but there was never a body, and no evidence whatsoever. Sneaking into her father's office, she once found the fateful letter. Typed front and back, it detailed down to the minute when his wife and Ed Thompson would check in and out of the Paradise Motel, situated halfway between Cuthbert and Havilah. She couldn't understand half of the acts it accused them of, but she knew they were perverse and depraved.

Later, when she learned to do searches on the computer, she plugged in every permutation of her mother's name she could imagine, but found nothing. It was as though Martha Wyman had never existed.

Chapter 29

After Butler left, Starr pulled a suitcase from her closet. Heavy and old-fashioned, it was an ugly blue-gray plastic box with a small grip instead of a shoulder strap. Wildly impractical, but it would have to do. She flung it open on the duvet. A cascade of clothes poured into it—underwear, bras, dresses, jeans, shoes—everything jumbled together in a pile. She fit smaller things around the edges, saving space for only a few sentimental objects: a snapshot of her and Clay as children, a small sheaf of letters he'd sent from Iraq. A pair of earrings her mother had forgotten in her own rush to escape. It all mixed together in a haphazard mess.

She didn't care about organizing. She had better things to think about. At last she'd be free! Free of this decrepit old house, free of her father's unreasonable demands, free of caring for the wreck of her brother. Somehow, she knew, Wyman would get Clay into a bright, clean facility where they could give him real therapy. In a year, perhaps months, he'd be whole again, and then she could tell him where she'd gone. Maybe he'd join her then, and she could help set him up in his own apartment, get him a job, and they'd be like normal siblings.

She cleared the shelves in the bathroom. Toiletries, homemade salves, tinctures, all went into the small train case that matched the bigger one. She lugged both downstairs and put them on the table in the living room, not even noticing that she knocked over a pair of plants. Her handwritten recipe books and a pair of references—Green's *Herbal Medicine-maker's Handbook* and *Culpepper's Complete Herbal*, marked up with her own annotations—went into the small case, cushioning the bottles so they wouldn't jostle each other.

She scanned the room, saw the overturned pots and righted them. Her poor plants. Wyman would probably order Sam to heap them in the garden and burn the whole pile. Nothing she could do to prevent that. But she'd start a new garden wherever she and Jase settled down. What if they ended up in the Deep South? Or the western desert? What kinds of new herbs would she discover? The world bristled with possibilities.

Her vision shifted, and the house became as it had been when she was growing up. She saw the ghost of the couch where she had hidden while her parents waged war. The floor was strewn with the scars of so many martyred ceramic figures. Maybe Wyman would burn the whole house down. Who would stop him? Chief Butler? Hardly.

The ceiling shook with Clay clumping around his room. She wondered how much of this he understood. Could he comprehend that it would be better in the long run to be in a hospital, with professionals instead of his sister caring for him? What arrogance had led them to believe that she could ever have helped him? Wyman had denied his son real medical treatment, not for love, but control. But if things worked out, Wyman was about to lose that control.

Shaking off the mirage of memories, Starr collected a few kitchen tools: her smaller mortar and pestle, her best shears, the wooden muddler. Nothing else fit in the case, but the rest could be replaced.

That night, she drifted off to sleep imagining a world beyond Cuthbert.

Tuesday morning, she had several more loose ends to tie up. She baked a special pasta casserole for Chief Butler with some fresh *Amanita phalloides* — the death cap mushrooms she'd spotted when she harvested the chicken of the woods the week before. True, there was a chance it might not kill him, but at the very least it would give him a miserable twenty-four hours of exploding fluids from both ends. More likely, once he thought he'd recovered, the poison would keep attacking his liver and kidneys. If he didn't drag himself to the hospital, and demand an instant liver transplant, he'd never sniff around a crime scene again. She tossed the leftover mushrooms in an otherwise delicious salad of greens from her garden for Ed Thompson. He deserved a nice cold dish, even if he never knew what it was for. He may or may not think twice about fucking another married woman like her mother, but he certainly would never be able to do it.

Next, she had to organize her final remedies. She skimmed her log to make sure she didn't miss any. Some black cohosh extract for Mrs. Demers's menopause pains. A lavender and peppermint tea for Sharon Tisbury's colicky infant. Ms. McAllister had been coming to her for years to treat the rheumatism that raged through her joints. Starr mixed a large batch of cayenne and coconut salve for her. The pepper burned her eyes. Poor Ms. McAllister probably wouldn't live long enough to use it all.

She ground, mixed, braided, and steeped another half dozen treatments. The sky grew red, then faded to deep blue. Carefully, she packaged and labeled the concoctions. She took the time to write out a few precise directions, or recipes. She didn't bother with Winter Wyman's licorice tea, didn't even leave a recipe. She couldn't care less if he ever screwed again, or not.

When she was finished, a triple row of neat paper bags stood like proud soldiers on the counter. She packed them in a cardboard box and set it on the passenger seat of her old Subaru. It took a couple of anxious tries, but it started up. One by one, she made her deliveries around town like a mouse in a maze. She made amiable small talk with Bill Butler, explaining in careful detail how to reheat the casserole, and even made plans for tea with Ms. McAllister that she knew she'd never keep.

At one point, she actually passed Jase as he made his own final preparations. She beeped and waved, but he was concentrating on the road, and didn't see her at all. She drove home, to wait out the last few hours in hell. It was too soon to do anything else, except look over her garden one last time.

The bells in the Church in the Woods chimed a quarter to seven, rousing her to act. Time to hide her things. It would be a slog through the woods dragging the outdated luggage, but she had no choice. With a quick glance to see if she'd missed anything, she hefted the cases, stepped into her gardening boots, and strode across the lawn toward the woods.

She tried to avoid looking at the soon-to-be-abandoned garden. If she did, she might be tempted to stay. Besides, it wasn't her last good-bye, not yet. Instead, she focused on the yellow butterflies that whirled from flower to flower, then squinted against the cloud of flies as she passed the compost. No question, there were more and bigger flies than in years past. But she assured herself no one would notice. She had a plan to keep Bill Butler from raking it out, and then there'd be no more suspicion. *Rest in peace, Jimmy.* She let out an explosive breath to keep the flies from her face.

The hike took almost half an hour, and the bells jeered her slow progress. Normally, she could slip like a fairy from rock to rock between trees and under low branches. But the suitcase banged against her leg, and the shoulder strap of the train case caught on limbs and spun her around. Her palms sweated and she kept having to change her grip, which only made it harder to keep her balance. By the time she stumbled into the open field around the tower, her legs were a welter of bruises and cuts. She regretted laughing at Jase when he had come out of the woods. Wasn't so easy when you added the unfamiliar, was it? But now she was halfway across the grass surrounding the bell tower, just as the drum turned to chime quarter past the hour.

Jase had said he'd arrive at ten. She wondered where he'd be until then, but that was beside the point. She had her gear ready, and they'd leave together just after midnight.

This was, Starr realized, the last time she'd see the Church in the Woods in daylight. She put the two cases by the door, and looked down from the edge of the access road at the expanse of Cuthbert. She thought she'd feel some sort of nostalgia. Her refuge, her retreat, and lately her bower. She called up images, but they fluttered away like the flies over Jimmy's tomb. In the end, she saw only the houses of clients in the roads below. If nothing else, Starr lived up to her responsibilities.

She turned at a sudden hum. A car was approaching. Not Jase's Mustang, not Wyman's Lincoln. She sprinted back to the Church, fumbling at the keys. She had stowed herself inside with the luggage, locking the door, just as the car reached the top of the hill.

From a corner of the window, Starr watched a teenage boy park an SUV and nervously climb out. Satisfied no one was around, he removed a sledgehammer, a heavy metal bar, and a shovel from the passenger seat. He selected a spot and dropped the tools on the ground, then drew a paper from his pocket and read it over. His eyes darted between it and the ground. He crumpled the paper back in his pocket and used the bar to measure out a square, marking it by the shovel blade. When that was done, he began to dig.

He soaked his shirt within minutes, but kept working like a demon. When he'd built enough of a pile, he shaped it into a rough block shape, and then alternated between doing that and digging the hole. Periodically he consulted the paper again, nodding to himself. Starr guessed he was trying to gauge both the depth of the hole, and the height of the mound. It was nearly eight o'clock when he seemed satisfied. Starr grew anxious. What if he didn't leave? How would she get out of the Church without being seen?

The hole was about four feet square and a foot deep. He'd been careful to make the sides straight. It reminded Starr of a book she had read to Clay when they were little, about a man and his beloved steam shovel. They were the best diggers around, but hadn't they come to a tragic end? Just another good intention gone wrong.

Now the boy set to finishing the mound, carving it into a rectangular block about two feet high and three feet long. He topped it with large divots so it looked like a lumpy billiard table. Next he used the sledge to drive the pole into the ground a few feet away. He surveyed his work, checked the paper one more time, then walked toward the woods. He returned with an armful of brush and branches. Understanding dawned on Starr. *This must be part of Jase's scheme. The kid was digging a fire pit. Was the mound some sort of altar? Now his interest in Wyman's religious beliefs made sense.*

On the boy's second trip to the woods, Starr took a chance. She eased the door open and slipped out. Before she disappeared around the corner of the building, she looked inside the back of the SUV and her eyes grew wide. *What the hell was that?* But she heard him coming, so she crept to the opposite side of the tower. While he arranged the kindling, she dashed into the trees, careful not to make a sound. Then she was invisible, lost in the shadows and leaves.

Back at the house, she checked on Clay in his room. More S&M

porn. Where did he get this stuff? Clay's pants were still on, thankfully, but he was pitching a massive tent.

Ignoring the obvious, she approached him, vying for his attention. "Clay? Clay, honey? We need to talk." He didn't respond. She stood at the end of the bed so she could see his face but not the television. She considered turning it off, but feared he'd get violent. Instead, she called him again. His eyes flicked to her before going back to the screen.

She gave him his meds, but there was no immediate effect. After a few seconds, she told him, "Clay, we're going for a walk tonight. Won't that be nice? A midnight walk through the woods? We're going to see Poppa." The last word stuck in her throat. It had been years since she'd said it. The slightest hint of recognition registered on Clay's face then faded away.

"And Clay, there's a little bit more. Poppa and I, we're going to get you some help. Remember that man from earlier? My friend? He's going to help me so I can help you."

She fought against tears. Was this really for the best? Or was she sacrificing Clay for herself? Probably, but even so, Clay needed real doctors. Wyman would probably disagree, but for once he would have no choice. Not if he loved his son.

She opened his closet and found his camo duffle. It reminded her of the day he had come home. She and Wyman had stood shoulder to shoulder, silent amid the crowd of jubilant relatives. As the soldiers reached the tarmac, wives, husbands, and children ran to embrace their loved ones. Starr saw tears and balloons and excited little children waving signs saying "Welcome Home Mommy" or "You're my HERO!"

But for Clay there was nothing. He walked mechanically through the knots of celebrating families, passing joyful reunions of all sorts without seeming to notice anything. Wyman held out his hand and said, "You have tasted war, and avenged the Lord. Now, son, let's go home. There's work to do." There had been no mention of missing him, of being proud of his service, nor an acknowledgment of his patriotic duty. The letter stripping Clay of his honors had yet to arrive. He followed dumbly back to the car, where Sam put his duffle in the trunk, and father and son sat in the back, while Starr, utterly forgotten, sat beside Sam in the front.

In the back of his closet, Starr found a box of their childhood games. Amid the scattered Monopoly money, Battleship tokens, and assorted colored dice, she spied the plastic cage from their old Mousetrap game. He had loved watching the complicated Rube Goldberg pieces push each other into action, and laughed whenever the cage fell, even if it was on his own piece. She tossed it in the bag. She doubted the nurses would know what it was, but she hoped that when Clay regained his mind, he would remember that she loved him, and always had.

When she was through, she kissed Clay's forehead, slung the duffle over her shoulder, and brought it downstairs. He never moved, never made a sound except to sigh as the televised torture grew more intense.

Chapter 30

The day of the New Moon, after a call to that pathetic lapdog Stephen Hutchins, Winter Wyman, leading citizen of the town of Cuthbert, Massachusetts, succumbed to the rage that filled his mind. Locking himself in the windowless *sanctum sanctorum* in his mansion, he stormed about in lunacy, venting his anger with inhuman yowls. To be humiliated by that unnatural hag! After all he'd done for her, for the town, for humanity! He was as a god to the people, and she mocked him like this! The unutterable gall of her, to flout him, right to his face!

His shrieks reverberated off the bare white walls of his retreat. It was clear now, the mistake in judgment he had made. He had to get his son out of her clutches, but how? And put him where? For there was still no chance of putting his precious Clay, son and heir, in one of those godforsaken institutions. An infinite loop played in his mind: his pure, innocent son, clutching himself like a rabid monkey. He'd strangle her—choke her with her own plants! He'd killed before, why not her? Who would dare to stop him?

For a minute, he luxuriated in his revenge fantasy, two women blending together into one wicked image. He watched her eyes bulge, her cheeks turn purple, then black. She'd brought this vengeance on herself. His righteousness was true, blessed by God in all His wisdom. *'Thou shall not suffer a witch to live.'* He imagined her strangled voice, desperately begging mercy, but unable to utter a single syllable through the mass of rotted stems that protruded from her bleeding lips. In his vision, she staggered, hands clutching her throat, until unconsciousness conquered her like the Red Sea sweeping over Pharaoh's armies. Her eyes rolled up inside her head, and she collapsed in a heap. He allowed her foot, her left foot, one pathetic twitch, before she was dead.

He replayed the scene some more, and when he looked up from her putrid carcass, there was his darling Clay, healed, a full man, watching in satisfaction. But then Clay said, in the voice Wyman longed to hear, "Now who will watch over me? Father, who will take care of me? Will it be you?"

The film stopped and bubbled and burned. Damn her! The miserable witch had certainly spun her charms. Much as he despised her and her methods, Wyman hated to admit he needed her. Unless the stranger's promise came true and the ivory panel could make Clay whole again. Yes! He made another pass around the room, wishing he had something to smash. Instead, he let out another howl, gripping his hair by the roots until blood flowed down his neck, soaking into his collar. *Another shirt lost. No dry cleaner could be allowed to see that.*

Shaking with his spent energy, Wyman released himself from his cell. Time to return to the mortal world. He forced himself to focus on preparations. There was so much to do. First, he had to change his shirt, before his company arrived. It would have to be a short visit, but he would be an excellent host.

With the energy of a man half his age, he bounded up the stairs. He stripped off the bloody shirt and made a mental note to burn it later. He was buttoning the cuffs of a new one when the doorbell rang. Looming from the top of the stairs, he watched Sam, one arm in a sling, answer the door. The girls bounced in. Behind them, the unwilling procurer Stephen Hutchins stood nervously on the front step. His clothes were stained and ripped, and his hair was slick with sweat. The stupid fool. What kind of reprobate would let his grandmother pimp for him? Only the most wretched of losers.

Wyman, calm now that he'd released his fury, made a dignified promenade down the steps. He bowed graciously to the girls, and ignored their simpering giggles. He didn't need their pity. In a few minutes, they'd be begging for his. He said to Stephen, "Have you finished your other errands, boy?"

The boy bobbed his head. "Yes, sir. Exactly as you said. I measured perfectly. And I found one that matched your instructions. I had a little trouble getting it in the car, that's how I got this cut on my cheek, but it's there, too. Everything is ready." Having such a sycophant made Wyman want to puke, but it was necessary. Soon he would have a proper servant, a successor of blood.

Wyman gave Hutchins his most disingenuous smile. "Good. Come back in two hours." He shut the door to avoid any more of the boy's prattle.

He said to Sam, "We'll be upstairs. You can finish cleaning the office, then attend to our other guest." He stroked Crystal's cheek, noting the shortness of her skirt. Amber pouted with one hand on her cocked hip. He ignored her distaste. She'd be paid enough to do whatever he asked, and tonight, he'd ask plenty. "We won't be needing anything else. Will we, girls?"

He ushered them up the stairs, and his hardness grew until he had to take the steps in a bowlegged gait. Two hours. An hour to each girl. Then, he would have his son returned to him. His wonderful, miraculous son, whole and as virile as he himself would now prove himself to be.

Chapter 31

Jase was headed to see Wyman for final preparations when the foolish woman drove past his car. Jesus, only an idiot would wave at him like that, showing everyone they knew each other. He shook off his anger and focused on the moment. He ticked off his makeshift crew: after his delivery, Mac was kicking the dust of the town off his heels; Rick Sutton was ready to do his part; and as a nice perk, Terry was ready to leave with him once he completed his mission and took possession of the tablet. Jase needed only to check that Wyman followed through on his end of the bargain. After that, no more errand boy status. He'd be a player. She promised.

He pulled up behind an SUV parked in front of Wyman's house. As he stalked towards the porch, Sam opened the front door. The light of the foyer pierced the ear of his silhouette. His arm was loosed from the sling, but he held it awkwardly at his side.

"Mister Wyman will be right down," the lackey said contemptuously. Only then did Jase smell ammonia wafting out of the office. With a smirk, he peeked in and saw a teenage boy sitting on the edge of the couch, his knee bouncing uncontrollably. His clothes were filthy, and blood streaked his arms. A nasty cut on his cheek was turning purple. Jase guessed he'd been the one Wyman sent to build the fire pit. Probably did the rest of the grunt work, too, since

Sam didn't seem to be up to the task.

"I'll just wait in here," he told Sam. The kid looked up sharply.

"Relax," Jase said, offering him a tumbler.

The kid waved it away. "Last time I had some of that, Wyman turned me into a pimp," he whimpered.

Jase shrugged and poured himself a shot. "It's almost over."

The kid shook his head. "Maybe for you. Me, I'm stuck. I thought I was working at a bank. Instead, I drive his whores between Havilah College and here, and make deliveries that I'm pretty sure are drugs. I think Mac Fletcher makes ecstasy in his basement."

"You don't know the half of it," Jase said with a chuckle. "What's your name?"

"Stephen."

"Well, Stephen, your days as a whoremonger and drug mule might be behind you." He checked his watch. "Past ten. Just over an hour to go."

"I still did it," Stephen said, and put his face in his hands. "Mr. Larsen, he knows. And they've got me using now, too. Forced pills down my throat, and now I actually want it. Just like my parents. Every time I try to pull away, they make me do something worse, or else they'll put me in jail. How the fuck am I ever going to get a job in this town? Why did my grandmother have to stick her nose in my business?" He burst into body-shaking sobs.

Jase hated to see a kid that age cry. He thought about his own mess of a life, traveling from one shitty motel to another, dragged by his mother until she disowned him at the gates of a paramilitary camp run by a bunch of borderline neo-Nazis hoping for a race war. Not one of them had ever seen real action, they just read endless histories of the Third Reich, re-enacting battles their idols had mostly lost, in search of the magic formula to do it right. By the time he found himself in that bar, he was ready to take an AR-15 to each and every one of them.

His new employer had saved him from them and that fantasy camp massacre. Her poise, her confidence, her apparent belief in him, had cast a spell that clung to him still. She was everything his mother wasn't, and offered him a stability he'd never known. It turned out that the training he'd gotten was good enough for what she had in mind for him—strong-arm collecting, shakedowns, the occasional manhunt—and he found satisfaction in pleasing her. It'd be a shame to cut ties with her, but that's what a kid had to do to grow up and be on his own. Funny, he had never thought about whatever happened to his real mother, but he'd said his goodbyes to her long ago, and he assumed that she'd drunk and drugged herself to death by now, likely in another anonymous highway motel no one else would look twice at. Everyone made their own choices.

He said to Stephen, "Listen, you're going to be all right. Once this is all over, get yourself to a hospital, ask for help. The worst thing you can do is pretend you can handle it yourself. Can you do that? Stephen, hear me? Can you do it?"

Amid the crying, Stephen managed to nod. It was the best Jase could do for now. He put the glass down and went to the foyer to find Sam.

"Where's Talis?" he asked.

Sam gestured to the basement door. "All cleaned up, like Wyman said to." Sam knew damn well that Wyman was only passing on Jase's own instructions, but he would never admit to doing anything except for his master.

Just then, an upstairs door opened. Jase looked and saw straight up the tiny skirt of one of Wyman's girls. She couldn't sit anywhere in public without getting arrested. The other one, a redhead, followed, but Jase turned away to spare his sight. He didn't share Wyman's tastes.

The girls flounced down the steps in bare feet, each of them hooking their shoes in one hand and gripping a pile of cash in the other. Jase shuddered to think what their last couple of hours must have been like. He stepped out of their way as they reached the bottom of the stairs.

"Hey, Stevie," crooned the dark-haired one. "Amber and me are ready to go."

The one called Amber leaned close to his ear and stage-whispered, "Come on, give us a *ride*." The boy shrank away from her.

Teases, or sincerely in need of normal sex? Jase couldn't care less.

Like a condemned man, the boy got up and the led the giggling girls outside. When the SUV was gone, Wyman appeared like a ghoul. He was dressed formally: dark suit, string tie, starched white shirt. A flush on his cheeks did nothing to make him look more human.

"Everything is ready," he said.

"And the panel...?

"Will be yours after the ceremony. Provided it performs as you say."

"That's between you and your faith," Jase said dryly. "But I have a feeling it'll all work out the way it's supposed to."

In the distance, the carillon played the first quarter of the Westminster chimes. Sam descended into the basement and returned minutes later with Talis in handcuffs. The prisoner swayed on his feet, and his cheeks were hollow under the scars from the hasty shaving of his scraggly beard. His eyes bulged horribly. But the cuts and bruises from his torture were beginning to heal and his clothes were new, though they hung loosely off his withered frame. In Wyman's terms, he would be a meet offering for sacrifice. Sam shoved him through the door, and the four men stood uncomfortably a moment before Jase broke the silence.

"Go time."

There were no witnesses to see Talis shoved into the trunk of the Lincoln, no one to see the strange little parade leaving Winter Wyman's house. Jase kept the Lincoln squarely in his headlights, ready to run it off the road if Sam decided to change course. They passed through town, past the dark and shuttered businesses. A blinking yellow traffic signal lit the square like a dying flame.

They navigated the switchbacks up Bell Hill. At the summit, Sam pulled over to allow Jase room to park. *Wasn't that kind of him.* Jase turned and backed in so the Mustang faced the road, all the better to make a quick departure. By the time he got out of the car, Wyman was already at the fire pit supervising Sam, who was trying to light the brush. The Lincoln's headlights flung his shadow onto the makeshift altar.

Sam paused in his attempts to light the fire and handed Jase the keys so he could free Talis from the trunk. Wrestling the old man from the car, he brought him to the pit, which was now starting to smolder.

"What's all this?" Talis said. His voice was a thin bleat. Sam got another spark going and a corner of the pit flared up.

"Sin needs to be expiated," Wyman said, putting a grip on his shackled arm. Talis tried to break free, but captivity and drugs had sapped his strength. Besides, Wyman's talons were strong as iron. As the tender flames spread across the pit, they revealed a glinting knife stuck into the altar. Talis moaned.

"Shut up," Wyman said. "Abraham didn't slit Isaac's throat, did he?" As if on cue, the tethered goat Stephen had liberated from Nephele Farms cackled.

Talis dropped his shoulders. "What am I here for, then?" he asked.

Jase stepped forward. "You're not the goat tonight," he said quietly. "More like a guinea pig." Sam gave him a small key and he uncuffed Talis's hands.

In the firelight, Talis went pale, and Wyman struggled to hold him upright. A rustling in the trees caught their attention, and Jase nodded as the woman stepped into the clearing. Her golem of a brother followed.

"My boy," Wyman crooned. "Soon you will be whole."

The raging pyre crackled and hissed like a living thing. It illuminated the whole area and sent sparks fluttering up to the stars. The woman and her brother stood behind the altar.

"Let's see the panel, Wyman," Jase said.

Wyman handed Talis's shuddering form over to Sam. From the Lincoln he removed a black laptop case. He unzipped it and pulled out the ivory slab. In the flickering light, the figure of Nimrod the Hunter sneered and rippled, straining to leap off the panel.

"Put it on the altar," Jase directed him, "and say the prayer."

Wyman, his head bowed, solemnly approached the altar and knelt before it. His face blazed and his white hair glowed like flames springing from his skull. His voice echoed through the smoke and sparks.

"Lord Almighty, accept this humble offering and forgive thus our sins. May your bounty flow like the blood of this animal. I pray that you accept this sacrifice, and grant its health to my son."

The monster grunted, and mumbled something that sounded like "Mine."

"Do it now," Jase said. He had to raise his voice above the roar of the flames.

Wyman beamed at his son, then pointed to the goat.

With a trollish grin, Clay approached the poor animal, which understood all too well what was about to happen. Wyman picked up the knife and it sparkled red in the firelight. The woman looked pleadingly at Jase, but he ignored her. Her role was nearly over in this little drama, and he had no further use for her.

Her brother wrapped one arm around the goat, impervious to its flailing hooves. With his other hand, he grasped the screeching animal by the snout and silenced it. It thrashed and bucked, but Wyman's ogreish offspring plunked it onto the earthen altar. Wyman gripped the knife in both hands, and the blade hovered over the animal's upturned throat.

"Do it," Jase barked.

Wyman slit the goat's neck. A gush of blood splashed across his face and drenched his white shirt. Gobs of it landed in the fire and spluttered. The animal freed its mouth to give one last dying wail, then went still. With a sign from Wyman, Clay lifted it by the hind legs and let the blood drain over the altar, onto the pearly white panel, into the sacrificial flames.

"Well?" asked Wyman in a pathetic voice. "Is its power restored?"

"Let's find out," Jase said. "Sam?"

Sam drew a syringe from his coat pocket. "Don't worry," he said to Talis with a cruel chuckle. "This is just what you've been wantin', isn't it?"

"No, no, I think I want to go clean," Talis whined desperately. His face, too, was streaked with the goat's blood. Jase pinned his arms from behind. Talis bucked and struggled as the goat had, but Jase slammed him against the car. He ripped open Talis's sleeve, then tied off the arm with a rubber tube he drew from his pocket. When the veins bulged, Sam put the needle in, and pushed the plunger home. Talis screamed miserably.

The overdose of heroin took effect in seconds. Talis fell limp. Suddenly he doubled up, clutching his belly, then snapped straight again. Jase eased his spasming body to the ground. A line of bubbles formed around his lips and oozed over his cheek. His breath came in raspy shudders, and his white skin turned blue. A minute after that, a fatal stillness enveloped him. A single, final sigh eased over the spittle that pooled in the hollow of his chin.

"Is he dead?" Wyman asked anxiously.

"Check for yourself," Jase said, standing up.

The old man crouched before the wasted figure and hesitantly put his finger to its neck. After a moment he said quietly, "He's a corpse. I'll have to purify myself."

"Never mind that. It's part of the ritual," Jase said. "Is the panel ready?"

For the first time since they appeared from the woods, the woman spoke. Jase was glad she knew enough to use the proper words.

"Here it is," she said, "with the blood of the sacrifice upon it." She carried it to him, unfazed by the dripping gore. Wyman and his son watched with awe. She stood solemnly before Jase. Then, like a priest, she raised it above her head, brought it back to eye level, then passed it on to him.

Jase bowed and accepted the offering. Then he knelt before Talis's body. He murmured what sounded like a prayer, pressing the figure of Nimrod onto Talis's belly, his heart, his face. It left bloody imprints on his clothes, scarlet figures that shone in the firelight.

Finished, Jase stood. He raised the panel to the sky.

No one spoke. The fire heaved billows of smoke over the monstrous scene.

A loud gasp shredded the silence. Talis sat up. His eyes spun crazily, independent of each other. The woman shrieked and backed away. Sam babbled, "Sweet Jesus, Mary, and Joseph!" The monster growled, either from disappointment or joy. Perhaps both.

But it was Winter Wyman who spoke. "He is Lazarus! The power of the Lord Almighty be praised! My son will be restored to me! Patton, give me the panel. Now!"

Talis clawed his way into an unsteady crouch, then, his strength returning, he breathed, "What happened?"

"You was dead," Sam said, his eyes wide. "I gave you a fatal overdose, and you fuckin' died." Horror spread across his face. He turned and bolted.

"Sam, get back here!" Wyman shouted, but his servant had disappeared into the dark.

Talis gazed around wonderingly. His ghostly face reddened in the firelight. "Is this hell?"

"Only something like it," Jase said.

He pointed to Wyman, who was kneeling again by the altar. The eviscerated goat steamed in front of him. He reached into the entrails, smearing new blood onto the panel. Next to him, his son intoned, "Mine, mine." He, too, was reaching into the mutilated carcass, but he looked to be doing it for sheer pleasure.

The fire had grown as the larger branches blazed. Jase watched a huge moth flutter out of the woods, circle the rising tongues of flame, then plunge into the inferno. In the heart of the pyre, its outspread wings disintegrated, and its furry body became ash.

It was time for the next act.

"Did you get all that?" Jase cried out.

"Every second!" cried a voice from the dark.

Wyman, his ghoulish face smeared with blood, looked up. His eyes were red embers, his hands bloody claws savaging the goat. His son cried in surprise.

Dick Sutton stepped into the firelight, a video camera against his eye. "This will ruin you, Wyman. You superstitious fool."

Wyman's face contorted in rage. He howled like a wounded animal and shook his fists.

"No! It's true. My boy will be whole!" He pressed the dripping panel against Clay's chest, but his son swiped it away into the dark.

Wyman scrambled after it. Sutton filmed it all.

In a flash, Clay jumped to his feet. He placed a foot on the altar and launched himself into the fire. A cloud of embers exploded around him. For a moment he looked like a demon chained in the fires of Tartarus. He ran through the shower of sparks, his murderous hands reaching for Sutton.

"No, Clay!" the woman cried, but it was already too late. As Sutton crashed to the ground, the camera flew from his hand and disappeared behind the cars. Clay was throttling him and nothing the woman said could slow him down.

Sutton battered his attacker's arm uselessly. In his thrashing, his hand latched on to a flaming branch. Ignoring his searing skin, he slammed it against Clay's head. But Clay just lifted him like a doll. He gripped the wrist that held the branch and spun Sutton away from him. The blazing stick drew an arc of flame across the sky, shattering the window of the bell tower. Sutton landed unconscious by the door. The woman hung from her brother's back, her arm clenched around his throat, but it had no effect.

Wyman was gibbering, "It's real. It's real. He was dead and rose like Lazarus. My son! My son!"

Chapter 32

The plant woman had been jabbering at him all day. He had no idea what she'd said. The television had been on. Someone was being beaten bloody, with whips and a stiletto. The screams had coursed through Clay's body like a sweet drug. He could almost taste the coppery tang of blood. It put a satisfying pressure on his cock, too.

The plant woman fluttered around the room, cooing like a bird, moving things. She said something about leaving. He wished she would, but for now he needed her. Needed her to bring him food. Needed her to give him the injections that allowed him to think more clearly.

The meds provided him fractured visions of his destiny. He glimpsed the moment when he would rise above all the puny wretches that surrounded him, the subhuman, mewling beasts that cried and chattered and shit around him. He would show them what a god was, just as soon as he broke free from the old man's chains and maddening voice.

The old man had placed a spell on him. Whenever the white-haired wizard entered the room, he saw flames in the man's eyes. Some kind of sorcery clenched Clay's chest. He couldn't breathe, and Clay thought his heart would explode.

But the plant woman calmed him when the wizard left, and then Clay would return to his study of pain. He devoured the videos, lapped up the agony of the brutalized men and women. They were alive, by the gods, never more alive than in the seconds before their hearts gave out. He would show them all what it meant to be alive.

His time was coming. He knew it and so did the others. That explained the movement all around him, the old man's increasingly frequent visits, the plant woman's tears. Was that a kind of pain, too? He never listened to her words, but he sensed the same brittleness in her voice as he heard the time in the desert when he had slid a scalpel across the farmer woman's eyeballs.

The peasant woman had screamed, but no one else could hear her above the pounding of artillery in the village nearby. He left her alive while his unit camped in her fields. For two days, he listened as her moans descended into the usual animalistic babbling. He wondered if she ate or slept in that time. Certainly, no one was left in the house to help her: he had surrounded her with the corpses of her family, arranging them like dolls at a child's tea party.

Then, abruptly, she fell silent. Clay feared she had killed herself, had ruined his experiment. But he was sent on patrol and couldn't slip away to check. Later, his patience was rewarded when she let out one last wild ululation, then died. It was a happy memory.

Gradually, he realized that the plant woman was packing his duffle. Was he being deployed again? He wouldn't go. He'd outgrown that part of his life. He focused again on the television until she was gone. Some time must have passed, but time meant nothing to him. When she returned, she stood him up. She said something about "Poppa." He felt the same pressure in his chest as he did when the old wizard put the spell on him. Why was that? But she gave him his meds, and then he was glimpsing his destiny again. The moment had come, she was saying, and Clay understood that she meant that now he would reveal himself to the masses.

The plant woman led him downstairs and outside. It was dark, and he felt a breeze on his face. She was crying and talking at the same time. She said something about "love" and "comfort" and "better," words that held no meaning for him. But when she said, "It hurts. You need to know, Clay, it hurts," the pressure in his chest relaxed. For those who had not reached his level of superiority, pain meant life. He would lead them to the truth.

They crossed the dark garden. By the fruit trees, he smelled the rot of the toy she had given him. Was it for his birthday? He remembered a time when there had been presents and a strange flickering stick. He remembered that he touched the orange light, but it snuffed out. A strange smell bit at his nose. The plant woman—she had been smaller then—pulled his hand away, and another woman had screamed. He wondered if maybe there was pain in that orange light, if maybe when he touched it others would be hurt, but after that there had been no more orange lights.

As they approached the pile of rot, a cloud of flies hurled themselves against his face, but he ignored them. Then they were in the woods. The plant woman warned him of low branches and moved him out of the way of trees. She said it would be all over when they came out of the trees. Then he would be free, she said. He felt the pressure building in his cock again. Freedom, to show others how to live. He would begin with the plant woman, reward her with the first gift of his reign.

They reached the top of the hill, and the trees thinned out. He saw more of the orange light. He remembered the word: *Fire. A great fire.* It truly was the day of his birth. The day when he would be reborn to wield dominion over the animals and teach them to enjoy pain as he did.

There were others near the fire. He saw the old wizard, and his deformed helper. And there was the new man who had hurt the plant woman. And another, bound and struggling. Clay smelled the smoke, and the fear. Then he heard the goat, and prepared to know joy.

They spoke strange words that Clay did not understand. But he knew it was a sacrifice in his honor.

"You will be whole," the wizard spoke. Yes, he would.

They slew the goat, and Clay felt its sticky blood on his arms as he reached into the shuddering cavity of its belly. Then they killed the bound man, and Clay felt his strength returning. The power surged through him, and his mind grew to unimaginable capacities. He saw before him countless means of delivering pain, and he knew he would experience them all. The old wizard and the plant woman were ready to release him at last.

The wizard put a white tablet against the dead man, who then lived again. So that was how they would break the final chain. His moment was at hand.

Another man stepped out of the darkness. He held a weapon to his eye. Aimed at who? Clay? The wizard?

He had to act. While the pathetic creatures remained still, Clay leapt across the fire, determined to kill the one who dared to interrupt his rebirth.

In two steps, he had the man by the throat. He throttled him, and felt the life draining away. The plant woman was holding onto his arm, onto his back, but he shook her free. No one would stand in the way of his rising. The man held a flaming stick and waved it against him, but Clay ignored it. He threw the man down, and watched the flashing light of the stick as it flew through the air.

But the plant woman was still on his back, shouting his name. She had her arm around his throat, and though he could not feel the pain, he did have to fight for breath. The fire dimmed, a shadow pushed in to the edge of his vision. The world fell silent, and the bright flames shrank, shrank, until they were no larger than a candle. That was the word: *candle*, on his birthday. He pushed against the plant woman's crushing arm, but he needed to rest first. Just a short rest, then he would crush her like she deserved. He no longer needed her. Today was his rebirth day.

His foot slipped, and he knew he was falling to the earth. He twisted his body, so when he fell, he would shake her off. Then, after a rest, he would show her.

He would show them all his superiority.

He would show them. But the shadow had swallowed even the candlelight.

He would show....

Chapter 33

Watching Clay splash through the fire pit like it was a kiddie pool terrified Starr. Then he grabbed Sutton, and her mind froze. If she interfered, she would ruin the plan. But she couldn't let Clay kill again, not now, not when everything was in the balance. Feeling her world slip from her grasp, she leaped onto his back and clamped her arms around his neck. He spun, trying to shake her off. But she clung with the strength of a woman who had nothing to lose. She jammed her elbow under his throat and tightened it until he staggered under his own bulk. He clawed at her arm, but was already losing consciousness. She pulled tighter, then rode his back like a surfer as he crashed to the ground.

She was caught underneath his body, the wind knocked from her. Jase wrestled the dead weight off her. The air rushed back into her lungs, and she let out a thundering scream. Jase gripped her arms but she threw him off, desperate to revive her brother.

"Here! Use this! Here!" Wyman shouted, emerging from the shadows back into the light. He thrust the cracked panel at her. Jase deftly relieved him of it and stepped back.

"Your son's just unconscious," he said coldly. "I'd suggest mouth-to-mouth, but maybe your breath is too cold to warm his lungs. Did you really believe an old piece of ivory would cure him?"

Wyman blinked and stuttered. The confidence drained from his eyes. "But Talis. He was resurrected!"

Jase shook his head. He held up a syringe with a large nozzle. "Narcan, courtesy of Mac Fletcher. The same stuff the prodigal son takes for depersonalization. I sprayed the mist into Talis's nose from beneath the panel. A birthday party magician could've done it cleaner, but you wanted to believe in miracles, so you fell for it. Sutton got it all on film. Something like that will go viral, and you'll be a laughingstock."

He pointed towards Sutton's prone body as he spoke, and it was only then they realized what had happened. While the light of the pyre danced on the exterior of the bell tower, an angry red glow pulsed in the darkness of its interior. Smoke seeped through the cracks around the windows, then drew back in, as if it were breathing: a sleeping dragon.

Starr followed Jase's gesture and saw her refuge, her beloved Church in the Woods, beginning to burn. She felt the searing in her heart. That was where she had learned to be herself, to be independent. It was where she had begun to love Jase. But as the fire took hold, she steeled herself. She decided it was fitting that the Church should be wiped from the earth. Starr refused to follow in the footsteps of the suicidal bell lady. All things must pass.

Then the present came rushing back.

"My bags!" she shouted. Worse than her clothes, she was about to lose her logbook. She might need that if it came to blackmail and her own Wyman letters. She ran to the door, but it was already outlined in living red. She battered at it and finally forced it open, but the sudden rush of oxygen exploded in a devastating backdraft. The force threw her across the grass, where Wyman caught her, almost by accident.

She lay stunned, both by the explosion and by the unfamiliarity of her father's comforting embrace. Did he, here at the end, actually love her? Had he reached out to save her, his instincts overriding the animosity they had flung at each other for so long? She let herself melt into his arms.

Meanwhile, Jase helped Sutton to his feet and moved away from the building. In seconds it had become a raging conflagration. Part of the roof gave way, and the flames twisted around the tower like vines reaching for the bells.

"I'll kill you, Sutton!" Wyman shouted over the roar of the fire. "I'll cast you into the flames of hell in front of your children!"

But Sutton didn't seem to hear him. He was laughing and dancing as another explosion, probably the machinery itself, ripped through the base of the tower. "I did it! I beat you all! No more bells! Ahahaha!"

The rest of them moved out of reach of the heat. Wyman still held Starr in a way that she could convince herself was tender.

"Why?" he asked Jase. "Why go through all this? You could have had the panel any time. Why did you have to destroy my son, too?"

Starr's illusion vanished. *Nothing about me?* Jase was right, she thought. Wyman was a vampire, and that embrace she had longed for all her life was nothing but cold iron against her skin.

"You don't get it, old man," she said, shaking herself from his arms. Now she saw her father for what he was—a weak, venal satyr who could never love her, or any woman. She retreated to Jase's side.

Wyman tilted his head questioningly. "What?" he said simply.

Feeling a surge of freedom, Starr felt like an empress. Looking down at his bloody, crazed state, she was no longer intimidated by Wyman. She knew what she wanted, knew what she was capable of.

"We are saving him," she announced. "Your son. My brother. Jase and I are leaving and you'll have to find Clay a real hospital. You needed to know that a miracle wasn't going to save him. But now Jase has the panel, Clay will get the treatment he needs, and I'll be gone with someone who loves me. The only one who loses is you."

Wyman shook his head. "But it has true power. It healed me."

Starr grinned wickedly. "The only recipe of mine you ever liked was licorice tea. Licorice and cottonseed oil and mugwort, every day. Each and every ingredient an all-natural inducer of impotence. There isn't a blue pill in the world that could get you hard through all of that. You never suspected it was your own thirst that kept you from indulging your perverted appetites. I only let you have those last flings with your whores to make you think that foolish artifact actually worked."

"Woe unto a daughter who knows of her father's intercourse," he moaned, but it sounded more like resignation than a curse. "But why involve Sutton?" He pointed at the wreck of a professor. "There was no need for that."

Sutton had found the camera and was filming the inferno. He sang, "Lady bird, Lady bird, fly away home. Your house is on fire, your children will burn!" over and over again.

Talis nodded in time with him, whispering, "I saw things. Wonderful things. Horrible ones, too. I'll tell you all of it." Starr wondered if the heroin was burning through the Narcan, if he'd collapse again into a second death.

"I lied," Jase told Wyman. "I wasn't sent by the Network, but it was easy enough to trace their steps. In fact, I was never even in Iraq. Hell, I only ever trained with a survivalist militia. For a while I was worried your son might have outed me, but that was before I realized he was in no condition to prove it. No, this was a job for hire, your past coming back to haunt you."

The flames lit the hilltop like it was day. Far below, the air horn at the Cuthbert Volunteer Fire Department began its whine. Jase handed Starr the soiled ivory and took an envelope from his coat pocket. He held it out to Wyman.

"Recognize the writing?" he said. "There were lots of letters like this once upon a time, weren't there? Everything you own was bought with blackmail, and it wasn't even your balls on the line. You had your wife do it for you."

Waves of heat washed over Starr, pounding her, making her dizzy. Survivalist? So he was nothing but a stupid weekend warrior, planning for an apocalypse that would never come. But what about the rest of the story? How did he know about her mother's letters? Blinking away the smoke and her confusion, she snatched the letter from Wyman's outstretched hand and ripped it open. There was no mistaking her mother's script. She wheeled on Jase and slapped him.

"She's alive! She's alive and you knew, and you never told me!"

She bent to read it, but a floating ember landed on the page. She had time to focus on only a single word, not even to wonder at its sudden appearance, before the paper flared and the hole spread toward her fingertips. She let it go, and the ghostly missive hovered before her eyes a half second until it went dark in a gust of wind.

"What did it say?" she choked through her tears.

"Not much," Jase said. He stared at Wyman. "Just that you should have expected this. Your wife built this empire for you, and you drove her out like a leper. You were so focused on your own woes, you never saw her coming."

Coming? Her mother was coming home?

The fiery wind twisted sparks and hair and flame in a speeding circle. A sudden crack sounded over the pounding thunder. Sutton fell in a heap. Starr spun and saw her old rival Terry, Ed Thompson's daughter. She wore a man's beater and an absurd pair of commando pants. Starr felt a sudden guilt. Why had she never considered the effects of her mother's letters on Terry's growing up? Terry carried a gun, and was stooping to remove the camera from Sutton's dead hand. What the hell was she doing here? Jase had never mentioned that she was part of the plan.

When Terry had the camera, she stepped over Sutton's body and joined them, the gun at her side.

"No need to worry, Wyman," Terry said. "Sutton's taken care of. Sam, too. In the end, you couldn't trust him, could you?"

With her arrival, Wyman seemed to gain new strength. He stood straight and chuckled.

"Thank you, Miss Thompson. 'That servant which knew his lord's will, and prepared not himself, neither did according to his will, shall be beaten with many stripes.' You have brought God's wrath unto a faithless servant."

Chapter 34

Starr gaped in disbelief. The ground shook beneath her, and she struggled to grasp the what was going on.

"You *work* for him?" she said.

"I put my trust in the Lord," Wyman cackled. "But in case He falls through, I make my own arrangements. If Clay can't take my place, Terry Thompson will. Now, girl, hand me the camera." He reached for it, but Terry held it back.

"Not so fast, Wyman. Sutton was an idiot, but he had the right idea on this. Besides, you said that panel would make me rich, and I have a plan for my newfound wealth. My father is a pathetic wreck because of you. I'll enjoy watching you suffer the same fate." She aimed the gun at Starr. "Hand it over, bitch. The game is through, and I won."

None of this made sense. Her mother was alive. Jase knew her. Was Terry working with Wyman or against him? Too many questions, but through it all, one truth was clear: Starr was left with nothing but a maniac for a father, a ruined shell of a brother, and a life subject to everyone else's needs but her own. Thank God she was leaving it all behind. Jase could bring her to her mother. There was still time to salvage everything, to start again. They would leave, and Wyman would be left to bring Clay to a hospital. Let Wyman and Terry have their own twisted partnership, some perverse father-daughter relationship. Starr would become an empress in her own right, the empress of a new land.

Terry, still holding the gun and the camera, stepped to Jase's side. Behind them, the Mustang glowed red in the fire, its paint starting to blister and crack.

"Jase?" Starr said slowly. "Jase, you said you would take me with you."

But Terry answered for him. "You dumb bitch. It was all part of the operation. Your mother never cared about you. Didn't you wonder why she didn't get in touch with you, after she made a life of sending letters to the rest of the town? She only wanted to bring Wyman down. And now he's finished, and I've got his business. And the guy."

"No," snarled Starr.

Her mind raced, making connections, breaking them, starting over. Permutations cascaded like molten rock through her imagination. Jase and Terry? Jase and her mother? None of it clicked.

She croaked the only thing she knew now for sure, "You loved Jimmy."

Jase reached out his hand. "Give me the panel, Starr." It was the first time, she realized, that he'd ever uttered her name.

She finally comprehended what he'd said. He'd never been to Iraq, never saw what he'd described. It was all an elaborate lie.

"How did you know all about the museum? The hidden passages? Were you involved?"

"It's amazing what details you can find on the Internet," he laughed. "Once I tracked down the path it took from Iraq to being collateral for the Network, your mother made sure I had the right credentials to insert myself into the story."

He wasn't a soldier, wasn't a hero, not like Clay. Not like the brother she had already damned in this insane scheme. Jase Patton was just a fortune hunter who told a good lie.

The fabric of his story had been torn and she clutched at the shreds, trying to knot them together. Nothing lined up.

She rearranged patches in the quilt, and it told a new story. Some of the edges were frayed, but she could make it work. With a new confidence, she whirled away from him.

She glared at Terry, and without another thought she said, "You do realize Jase killed Jimmy, right?"

"What?" laughed Jase uneasily. "I never even met him."

But Starr spoke over him, the lies forming easily, like a spell she'd practiced all her live. She gazed into Terry's smoldering eyes, which tried, but failed to stare her down.

"You did it, Jase. You told me everything. There's no use lying now."

The words tumbled out of her like an incantation. She swayed with their rhythm, and soon, Terry did, too.

"You needed to get Jimmy out of the way to get close to Terry. So you killed him, and hacked him up. You asked me for help, and I put the pieces in the compost pile. Wyman, isn't that true?"

Caught off guard, the old man didn't answer at first. Then he glanced at Clay, and the light returned to his eyes.

"Yes," Wyman said. "Jimmy is there. Under the compost, in pieces the way Patton told you to do it."

Terry looked at each of them suspiciously.

"You're lying," she said unsteadily.

Her gun hand moved between Starr and Wyman, but she took a step away from Jase to include him in her aim as well.

Starr wound up the threads of the spell. "Then why did he disappear just when Jase came to town? Cut through the woods there, and you'll find him under the apple tree. Every part."

"Then you killed him, or Wyman did."

"Why would I kill him?" Wyman said, regaining some of his lost authority. "He worked for me, always did what I said."

"Terry," Jase pleaded, "it's not true. I never heard of Jimmy until you told me about him."

"And who do you think killed Patty?" Starr gibbered. "Not that guy from Havilah. He was fucking me that night." *That was true. But where had Clay been? She knew exactly where, taking his revenge on Patty for flirting with that stranger Mike Harris. She had found Clay, kneeling by the shower, soaked with water and blood, both hers and his own. One glance told her that there would be no saving poor Patty. Starr's only hope was that she'd given up the ghost before the worst of Clay's blows.*

Still, her loyalty was to her family, even then. She had got Clay out before he was seen. Years had gone by, but the last few days' events might re-open someone's curiosity. In case anyone asked, this would clear him. "It was Jase."

"I wasn't even in town…" Jase began. His desperate tone was the last ingredient Starr needed to bind up her charm.

Terry's mesmerized expression showed it had worked. Her mind was transfixed, unable to see anything except the illusions Starr had created.

"Why?" Terry said, in a voice that belied her denials. "Why would he do it? If he was working for your moth—"

Starr summoned her power from the betrayal and pain that coursed though her veins. It enveloped her, choked out her humanity like a poisonous vine. Its sap replaced her blood, and burned like fire. "That was just a front," she said.

While Terry struggled to keep up, Starr continued, "Jase was out to get you the whole time. It was all about you, Terry. All your life it's always, always, been about you. Of course I knew that Jase and my mother were working together. She wanted revenge on your father, too. For letting out their secret. For screwing everything up.

Jase killed your friend Patty and your lover Jimmy. He took it all away from you. You found Patty's body all beaten and bloody. Jase is *trained* to hurt like that."

"No!" Terry shrieked. But Starr's words had struck home. She turned the gun on Jase, whose winning smile drooped like a lopsided mask.

"How could you believe a word of—"

But he never finished the question. The shot rang out just before the Mustang's interior caught fire. Jase fell without a sound, a crimson hole blooming in his gut.

The sirens drew closer. The windows along the spiral staircase of the bell tower burst one by one. Wyman knelt protectively over Clay, while Starr and Terry eyed each other, ignoring the rain of molten glass.

"Give me the ivory," Terry said, tears glistened on her cheeks, her pistol aimed again at Starr's heart. "I still have the gun, and I can still win."

Starr held the panel over the fire pit. "If you shoot me, it's gone. You want it, you'll have to drop either the gun or the camera, and I don't think you can afford to do either." Her eyes bored into Terry's. She couldn't help thinking, ridiculously, that the girl's hair was still perfectly smooth, like a helmet.

Starr went on, "What are you going to do, Terry? Shoot me and grab the panel? Send the video to the Network and take Wyman's place as the Godmother? It's all over. Jase killed Patty, then he killed Jimmy. He betrayed you over and over again."

Terry shook her head. "I thought you were in love with him. But you're pretty eager to let him die."

Starr took a step closer to the fire pit. "He served his purpose. And so have you."

The flames licked her skin, but she lowered her arm, put the panel closer to the heat. "I'll let it burn, Terry. Back off."

Instead, Terry moved forward, close enough for Starr to lunge at her. With her free hand, Starr wrenched at Terry's gun hand, and at the same time brought the corner of the ivory panel down at her eye. Together they tumbled to the ground, each scrabbling to get at the other's prize. Terry let the camera go, and it rolled toward the pit, its edges melting almost instantly.

Terry was wiry, but Starr had the advantage of her father's height and the tenacity from working outside in any weather. She pinned Terry with her knees, crushing her at the waist, but Terry's lithe body wriggled out of her grasp and scrambled to her feet. Terry grabbed at the ivory, but Starr clung to it and simultaneously clawed for the gun. It was out of reach, but her efforts forced Terry to aim the gun away from her.

The struggle wore on, and Starr felt the smooth panel sliding out of her grasp. She gripped harder, afraid to lose it, but she knew she was losing the battle. What then? She might survive, but how would she stop Terry from blabbing the whole thing? Would anyone believe Starr if she said Terry had killed Sutton and Jase? If Bill Butler was lucky enough to survive the mushroom casserole, he'd be arresting Starr, not following one of her tips. A moment ago, Starr had felt like an empress. Now she was the empress of nothing.

And then, she lost her hold. Terry exulted in her victory, raising her hands in triumph.

Starr leapt forward one last time, using Terry's gloating as a distraction. Both hands reached for the gun. It went off, once, into the flames. Then Starr threw all her weight onto Terry's body, slamming her into the ground. Terry's wind caught in her throat, and Starr easily, too easily, turned the gun to Terry's ear.

Unable to breathe, Terry opened her eyes wide, then smiled.

She mouthed, "Fuck you," and pulled the trigger herself. The rumbling of the firestorm drowned the sound of the report. Her dead hand dropped the ivory into the fire pit.

Starr nimbly pulled it out. The ivory was scorched, but it had survived upheavals throughout its history. She knew that it would clean up, hardly damaged at all. And she had the damaged camera, too, though she wasn't certain the video had survived.

She stood shakily and surveyed the hellish landscape around her. The bell tower rose like a brilliant tornado. The lower building had caved in on itself. Her bags, the futon where she and Jase had slept together, the comforting ratcheting of the drum mechanism, all had been devoured.

Burning bits of wood and paper floated through the air, and had ignited small fires in the grass all around. And there were bodies: Sutton, Terry. Sam was out there somewhere, too. Maybe Talis? And where was Jase? Not where he'd dropped. She looked toward the Mustang, but its interior was engulfed, and the windows had shattered in the heat. It wouldn't be long before the gas tank went up. If he'd gone there, there was no rescuing him. She had to admit she'd lost him. Her world had grown small again, reduced to only herself, her brother, and her depraved father.

She found them near the altar. Somehow the old man had dragged his son across the grass to the edge of the flames.

"We have to get out of here," she said. "I'll help you get him in the car."

But the events of the night had stripped Wyman to his basest thoughts. "Leave us alone, Jezebel!"

"We don't have time for insults," she said. "Let's get him to safety."

"What do you know about too late?" Wyman scoffed.

And then she saw. Clay's open eyes were as dead as the desert.

She looked from Clay's corpse to Wyman's kneeling form. "What happened? Poppa, what happened?"

Her father was weeping. The tears mixed with the blood on his face.

"He was my only son, flesh of my flesh. But we all must pay the wages of sin."

"Poppa, what happened?"

"If he had awoken, he would still have been ruined. God smote him early, and never would He repent. Clay would never have healed. So… so I helped him sleep. With my own hands on his nose and mouth, I helped him to sleep forever. Lord Almighty forgive me. What have I done with my life?"

She refused to answer him. Her world was shattered. Wyman was still weeping over Clay's body, the sirens were cresting the hill, and for the first time in her life, there was no reason for her to remain. Her brother Clay was dead, killed by their own father. Nothing could ever redeem them. There would be no miracle, no return to the distant past when her family had flowered with love. That flower had been torn up by the roots long ago.

"Help me commit him to the flames," Wyman choked. "Give him a hero's farewell. Make a burnt offering for all my life's trespasses."

But she'd already turned her back. She strode to the Lincoln. She discovered Jase, barely conscious, slouched in the passenger seat. Weakly he held up the keys. She snatched them and tossed the panel on the backseat. She adjusted the mirrors. A moment later, she was hurtling the car through a wide arc, slaloming around the patches of flame.

Her final sight of her old life was the pathetic vision of Wyman rolling Clay's body on to the sacrificial pyre. A plume of sparks burst around them, like a swarm of bees. She hoped that something good of Clay's might have passed into that living fire, and would pollinate the world. He deserved that much.

She veered to the shoulder to let the fire engines by. Her headlights revealed Sam's prostrate body. He got no less than he deserved: Terry must have shot the coward in the back as he fled.

She pulled back onto the road. In the rearview mirror she watched as the tower collapsed. Even with the windows up, she heard the last shuddering tolls of the bells as they crashed to the ground. Light flared all around her, and she smiled when she saw a pillar of holy fire scouring clean the last of Wyman's world. In her imagination, the fire spread to include Jimmy, rotting beneath the dark heat of the compost pile.

The Lincoln had a nearly full tank of gas, and she aimed it toward the highway, past the town center, past the Rhode House, north toward Havilah and beyond. Wyman had often told her that the Bible says there is gold in Havilah, but she thought the piece of ivory might bring far more riches somewhere beyond that tiny college town. It had brought her and Jase together in the first place, and if her skills, even with store-bought medicine, could save him, he would show her how to sell it. He would take her to meet her mother, and they would live as she knew they were meant to, like a seedling transplanted from planter to plot. Then she'd have all that she had ever dreamed of: her mother back and a man who would give her love, not disdain.

And if he died, she still had one thing left: the single word she had read on her mother's letter, the name of a city. Wichita. All in all, she had a lot to look forward to. She just might put down some roots.

Acknowledgments

While this is a retelling of the ancient tale of Medea and Jason, many of the details are rooted in real and current details. For example, Jase's story of the looting of the Iraqi National Museum, a series of thefts perpetrated against all cultures, draws heavily from the article "The Casualties of War: The Truth About the Iraq Museum," published by Matthew Bogdanos in the American Journal of Archeology, vol. 109, no. 3 in July 2005. It is a heartbreaking account about the acts of vandalism and profit-seeking that devastated 5000 years of human artistic expression.

The panel itself is a fictionalized version of several ivory panels in the "Nimrud Treasure" that was sacked during the war. The trafficking of such antiquities in boxes marked "decorative tiles" is well-reported and even touched on a prominent chain of stores several years ago.

A number of people have helped shape and polish this manuscript. Mary Pierce and Judy White workshopped this in its earliest, messy stages, and gave me the encouragement to stick with it. Karen Salemi gave it a thorough polish, and made it shine. And since mistakes are like gremlins or bio-hacked triops, Dale T. Phillips —without whom this book would not have seen the light of day— was able to hunt down a few more bits that needed correcting. Next, Maureen Milliken saved the day by uncovering some serious timeline issues. Whatever is wrong at this point is entirely my own failing.

Most importantly, I want to thank my family for their constant support. Mayre's invaluable insights into characters, plotting, and all-around book-world wisdom are the only reason this book even exists in finished form. She and Nick had to endure endless hours of my absence as I researched, wrote, revised and talked, talked, talked about the book. Thank you both for your love, support, and smiles.

J.M. TAYLOR cooks up his sinister fantasies in Boston where he lives with his wife and son. He has appeared in *Crime Syndicate, Thuglit, Out of the Gutter, Wildside Black Cat,* and *Tough,* among others. His first novel, *Night of the Furies,* was published by New Pulp Press and was listed in *Spinetingler's* Best of 2013. When he's not writing or reading, he teaches under an assumed name. You can find him on Twitter at @taylorjm7 and like his Facebook page Night of the Furies.

Also by this author:
Night of the Furies (New Pulp Press)